Desire's Edge

Eve Berlin

BLACK
LACE

1 3 5 7 9 10 8 6 4 2

First published in the United States of America in 2011 by
The Berkley Publishing Group, part of Penguin (USA) Inc.
Published in the UK in 2013 by Black Lace,
an imprint of Ebury Publishing
A Random House Group Company

The Random House Group Limited Reg. No. 954009

Addresses for companies within the Random House Group
can be found at www.randomhouse.co.uk

A CIP catalogue record for this book is
available from the British Library

The Random House Group Limited supports the Forest Stewardship
Council® (FSC®), the leading international forest-certification
organisation. Our books carrying the FSC label are printed on FSC®-
certified paper. FSC is the only forest-certification scheme supported by
the leading environmental organisations, including Greenpeace.
Our paper procurement policy can be found at:
www.randomhouse.co.uk/environment

Printed and bound by CPI Group (UK) Ltd, Croydon, CR0 4YY

ISBN 9780352347275

To buy books by your favourite authors and register for offers visit
www.randomhouse.co.uk
www.blacklace.co.uk

To my friend K. B. Alan, who knows why.
And to my darling R. G. Alexander,
always—and you know why, too!

one

There was no reason for Kara to be thinking about being spanked at her best friend Lucie's housewarming party—or about the diary entry she'd made the night before. Except perhaps that she'd had too much wine because she was feeling sorry for herself still, nearly six months after her breakup with Jake. She poured herself another glass anyway, and was taking a sip when she spotted him across the crowded room.

Dante De Matteo.

She hadn't seen him since the last week of her junior year in high school. Not long after he'd knocked her louse of a boyfriend at the time on his ass. Brady had deserved it. She'd caught him cheating on her, and when she'd confronted him, he'd gotten ugly about it, grabbing her arm, bruising her, yelling in her face. And if she hadn't already had a mad crush on Dante before then, his coming in to rescue her like her own personal white knight had certainly sealed the deal.

She remembered Dante's face once Brady was moaning on the ground and two teachers had run up and grabbed him, probably to keep him from hitting Brady again. She remembered his dark eyes, how shadowed they'd been. Fierce. Vulnerable, as he'd looked at her, which had surprised her. She'd wanted to say something. To thank him. To ask him why he'd done it. But she'd been too young to know how to handle it.

Then Dante had been suspended. And soon after that he'd left for college and she hadn't seen him again.

It had been more than twelve years, but she'd know him anywhere. He still had those chiseled good looks, all broad shoulders and long, lean muscles, but everything more refined, streamlined. The dark brown hair that used to fall into his face but was cut short now. And those eyes . . . She supposed most people would call them brown, but she remembered how they could flash gold in the sun.

She went warm all over so fast, it was like being engulfed by flames. Sensory overload. She had to look away. To get out of there.

I've sworn off men. Sworn off!

She ducked her head and made for the back door, her wineglass clenched in her hand. She was not going to think about how hot she'd been for Dante all those years ago, all through high school. And apparently still was, from the way her pulse was racing.

Outside, the early January night was cold and damp, but she was used to that having grown up on Mercer Island, just across the bridge from Seattle, where Lucie and her roommate, Tyler, lived now. And she needed the cold to settle her body, her head.

No men right now.

Her life had been so much calmer since her last relationship was over. No more drama. No more expectations. Everything nice and peaceful, and she liked it that way. Or, that was what she told herself, anyway. How she explained to herself why she hadn't even dated much since the breakup, which was not like her. She'd been with plenty of men before Jake. She didn't want to think about how that relationship had affected her. Had ground down her confidence.

So, her vibrator was her current best date. So what? She could go home, take out her pink plastic friend, and imagine it was Dante De Matteo between her thighs . . .

She shivered, squeezed her legs together, sighed.

She sat down on the porch swing, the wooden slats biting into the backs of her thighs through her knit wrap dress. Settling back onto a small pile of pillows, breathing in the crisp evening air, she took a long sip of her red wine and crossed her legs.

She was just buzzed enough to easily slip back into brooding about being alone. All of Lucie and Tyler's friends were happily paired off, it seemed, the house full of nuzzling couples. Until Dante had arrived. She'd noticed he appeared to be alone. Like her.

Not that she wasn't better off by herself right now. Maybe forever. It was still too soon after the disaster with Jake for her to feel any differently, to want to be in a relationship again. She hadn't completely shaken her bitterness yet.

She brooded for several minutes more, ignoring the jump start to her nerves she'd had inside, seeing Dante again. Or pretending to. Until she heard a footstep on the creaky boards of the porch. She looked up and saw a tall silhouette, a dark outline against the light coming through the doorway. Tall and well muscled and sexy as hell.

Dante.

Her whole body surged.

"Kara? Is it really you?"

"Dante. Hi. What are you doing here?"

He stepped closer, into the light of the porch. He was well dressed, in dark slacks and a sweater that fit him like it was custom-made for his body. Maybe it was. He looked too damn good.

"I ran into Lucie a few days ago and she invited me to the party. I haven't seen you since I left high school. Did you ever get that degree in art you wanted?"

She shrugged, trying to look cool. To keep cool. But seeing those same eyes looking at her now with unabashed appreciation, in a way she'd fantasized about since she was fourteen, was almost too much.

She took a breath, tried again.

"I took a lot of classes in college, but my parents didn't exactly approve of me pursuing art. I dropped it after a while."

"If I remember correctly, you were a good painter. Didn't you show at some state competition in high school?"

"I can't believe you remember that." She felt her cheeks going warm.

He leaned against the doorframe, one of those poses only the most confident of men could get away with and still look completely natural and relaxed. "I remember a lot about you, Kara."

"Do you?"

He smiled, his dimples flashing. How was it any man could look so smooth and so boyishly charming at the same time? She could see the teenager he'd once been beneath the more masculine planes of his face. Under his sophisticated looks, his immaculate clothes, he was still the old Dante, she was certain. He'd always been kind. Even in high school, when boys were mostly jerks. Dante was the sort of guy who would talk to anyone at school, not just the jocks or the cool kids. Who would stand up for the smaller boys who got picked on by the bullies. He had stood up for *her*. And she was just as charmed by him now as she'd ever been.

"I remember you used to drive that old VW Bug," he said, moving closer. "It was baby blue. Do you still have it?"

"What? No, of course not." She laughed.

God, he looked good. Gorgeous. The sweater fit his broad shoulders perfectly, outlining the breadth of them. He definitely had some muscle under there.

"It'd be worth a lot these days," he said.

"I sold it after high school and got something more mature," she told him, smiling.

"I did the same. Sold my old Camaro and got a small sedan right after college. It's funny how we all have these ideas about what being an adult means. I wish I had that car now."

"What did you do after college besides sell your muscle car?" she asked him. "You were going for a law degree, right? And I think your whole family moved away?"

"I went to Yale, got my law degree there. I lived in New York for a while, worked at a firm there. My folks retired and moved to

Colorado right around the time I finished school. But my brother, Lorenzo, is still here in Seattle. Do you remember him?"

"He's a bit older than you, isn't he? I think he graduated at the end of my freshman year. He looked a lot like you."

Dante nodded. "He's a civil engineer, married just last year. We're pretty close. I moved back to Seattle a couple of years ago. I thought it'd be nice to be close to family. Is your family still here?" Dante asked.

"My parents never moved away from the island, although they both still work in the city."

"You never had any brothers or sisters, did you?"

"No. Just me."

Her mother, owner of one of the top architectural firms in Seattle, had never had time for more than one child. She'd never really had time for Kara. And her father, a stern and disapproving man, had his own law practice, which had always meant long hours. Even if their personalities had been conducive to parenting, their jobs certainly weren't.

She had chosen a man just like her father when she'd gotten together with Jake. Harsh. Judgmental. Just like Brady back in high school, come to think of it. Apparently her father had ruined her ability to pick a man. Another good reason to have sworn off them. And she would stick to it. Even if Dante De Matteo, her crush since she was a teenager, was standing so close to her. Talking to her. Watching her with an appraising gaze and smiling. Making her tingle all over.

"So, no art degree, Kara? What are you doing now?"

"I ended up with a law degree, too, actually. I'm surprised we haven't run into each other."

"So am I. And that it took so long for me to run into Lucie. But I'm glad I did." His dimples were flashing at her again. "I'm glad she invited me here so I could run into you, finally." He gestured with his chin. "Mind if I sit with you?"

Her body gave another surge of heat.

"Um, no. Go ahead."

He moved across the porch and was in front of her in a few long strides, settling his lanky body next to her on the porch swing. She caught his scent, something dark and male, with a hint of musk that made her shivery inside. And she could feel the heat emanating from him. Or maybe the heat was her own, building, spiraling, with him next to her.

"Are you practicing law"? he asked her; then he shook his head. "I really always have thought of you as an artist."

"So did I, for a long time . . ."

It was so strange, hearing him say these things to her. An artist . . . It was what she'd always wanted. How did he remember how important art was to her? The idea made her heart beat a little faster.

He was watching her, his gaze dark, intense. "You should go after whatever you want, Kara."

She crossed her legs, draped a hand over her knee where her wrap dress revealed a few inches of bare thigh between the hem and the tops of her high, brown suede boots. "Do you think so? It's not always as easy as it sounds."

She had the distinct impression he was flirting with her. And she was definitely flirting back.

He nodded. "A missed opportunity only leaves behind regret."

"I agree."

"I always liked you in high school," he said suddenly, his tone lowering.

"Did you?"

"Yes. Always. I remember you when you were fourteen, fifteen. You had the longest legs even then."

He moved his knee, tapping it against hers. She went warm all over, a lovely rush of heat.

"Hey, you two. Anyone need a refill?" Lucie had a wine bottle in her hand. Her blond hair was piled on top of her head, her cheeks pink, glowing with the chilly night air and probably a few glasses of wine. "I almost forgot you guys would know each other from school."

"We were just talking about that. And I'm not drinking tonight. Kara, more wine?" Dante offered, taking her glass, his fingers brushing against hers. He took the bottle from Lucie, filled Kara's glass, handed it back. This time he paused, his fingertips lying against hers for one long moment. He smiled at her. She heated all over, a furnace blast of pure desire.

"Okay, then . . . I'll just . . . go on back inside," Lucie said, disappearing back into the house.

But Kara hardly heard her. She pulled in a deep breath, took a sip of the wine.

Need to calm down.

He had a dazzling smile. There was no other word for it. His face was all masculine planes and angles: a finely sculpted jaw, high, almost sharp cheekbones. But his mouth was nothing short of lush. Generous. And the dimples . . . When he smiled, her entire body melted. She felt like a teenager all over again, dumbfounded by that smile.

She lifted her glass and sipped, realizing only when the wine was all gone that she wasn't nearly as buzzed as she'd thought she was. Maybe the shock of seeing Dante, her reaction to him, had sobered her up.

"You're still as pretty as ever, Kara," Dante told her out of the blue, that golden-brown gaze on her. "I hope you don't mind my saying so."

She shook her head.

Speak, Kara.

"Thank you."

"Beautiful, really," he murmured.

He was staring at her. Her cheeks heated once more, that warm and needy place between her thighs.

"Will it make you blush more if I ask you if you're single?"

She sighed. "Yes."

"Ah, I'm sorry. None of my business. Forgive me."

He was all old-world manners. He always had been—a gentleman, even in high school. She'd loved it then. Loved it now.

"No, I mean, yes, I'm single," she told him. "I broke off with someone about six months ago. Well, he broke up with me."

"He was a foolish man."

She shrugged. "Maybe. What about you? Married?"

"No, I've never been married. And I'm . . . on my own."

"Ah." She felt awkward, suddenly. She usually had no trouble talking to people. She considered herself outgoing. She was a trial lawyer, for God's sake! Why couldn't she put two sensible sentences together?

"Kara, am I making you uncomfortable? I don't mean to ask such personal questions. It's just been so long since I've seen you. I'd really like to catch up."

"No, it's fine. I'm fine." She let out a small laugh. "I don't know what's wrong with me. I've had a little too much wine, maybe." It was a lie—she still felt only the slightest hint of a buzz—but a convenient excuse. "I'd like to catch up, too."

He smiled at her, his dimples creasing his cheeks, making her pulse race once more. Then he reached out and brushed the backs of his fingers over her wrist, almost absentmindedly. Except that when she looked up at him, he was watching her, that golden gaze on hers. There was an odd expression on his face, and it took her a moment to recognize the naked desire there. And even through her clothes she swore she could feel his heat, arcing like a small shock from his hand through her arm.

She pulled in a breath, dizzy with sensation.

This cannot be happening.

Except that it was.

It was just chemistry. She'd had a crush on him for years, and now here he was, as if by magic. Looking better than ever. And he was nice. Smart. Easy to talk to. It was a perfectly normal response. Any woman would have to be blind and completely frigid not to respond to Dante De Matteo.

She was pretty sure he had never touched her before. She wanted him to do it again.

She focused on his mouth for a moment, then lifted her gaze back to his. Oh yes, hunger there. And something else . . . like an unasked question.

She swallowed, looked away into the darkness of the yard, and beyond it to the street, the amber glow of the streetlights illuminating the fog.

"Kara? Did I say something wrong?"

She turned back to him. "What? No, of course not. It's just . . . it's a little strange, seeing you again."

"Yes. Strange, but good."

He smiled, a thousand-watt smile. There was invitation there.

She was beginning to forget exactly why she'd sworn off men. It wasn't as though she was going to get involved with Dante. She was definitely not in the market for a relationship. And she was no shrinking violet. Maybe it was time for her self-imposed dry spell to end. If he was interested and she was interested, then she didn't see anything wrong in a little flirtation. Maybe leading to something more . . .

She watched him watching her. And was glad she was a habitual lingerie girl. She decided then that if the evening ended with her taking Dante home with her, perhaps that was better than sitting around feeling sorry for herself. And with Dante around, there would be nothing to be sorry for.

She smiled back, letting her own invitation reach her eyes.

Eyes like they were made of metal. Silver and gold and edged in green . . .

Dante felt stunned by her. He hadn't seen her for twelve years, yet his body was responding exactly the way it had when he was a teenager. His pulse was hot, racing. He had to force down the arousal in his system, try not to get hard. But the girl he'd dreamed about through the last two years of high school was sitting right next to him.

He remembered suddenly the shock on her face when he'd punched out that punk Brady Metcalf. And the way that shock had warmed into a brilliant smile, just for him. That had made it worth it—getting suspended in the final week of his senior year. He'd have done it anyway. Brady was getting rough with her, and he sure as hell wouldn't have let anything happen to her. But he'd never forgotten that smile . . .

She'd been too young then, and he'd never pursued anything with her. She was still in high school while he was getting ready to go away to college. But she was all grown up now. Warm and female, her pale skin luminous in the amber light of the porch. As they'd talked, she'd begun to lean toward him, sending a subtle signal. And now her smile—sweet and sensual and reflecting the same desire he felt like a sharp current in his system—just about knocked him out.

Her light brown hair was long, as it had been in high school, a smooth, heavy sheaf of shining strands. He wanted to touch it. He wanted to touch *her*.

He *wanted* her.

Slow down, buddy.

His body didn't want to. But this was someone he'd known years ago, not some girl to pick up in a bar or at the Pleasure Dome, the BDSM club he'd frequented the last several years. Not a woman to have a brief fling with then never see again. Kara was the girl next door. Literally. And he was always especially careful with the vanilla girls. Not that he couldn't enjoy sex with a woman who wasn't interested in the rougher games he played. He could. He often did. But that taboo edge made things more exciting. Revealing that to someone new was always a delicate situation. Revealing that to someone he'd known when they were just kids . . . But they weren't kids anymore.

Jesus, he was thinking as though she'd already offered to sleep with him, offered herself up to him on a silver platter.

Not that he'd mind if she did.

He went hard thinking about that. He couldn't help it.

Calm down.

He pulled in a long breath of the cool night air, exhaled.

"Would you like me to get you some more wine?" he asked her, thinking a short diversion might be a good idea, a moment inside the house where he could cool off.

"No, I don't need any more. Thanks."

She set the glass down on the floor of the porch. Smiled at him again. That sweet mouth. Her lips would be so soft . . . and suddenly he couldn't think of any reason not to just lean in and kiss her.

He did—one hand going to her cheek, he moved in a little at a time, giving her a chance to pull away. But all she did was part her lips, her big hazel eyes on his, then fluttering shut as he got closer.

Her lips were soft, softer than he'd imagined. And she was going soft all over, her body yielding, leaning into his. Yielding was one thing he recognized easily. And this woman had it, that ability to give herself over, whether she was aware of it or not.

She opened her lips and he slipped his tongue inside. She tasted of wine, liquid and sweet. And she was kissing him back, her mouth welcoming him. Drawing him deeper.

She moaned quietly, and it went through him like a shock. He kept kissing her, just kissing her, and he was as hard as if she'd had her hands on him, or her gorgeous mouth.

Jesus.

He pulled back, and she held perfectly still, her eyes closed, her mouth still slightly parted. Her lips were plush, a little swollen from his kiss. He wanted to kiss her again. But he was actually afraid that if he did, he might push her too far, too fast. Because the truth was, he wanted to strip her down, push her onto her back right there on the narrow porch swing, and sink into her. Do every dirty thing he'd ever imagined back in high school. And a few more things he'd learned since.

He groaned.

Her lashes fluttered; her eyes opened.

"Dante?"

"Yeah. Do I need to apologize?"

"No. That was as much my fault as it was yours."

"Does anyone need to be at fault here?" he asked, needing to know, to be certain he wasn't imagining she wanted him.

"Maybe not."

That sweet smile again. God, she was something.

He realized he still had his hand on her face. Her cheek was smooth beneath his palm, the skin silky and cool in the chilly night air.

"Are you cold?" he asked her.

"No, I'm fine. I'm good."

She looked a bit dazed. She looked exactly the way he felt. Overcome by lust.

No woman had ever had this effect on him, not that he could remember. Could it be the reawakening of those long-held teenage fantasies? Or was it simply *her*?

It bothered him a little. But not enough for him to walk away. All he could think of was her naked body under his. Even better if she'd let him do the things to her he loved best. Spank her. Bring her to orgasm with that excruciating combination of pleasure and pain. But how to bring it up with her? It was so much easier with the women he met at the Pleasure Dome. There, everyone knew exactly what to expect. No one went to the city's biggest and finest BDSM club without having at least some idea of what went on there. Without sharing the same kinds of desires.

But the fact was, he was so turned on by her, he wanted her with or without all the extreme sex. It didn't matter right now nearly as much as it normally did. As much as it should.

What did that even mean?

He didn't want to question it too carefully. He just *wanted* her. Out of control, like some hormone-driven teen. Wanted her in a way he'd never desired another woman before. After fifteen minutes of talking to her. After all these years.

Have to have her.

He'd figure out what the hell was going on with him later.

"Kara. I'm going to ask you something, and I don't want you to get offended, but I'm going to be blunt."

"Okay . . ."

He leaned in, keeping his voice low.

"I can't believe I've run into you tonight, after all this time. But I have to tell you, if we were still in high school, this would have been my dream come true. Just kissing you. But I'm all grown up now. So are you. And I want more."

Her eyes went wide, her breath coming out in a small puff of warm air. Then she smiled again, and he knew it would be all right. She leaned into him, looked up at him from beneath her long, dark lashes. It was the look of a seductress, yet there was still something sweet, almost innocent about her.

"We *are* all grown up, Dante. What is it you want?"

He took her hand, wrapping his fingers around hers. "I want you. I want you so badly, I can't wait for all the usual polite talk. And this is not some well-practiced line. I don't believe in that crap, frankly. I just . . . want you."

Kara's breath went out of her. The blunt honesty was like some sort of wild aphrodisiac. That and the way he was looking at her, his plush mouth loose and still damp from kissing her.

The man could kiss. No doubt about it. She wanted him to do it again. She wanted him to do more than kiss her. And she wanted it now.

She shrugged, trying to appear casual about it even as her pulse thrummed with need. "Then have me, Dante."

He smiled at her, all heat and a slow, simmering pleasure.

He stood, helped her to her feet. He was even taller when he was standing next to her, dwarfing her five-foot-eight frame. She loved that, loved feeling small and feminine next to him. She drew in a deep breath, inhaled the dark, musky scent of him. A shudder ran through her, pleasure trembling like some long, drawn-out note through her body.

Yes, they were all grown up. And maybe this was exactly what she needed. Maybe *he* was. She'd brooded long enough.

Dante De Matteo, after all these years. A fantasy about to come true.

two

A part of her couldn't believe she was doing this—leaving a party with a guy she hadn't seen in years. A guy she hadn't known all that well in high school, and whom she no longer really knew at all. But she felt safe with him. Inexplicably, maybe, except that Lucie and Tyler knew him, too, which made it a little safer.

Kara had caught a ride to the party with another friend she and Lucie had known for years, so she'd said a quick good-bye and gotten into Dante's silver BMW. The car fit him. It was sleek. Sophisticated. Fast.

She turned to look at Dante's profile as he drove across the bridge and back into the city. He was very European-looking, with his dark hair and olive skin, the strong, clean jawline. He would make the perfect *GQ* model. There was almost a prettiness about him, except that his features were so angular. So purely male. The dimples in his cheeks softened his look, though. And his mouth . . .

She shivered, wanting to reach out, to touch his full lips with her fingertips. Simply wanting to touch him.

Oh, but she was going to. And he would touch her . . .

She rubbed her hands over her thighs, the purple knit of her dress soft against her palms.

Calm down.

"Are you warm enough?" he asked, turning up the heat in the car.

"Yes, I'm fine." Too hot, maybe. "The seat warmers do a good job."

He turned and smiled at her for a moment before looking back at the road. God, even the way he downshifted the car as they reached the Seattle side of the bridge was sexy. Her entire body was humming with anticipation.

"I hope you don't mind that I'm not talking much," Dante said, shifting once more to speed up. The highway was mostly empty, the sky outside a series of dark layers of cloud. It would rain soon. "It's not that I don't want to talk with you."

"I don't mind. You have to pay attention to the road."

"It's not that."

"No? What, then?"

He glanced at her once more, just a quick flash, his eyes gleaming darkly in the amber light coming from the dashboard. There was a small grin quirking the corner of his mouth. "To be honest, if I try to make small talk, I'll fail miserably. And I don't want to say anything so stupid that you'll change your mind."

"You don't strike me as the kind of guy who would have any trouble making small talk."

"Not usually, no. But I have to tell you, Kara . . ." His tone lowered, a deep rumble of smoke and desire. "If I don't get you to my place soon, if I don't have you in the next few minutes, I'm going to lose my mind. So I'm keeping my mouth shut until I can get you home. Get you naked. Get my hands on you."

"Oh . . ."

She didn't know what to say. She was stunned by the need filling her body. So fast, so sharp. She was dazed by it.

Get you naked. Get my hands on you.

Oh yes, that was exactly what she wanted. But she couldn't say it. She was wet, aching. And in her head was one message, repeating itself over and over, until she really couldn't think of anything else.

Need him now . . .

He was watching the road carefully as they raced across town. They were both quiet as he got off the 90 and made his way north. She didn't mind that they weren't talking. There was nothing uncomfortable about it, as there might be with someone else. She didn't know why. All she knew was that the silence and the expectation were mixed together, making her feel as though they were in some sort of bubble. Cut off from the rest of the world. And she liked it.

The rain started as they drove through the streets, passing office buildings, restaurants, bars. The streetlights shone on the dampening pavement, casting light and shadow across the car windows. And the seat warmers, which had been comforting at first, lovely, were almost too warm now as need rose in her body, heating her through.

Finally they pulled into a parking garage in one of the newer high-rise buildings on Elliott Avenue. The real estate here was pricey. She remembered vaguely that Dante had been one of the rich kids in high school. Not that he'd ever flaunted it. But Mercer Island was a small community, and everyone in their school had known something about everyone else.

None of that mattered to her one way or another. She'd never dated a man for his money, although she preferred a man with some ambition. But right now all she was interested in was parking the damn car and getting inside. Somewhere private. With *him*.

When had she ever felt this sort of urgency with a man? One who hadn't even kissed her, touched her, for almost an hour. Normally, that sharp edge of desire would have worn off by now. Not tonight. Not with Dante.

He pulled into the garage and into a parking spot, turned the engine off, then turned to look at her. One quick glance, that small, devastating grin; then he was out of the car and opening her door, pulling her into his arms.

She could smell him again, that dark, lovely tang of clean male flesh, mixed with a little exhaust, the scent of motor oil and tires from the garage that only made him seem more essentially male.

He was so tall, and he was holding her so close, she had to tilt her head back to look him in the eye. His were full of the same driving need she felt in her body. Tingling. Electric.

If only he would kiss her.

"Let's get you upstairs."

His arm never left her waist as he led her to the elevator and they rode up, floor after floor. He watched her face the whole time, his golden-brown eyes hot on hers. Mesmerizing.

He leaned into her and murmured into her hair, "Almost

there. You have no idea how badly I want to touch you, Kara. I don't even dare kiss you yet. If I do, it'll have to happen right here in the elevator."

"I don't think I'd mind," she said quietly, smiling, dazzled by him.

He laughed, a low, husky sound. "Maybe we can save that for later. After the neighbors are all in bed. But I love that you aren't opposed to the idea of sex in the elevator. Someplace where we could get caught."

"It sounds . . . exciting."

Anything with Dante sounded exciting. Everything.

The doors opened, and she was nearly breathless as they moved into the hallway, as he unlocked the door and led her inside.

His place was one of those open loft spaces, with floor-to-ceiling windows overlooking the city. The apartment was dark, but enough light came in from the city below to illuminate the silhouettes of the furniture. But she didn't have time to look, wasn't really interested. Dante had his hands on her, was pushing her back against the front door. And all she could think was, *Yes. Now*, as he bent his head and kissed her.

His mouth was hard and soft all at once. Plush lips, wet tongue pushing into her mouth. Her hands went to his shoulders, her mind buzzing. She was weak with desire, her legs shaking immediately. She hung on while he backed up enough to pull their coats off and drop them on the wood floor, his mouth never leaving hers.

He kept kissing her, kissing her, and she braced her hands on the door behind her as he pressed against her. His body was all hard muscle: his strong thighs, his chest, his broad shoulders. And that one hard ridge pressing into her belly. Hard and big and oh . . .

She was panting by the time he released her mouth and began to undress her. In moments, it seemed, she was left in her bra and panties, not even knowing how it had happened, exactly, her dress and her boots in a pile on the floor.

"Hold still," he told her, his voice a low command, and something in her responded, reverberated with it.

He stood back and pulled his own clothes off, watching her. She could barely make out the dark gleam of his eyes. But she felt them on her like a burning coal, heating her skin, scorching her.

"Dante . . ."

"Shh. I know what you need, Kara. Just stay there; let me look at you. Touch you. I'll do the rest."

She felt her body go loose all over. There was something about what he was saying to her, the way he said it, that made her feel . . . released. It was odd. She was normally fairly aggressive sexually. But with him, she didn't feel any need to be. None at all. As if she could easily do as he said. Hold still. Let him do everything.

She didn't understand it. She didn't need to.

The air was cool on her nearly bare skin, the wood of the door hard and cold behind her. But the contrast only added to the heat of his fingertip as he traced a long, slow line down her stomach. She shivered, trying not to move. He reached the top edge of her panties, and she sighed quietly.

"Do you like it when I touch you, Kara?"

"Yes," she whispered.

"Kara. Say it so I can hear you."

"Yes," she said, her voice echoing in the high-ceilinged apartment, sounding too loud to her ears.

She was melting inside. Some strange sensation linked to the way he was treating her. As though he were completely in charge.

He was.

She knew it. And something in her loved it.

Don't think about it. Don't question it.

His hand moved up, over her ribs, higher, until his fingertip rested in the narrow space between her breasts. Her nipples went hard.

"It kills me not to touch you. Really touch you. But there's something that's just too good in torturing myself a little this way." He paused. "Do you feel it, Kara? That nearly unbearable pleasure in waiting?" He paused again. She couldn't catch her breath enough to answer. "You don't need to tell me. I can feel it in the tension in your body. In how quiet you've become. I can feel it in the heat of your skin."

A hard ache had started between her thighs. Yes, nearly unbearable.

"Dante, please . . ."

"Please what?" he asked, his voice so soft she could barely hear it.

"Please touch me now."

A small chuckle from him then. But there was nothing condescending in it. He was merely pleased. And it warmed her to know that he was.

What was going on with her?

"You ask so nicely," he told her. "So sweetly. But your body will be even sweeter under my hands. My mouth. And you're right here, just waiting for me . . ."

One breath, then two, while they both stood perfectly still. All she could hear was his breath and her own. Then he was on her. One hand went into her hair, gripped the long strands right at the scalp, pulling her head back. His lips went to her throat, hot and soft, then wet as his tongue flicked out, licking at her skin.

"Ah, Dante . . ."

He moved in closer, his body pressing into hers again, and through the soft cotton of his boxer briefs his erection was solid, pressing against her flesh.

God, to feel him inside her . . .

But right now she was almost too distracted by what he was doing to her: sucking on her neck, licking, his teeth sinking in just hard enough. His hands were everywhere: on her sides, her thighs, then slipping her bra off. He filled his palms with her flesh, and she arched into him, her hard nipples against his palms.

"Jesus," he muttered, pulling his mouth from her neck, pausing to look at her breasts for several moments. Then he lowered his head and took one nipple into his mouth.

"Ah, God, Dante . . . Yes."

Her hands went into his hair, and it was soft and silky. She held on, held him to her breast as his tongue moved over her aching flesh. He lapped at her, over and over that hard nub, sending desire like lightning through her system. Her sex was wet and hurting. *Needing*.

"Come on, Dante."

She wasn't even sure what she was asking for. Just *more*.

"Shh. Quiet, Kara."

The command in his tone made her limp, her muscles loose and warm. Yes, just to hand it all over to him. To let him take charge . . .

He pushed her against the door with his hands, one on her shoulder, one on her belly. Then he moved his hands lower to slide her panties off.

"You are so beautiful," he said, his tone low. "So, so beautiful."

He knelt down, and, holding her hard against the door once more with his hand on her hip, he used the other to push her thighs apart.

She could feel his breath warm at the apex of her thighs. And as he leaned in, her sex squeezed in anticipation.

"Do you want my mouth on you, Kara?" he asked her.

"Yes, Dante . . . Oh . . ."

His tongue flicked out, one brief flicker against the hard nub of her clitoris.

"Ah, God . . ."

He held her harder against the door. Leaned in and licked. One long, slow stroke up the length of her soaking cleft.

Pleasure hummed, a sharp current arcing through her. From sex to belly to breasts. He licked again, and once more it was like a jolt of pure pleasure.

"You taste like honey, Kara. I swear it," he murmured against her needy flesh.

He licked again. And again. His tongue was soft and silky and hot. Burning her up. With pleasure. With a need that was spiraling, climbing higher and higher. His tongue moved faster, sliding over the lips of her sex, over her hard clit. But she needed more. And without her saying anything, he seemed to sense it.

Pulling back, he told her, "Spread for me now. Yes, that's it. Perfect. You're so damn wet. So perfect."

He used his fingers to spread her pussy lips, and even the hard press of his fingers on her flesh was exquisite.

Even better when he bent his head once more and took her clit into his mouth and sucked.

"Ah!"

She thought he'd pause. Tease her. But instead he really went to work, sucking, sucking at her clit. His tongue swept over the hard tip, back and forth. She was going to come any moment.

When he pushed two fingers inside her, the sensation was shocking. Intense. She had to hold her climax back, wanting simply to feel it all: his mouth, his fingers inside her, beginning to pump now, like some small cock.

She pulled in a breath, trying not to come. But she was overwhelmed by sensation. He drove his fingers deeper, sucked her in, *drank* her in. And her climax roared through her like a freight train as thunder clapped outside the windows. Pleasure and pleasure. Sensation upon sensation. All of it deep in her sex, her belly. She shuddered, her legs almost too weak to hold her up, if Dante's hand wasn't still on her hip, pressing her against the door.

Was it the sudden storm shaking the door? Or was it her? Coming and coming still in tiny, shivering coils, shimmering through her body.

"Oh my God," she muttered, her head falling back against the door.

"Again," he demanded.

"What? I can't. Come on, Dante. Take me to bed."

"Not yet. I want to make you come again. Here."

"Oh . . ."

She wanted to argue. But his mouth was on her once more, one hand caressing her breast, taking the full flesh and kneading gently. And his mouth . . . his tongue was softer on her this time, as though he knew she was acutely sensitive after her climax. A gentle lapping at her clitoris, then moving lower to push inside her. She opened her thighs farther for him, held on to his shoulders to steady herself. She was aware of how amazingly soft his skin was beneath her hands. She wanted to touch him: his chest, his cock. But later. After he was done with her. After he made her come again. It was going to be soon.

His tongue was moving inside her, pushing in, slipping out. The sensation was amazing. The pleasure was undeniable. Then he did something she'd never experienced before. He pushed his fingers inside her again, angling them against her G-spot. Her hips arched, and she moaned. Then he slid his tongue right up against her opening, so that it was hard to tell where his fingers stopped and his tongue began. He moved them both, soft, undulating motions. Her hips arched in time with him. And the pleasure built once more, quickly, but in some softer fashion.

When she came this time it wasn't as sharp as it had been before. But it was deeper, rumbling through her, her clit pulsing with it. Pleasure was like a solid core in her body, thick and sweet, like honey moving through her system. Taking her over.

"Oh . . . Oh . . ."

All she could do was moan, her hips moving against his finger, his mouth. She was dazed. Helpless. Her legs went weak, and she felt herself begin to crumple.

"I've got you."

He caught her, somehow. Pulled her to the floor so that she was lying across his knees. His arms were tight around her. She was still shuddering with her orgasm, as though it had left something behind. Some spark of light traveling through her, lighting her up inside.

She looked at him in the mostly dark room. His gaze was hot, burning in the dim light coming through the windows. His skin was hot to the touch, his body solid muscle. She could only lie in his arms, trying to catch her breath.

"Jesus Christ, girl." The words came out on a panting breath. Full of desire. Low and smoky. "That was beautiful. I need to do it again. To fuck you. To make you come. Over and over. Yes . . . I need to make you come again."

All she could do was moan.

He held her as he got to his feet, taking her with him. And before she could protest that she really could walk, he was carrying her across the room. She could hear the soft scuffing of his bare feet against the polished wood floors. She caught once more the breathtaking views from the windows as he carried her behind a screen and laid her down on a big bed.

"Hang on."

He leaned over the bed and pulled the covers back, moved her onto the cool sheets, then climbed in with her, laying his now-naked body over hers.

"I need to be inside you, Kara. Just fuck you hard. Can you take it?"

"Yes."

"Tell me you want it."

God, his body was like burning silk against hers. His skin so smooth. His cock so hard, resting between her thighs.

"Kara. Tell me," he commanded.

"Yes, I can take it. I want it hard. I like it hard."

"Hard fucking? Or more?"

"More?" Why did her breath catch in her throat when he asked her that? Was he asking what she thought he was? "Dante?"

He kissed her neck, his lips firm yet soft. He nipped at her with his teeth, and the pain was nothing more than sharp pleasure. He was tracing her lips gently with his fingertips, and she could smell her own ocean scent there. He was all contradictions, this man. She loved it. Loved that he touched her all over at once. Sensation overload.

"I like my sex a little rough," he told her, kissing her neck once more, then the curve of her jaw.

"Oh . . ."

"Does that shock you?"

"No. Not much shocks me."

"Do you like the idea, Kara? Because I think you do. As soon as I said it, your whole body let go."

"God, Dante. I . . . Yes. I like it. It's what I want. Exactly what I want."

It was his turn to moan. "Ah, you are perfect," he said. Then after a few breathless moments he said again, "I like it rough. I like to really pump into you. To bite you. To pinch your nipples."

"Yes . . ."

God, was he really saying these things to her? Her wildest fantasies come true. The ones that had sent her ex, Jake, running in the other direction. Telling her she was crazy. Some sort of weirdo. But she didn't want to think of him now.

Dante said quietly, "What I really want to do is spank you."

"Oh!"

"Now I've shocked you."

"No. It's not that."

"What is it?"

"It's just . . . what I've always wanted. Craved."

She felt a shiver go through him. Then there was a long pause before he said, "This is going to be very good, then. I promise you, Kara."

She was shaking all over. Waiting. She was absolutely soaked. Wanting. Dazzled. And it hadn't even happened yet.

But it was about to.

Dante watched her closely, but all he saw in her, felt in her, was pure desire. Her body was blazing hot under him. Her breasts, the shallow curve of her stomach. Her hot little sex was wet. Ready for him. He was as hard as he'd ever been in his life.

He wanted her to come again. Again and again. Nothing turned him on like seeing a woman come. Feeling that pulse beat deep inside her. Hearing her moans, her cries of pleasure. And never more than with this woman.

Kara.

Maybe it was the years of a schoolkid crush. He didn't know. Too damn difficult to think about it now, with her body right here. No, now he had to just touch her. Taste her skin. Slide into her and fuck her until she screamed . . .

He reached down between them and swiped his hand over her sex, making her gasp. She was so damn wet. He could hardly stand it. The scent of her come . . .

Again.

Yes, he'd make her come again.

He slid down her body, opening her sweet thighs with his hands. And she let him do it, didn't try to fight it, to control anything. Perfect.

He paused over her open sex, looking at her in the low, misty light of the moon, piercing silver through the cloud layer, the dim glow of gold from the streetlights.

She was mostly shaved. Just that one narrow strip of hair, which was exactly how he liked it. Nearly naked. Tempting. And when he used his fingers to spread the plush, pink lips, he could see her glistening inner flesh.

"I love the way a woman looks," he told her, his voice coming out on a rasping breath. "So damn beautiful."

He leaned in, ran his tongue up her slit, loved her answering shiver. He loved to go down on a woman. Loved that smoky flavor of desire. He licked her again, softly. He knew she'd be tender, a little overstimulated. But he could make her come again, if he went about it the right away.

He *would* make her come again.

He pressed his tongue against her clit, swirled it in slow circles. As he did it, her thighs tensed, her hips rising to meet his searching mouth. He let his tongue dip inside her, then slide out again to run over the hard nub of her clit. Then again, and again.

He heard her panting breath, felt her hands go into his hair. And when he pushed two fingers inside her, she came, crying out. Her body shaking. He loved the taste of her on his tongue, hot and sweet and tangy.

Finally she stopped clenching around his fingers. But she was still that smooth velvet inside. Unbelievably hot.

If he wasn't inside her in the next few moments, he was going to lose his mind.

He sat up, reached over her limp and panting body to pull a condom out of the lacquer box he kept on the nightstand. Holding himself up on his knees, he sheathed himself. She was watching him, her eyes going from his face to his hands to his cock. She licked her lips. They were dark, swollen, even though he hadn't kissed her much. Not nearly as much as he wanted to.

When had he ever had this driving need to simply kiss a woman?

Just fuck her. Get inside her. The rest will work itself out.

And get himself under control. Get *her* under control. Under his command.

He gripped her thighs, his fingers pressing into her flesh.

"Are you ready for me, Kara?"

"Yes, I'm ready."

"Tell me what you want."

He'd said this to women before. Why did it feel like some sort of test now?

"I want you. I want you to just . . . sink into me. To fuck me hard. To . . . do some of the things you talked about. Bite me. Pinch me . . ."

"Spank you?"

She was quiet for one moment, and he waited for her answer as though they were suspended in time.

It was too important, damn it.

Finally she breathed, "Yes, Dante. I want it. I want you to spank me. I've never done it before. It's something I've always wanted. Always."

A small groan escaped him.

This girl was going to be fucking perfect. He'd sensed her submissive tendencies. He was usually right. But with Kara, he'd been a little unsure. Thrown by the power of his attraction to her. The sex would have been good even without the rest of it. The kink. The power exchange.

But now he knew. She wanted it. And it was going to be fucking perfect. *She* was going to be.

three

Kara was spent. Weak. Yet somehow she wanted more. Especially if he was going to spank her . . . Oh yes, that lit her up inside like New Year's Eve, all brilliant heat and sparkling light. Just the idea of it.

She moaned softly as Dante turned her over. So easily, as if she were a doll in his large hands. He put a pillow under her stomach, laying her over it.

"Open for me, Kara. Yes, that's it."

He helped her part her thighs. She was aching already for him, even though she'd come over and over. So many times already, the climaxes were melding together. One endless moment of sensation. Intense. Dazing her.

But this would be something else altogether.

Finally.

His hands stroked her buttocks, in between her thighs, brushing against her sex. She realized she didn't know if he would spank her or fuck her first, which made it even more exciting. It made her nervous, too, but in a good way. She couldn't think straight.

"Kara, listen to me. Take in a breath. Nice and deep. Let it out. Good. Again."

His voice was soothing, helping her mind to calm. Smooth and deep, as if she could just fall into that sound. And his hands were moving over her body, heating her skin, her sex.

He was kneading the firm flesh of her buttocks and thighs now, his hands strong. As commanding as his voice.

"I want you to hold still for me. No matter what I do," he told her.

Was there a small threat in there somewhere? But it was lovely. Thrilling. She took in another deep breath, exhaled. She was shivering in anticipation.

"I'm going to spank you now," he said, his voice low. And before she even had time to comprehend it, his hand came down in a loud smack on her flesh.

"Oh!"

"Did I surprise you, Kara? That's exactly what I want. For you to wonder. To wait in expectation. And to take it."

He smacked her again, a small slap that rang in the still, cool air. And even though there was a little pain, the pleasure was even stronger, a tiny, electric arc shimmering over her skin.

"Breathe, Kara. Keep breathing."

She did as he asked, not even questioning it. Nothing in her wanted to question him, defy him.

Another spank, harder this time. But she simply pulled in another breath, waited for the sting to convert to pleasure.

"Beautiful," Dante murmured, stroking her skin once more: her ass, her thighs, dipping down in between them. "You are so beautifully wet. Beautiful girl."

He pressed two fingers into her so suddenly she jumped.

"Ah, hold still, Kara. Good girl."

She could barely manage it. The pleasure was too keen. Too new. Pain and pleasure mixing in her body in a way she had only ever fantasized about. And something was happening inside her head. Something she didn't want to think about. A letting go. A strange kind of trust.

His hands were soft on her skin, sliding, moving. She was lulled by it as he caressed her. When he leaned in and laid a kiss at the small of her back, goose bumps ran up her spine. She shivered.

"You are so damn responsive," Dante told her, his voice a low whisper. "Unbelievable for someone who's never done these things before."

His hand came down so hard, so unexpectedly, she jumped again. She couldn't help it.

"Oh!"

A small laugh from him. She could hear in it that he was pleased with her, and the idea warmed her.

"How are you doing, Kara? Good?"

"Yes. Good. I . . . want more."

"So do I. I want *you*. Don't move."

His hands on her thighs, spreading her wider; then he was behind her, his hips pressing against her, his rigid shaft poised at her entrance. She would have surged back against him—wanted to—but she felt immobilized. By his wish for her to remain still. By her own desire for him.

He pressed, and his cock slid in. Just the tip, but pleasure went through her like a shock.

"Oh, that's good . . ."

"Shh," he told her.

He held still for one breath, two. Then he ground into her. All at once, driving home. Hard and powerful, filling her up.

"Ah, God, Dante!"

"So damn good. You feel so good, beautiful girl."

They were both panting. Then he began to move. One hard stroke after another, his cock thick and lovely inside her. Hurting a little, he was so big, but driving pleasure ever deeper. He kept one hand on the small of her back, holding her down. She loved it, loved it all.

He thrust harder, and she was helpless beneath him. Limp, even as her insides coiled, tight with desire, bringing her to that edge once more.

A hard smack on her ass, and it nearly sent her over the edge.

"Ah, Dante!"

He really started to spank her then. A series of small blows using the same rhythm as his hips. He was fucking her, spanking her. She was going to explode.

"Dante . . . please . . ."

"Please what?" he panted, his voice a ragged growl.

"Please . . . don't stop."

"Ah, I won't."

He drove into her, his cock like some heavy point of pleasure in her body. The spanking was burning her skin. But she loved it. Needed it.

One more hard thrust, one more hard smack, and she fell, tumbling, into that dark place. Lights flashed behind her eyes. Pleasure roared through her system. And as her sex clenched in exquisite agony, Dante tensed behind her.

"Ah, God, Kara . . . I'm coming."

He pumped into her. His hand pressed down on her back, and she loved hearing his groans and cries. Knowing he was coming into her.

When it was over, he fell on top of her. His breath was warm at the back of her neck. She was half-numb. Barely able to think. Unable to move.

After several minutes, he shifted, rolling onto his side, pulling her with him. He settled her head on his chest. His heart was a hammering beat against her cheek.

Had this really happened?

This was, by far, the best sex she'd ever had in her life. And part of it was the realization of her fantasies: Sex with her girl-hood crush. The spanking. But part of it was simply *him*.

Dante.

Don't get all mushy.

No, she wouldn't do that. Not for a long time, if ever again. She'd paid too dearly for it in the past. With her sense of self. She wasn't willing to surrender that to any man. But her body . . . Well, that was something else. That, she had loved. More than she'd ever imagined.

What did that say about her? But she was too tired, too entirely spent, to think about it. To think about how much she had trusted Dante, to allow him to do these things to her. She didn't understand it. But now she wanted to simply enjoy being there, Dante's warm, solid body next to hers. His scent in her head. The scent of sex.

There would be plenty of time to question it all later. Tomorrow, if he let her stay the night. He didn't seem inclined to take her home at the moment. Which was just fine with her. She was happy there.

Happy . . . for the first time in a long time.

When she opened her eyes it was because the sun shone, pale and golden, through her closed lids. She opened them slowly, letting them adjust to the daylight.

It was a bit gray outside, the Seattle sky heavy with clouds, but with the morning sun piercing through here and there. Nothing unusual for January in this city. What was unusual was the way she felt.

She was a little sore, inside and out, but it felt good. And Dante's body next to hers felt even better. Even stranger was the fact that she'd slept through the night. A deep sleep, uninterrupted by dreams. She wasn't a good sleeper. It was worse, usually, when she tried to sleep with a lover. She'd lie awake for hours, wake up half a dozen times in the night, hyperaware of every movement, the sound of the other person's breathing. How odd that she'd slept so soundly with Dante.

Dante.

She turned onto her side, facing him, and found him looking at her.

Her pulse sped up.

There was even more gold in his brown eyes in the light of day as he looked at her. Tiny golden flecks surrounding the darker centers, which were a rich whiskey brown at the edges of the pupils. And his lashes were so dark, so thick . . .

"Hey." His voice was rough with sleep.

"Hey."

She smiled. She couldn't help it. Couldn't even consider that this might be one of those awkward morning-afters. But he smiled back. Her body surged. Need and a sudden, aching warmth that had nothing to do with sex.

Did it?

He propped himself up on one arm, looking down at her. She had one moment to wonder what her hair must look like, if she had marks from the pillowcase on her face. But she was too dazzled by him, by the dimples flashing in his cheeks, the dark stubble shadowing his jaw, making him even more handsome, more masculine, than ever. It was hard to think about anything else. Hard to be self-conscious under his gaze.

Those golden-brown eyes were full of desire. And even as she realized it he pulled her closer with a small growl, his erection pressing against her hip.

She was wet in an instant.

"Kara . . ." He kissed her cheek, her lips. "I hope you like morning sex."

She laughed, turned on her side, and arched her hips into his.

"I'll take that as a yes," he said. "But tell me, are you sore?"

"I won't be sitting comfortably for a day or two, but I don't mind it. I like it. I feel . . ." She paused, trying to figure it out. "I feel like the soreness is . . . a badge of courage. Does that sound silly?"

"Not at all. It is. I may have bruised you. Marked you."

"Oh . . . I hadn't thought of that."

She twisted, trying to look over her shoulder, needing to see.

"Does that concern you? Should I have been more careful with you?"

"No. No, it's fine."

How could she tell him she *hoped* to be marked? That she loved the idea of it? That she loved even the word?

He reached for her and turned her onto her stomach, ran a hand over her bare buttocks. "There are a few small bruises." He brushed his hand over her again. His voice was low, quiet. "I can feel you shiver when I touch you, Kara. When I touch the marks I left on your skin."

"I like it. I don't know why."

"I think I do."

He rolled her over until she was facing him once more. His mouth was soft and lush. There was desire there. And something else. Something she couldn't identify, but that beat through her own system.

"Kara, I should tell you, should probably have told you last night, that I'm more than just into the spanking."

"What do you mean?"

"I'm a dominant. A sexual dominant. This is something I practice. I have for years. I didn't want to scare you off. But I should have been open with you as soon as I found out you had some desire to be spanked. It's more serious than that for me— not just some bedroom play to spice things up. I go to the clubs.

The Pleasure Dome, here in Seattle, in particular. I have friends there. A community. That's where I met my best friend, Alec, a few years ago."

Were they really lying there in his bed, having this conversation? But she was fascinated.

"It doesn't frighten me, if that's what you're worried about."

"Good. I'm glad to hear it. Do you have questions about it? About what I do?"

Where to start? She'd done some reading. A lot, actually. But she wasn't sure how the titillating fiction she'd read translated to real life.

"I don't know very much about what that means, to be a sexual dominant. The kind of person who goes to those clubs. But I've gathered from stories I've read that it means something a bit different for each person."

"That's true."

"What does it mean to you, Dante?"

"For me it means that I am honest with myself about what my desires are. Desires I've been aware of having since I was a teenager, and in odd ways even earlier. There was that small thrill in playing pirates as a kid. In tying someone to a tree. Telling other kids to walk the plank, or whatever the game was. There are a lot of people who are into the BDSM scene who have similar stories. It doesn't mean we sexualized these things as children, necessarily; that usually comes later. But as I said, that thrill was there all along."

"I think I had some of those same experiences early on. I know just what you mean."

It was a revelation to her. It explained so much about the way she'd perceived certain things in her life.

"A lot of people let it end there," he said with a shrug. "Maybe have an active fantasy life. But for me, it's something I actively seek out, although I don't require it."

"But you prefer it. To have your sex with some . . . I'm not sure what to call it."

"Power play. Power exchange. Because it *is* an exchange. It's not simply about me as a dominant, a top, wanting to spank you, or whatever the particular desire may be. A BDSM scene is not a solo act. The bottom's needs, their power, comes into play every bit as much as my own. More, actually. That's where the real thrill is. The real power."

"I've heard that term, 'bottom.' Submissive. Is that what I am, then? Because I like the . . . spanking?"

"I don't think you have to label yourself, if you don't want to. You definitely have submissive tendencies. I saw it in you right away. I felt it from the moment I first touched you. But how far that goes remains to be seen. If you decide to pursue it."

She nodded. Her head was spinning a bit. It was a relief in some way to have a name to put on her desires. A way to identify it. A way in which other people identified similar yearnings. It made her feel less alone.

"Thank you, Dante."

"For what?"

"For . . . allowing me to explore this. For making it so good for me."

He grinned then, a grin full of dimples and boyish charm. Strange, how he could be so utterly masculine, so dominant, and still have that boyish aspect shining through. It was part of his charm. Devastating.

"Dante . . ."

"Yes?"

"I'd like to do it again."

"Ah, so would I. Right now."

He ran his hand into her hair, his fingers grasping, pulling just tight enough that she had the sense once more of his absolute command over her. Pleasure ran through her, a shiver of light and heat.

He pressed against her again. He was still hard. Her sex pooled with desire, just thinking about him pushing into her. When he thumbed her nipple her insides clenched.

"Dante . . . come on."

He chuckled. "Soon enough, beautiful girl."

She knew then that he would tease her, draw it out. Control the pacing.

Yes.

She pulled in a gasping breath when he pinched her nipple, pleasure racing through her like a lovely shock.

"Have you ever come just from this?" he asked her, gravel in his tone again. "Just from having your nipples played with?"

"No." God, she could barely breathe already. Just to have him ask her this!

"Shall we try?"

All she could do was groan as he got up on his knees beside her so he could use both hands. His naked thighs were strong, muscular, covered in a bit of soft, dark hair. And between them his cock was a rigid shaft of gorgeous golden flesh. She couldn't believe that he was hard again. The sight of it, that solid flesh, made her mouth water. But she was too distracted by his hands on her breasts.

He was caressing the flesh: the undersides, the rise at the tops of her breasts, tracing the outline. Keeping away from the nipples. They ached with the need to be touched. Tortured. But he kept feathering his fingertips everywhere but there.

"Dante." She arched, her body surging into his hands.

"No, Kara. Hold still. Breathe. Relax into it."

She almost wanted to whimper. But she loved the authority in his tone too much not to do as he said.

She pulled in a breath. He kept stroking her skin. Unbearable. But wonderful. Her nipples throbbed. Her sex throbbed until it hurt, engorged and full of need. She wanted to squeeze her thighs together to ease the ache. But she bit her lip and held still.

Finally, he brushed his fingertips over both nipples, and she gasped.

"Good?" he asked.

"Oh yes."

"I don't want you to worry about it. About whether or not you can come. I want you to simply enjoy it. To focus on nothing but the pleasure. We'll see what happens. Just let it happen, Kara."

His golden gaze was on her breasts. His tongue darted out to lick his lip, and she wanted to put her own tongue there. But she didn't dare move.

He brushed her nipples again, the lightest of touches. Pleasure was like a slowly burning flame, building and building, a low, hot pulse beat inside her. Unbelievable how intense it was, simply from him touching her breasts. Being so much the center of all his attention. She couldn't remember any man ever focusing on her this way. She didn't know how she'd gone without it.

She kept her gaze on his face. He was the most beautiful man she had ever seen. And that only added to her desire.

He kept at it, his fingertips soft, but eventually her nipples were so hard that even the smallest touch felt like an abrasion. But lovely, wonderful. Sensation rose, intensified with each caress. She moaned.

"Is it building?" he asked.

"Yes. Yes . . ."

"Good."

He pinched her, suddenly, hard, and her body arched up off the bed.

"Oh!"

The pain was followed by a flood of pleasure.

"You like that, don't you, Kara?"

"Yes. Please, Dante. I want more."

He smiled, pinched again. And again, her body rose from the bed, pleasure like an electric current. Shocking. Leaving her tingling all over. Intensified when he used one hand to hold her down on the mattress.

She loved that sensation of being controlled. She couldn't think about why. It made no sense to her. But she was too lost in it to really question it. All she knew was that it was *good*.

He leaned in and whispered, "I'm going to take them into my mouth now." And he did just that, touching the wet tip of his tongue to one nipple, then the other, before sucking the hard flesh in.

His mouth was hot, silky. Her nipples were rock-hard. Pleasure was even harder, like something solid moving through her. Her sex pulsed deep inside, a strange sensation, unlike anything she'd ever felt before. Some odd combination of him teasing her nipples and the sense of being under his hands. Under his command.

He kept at it, sucking, biting, pinching the undersides of her breasts. She didn't know how long it went on—it could have been an hour. Her skin was damp all over, her breath a panting rasp in her ears. Sensation crested in her body. Unbelievable.

She was going to come.

"Dante . . . I'm so close . . ."

He sucked harder, pain and pleasure mingling until she didn't know where one began and the other ended.

"Oh God . . ."

Her body hovered on that exquisite edge.

"Please, Dante . . ."

He lifted his head and murmured, "You've done very well, beautiful girl. Come now."

His mouth went to her nipple once more and latched on. And his hand went between her thighs, taking her clitoris and rolling it between his fingers.

"Oh God!"

Her climax shot through her, hard, intense. Almost too much to take. She yelled, her entire body arching, writhing in pleasure so intense she could barely stand it.

She was still shivering with it when he climbed onto her, his sheathed cock slipping between her thighs and inside her.

She felt helpless beneath him as he began to pump into her. Beautifully so.

His thrusting cock was a solid shaft of flesh. Exactly what she needed. And as he had the night before, he set a hard, driving pace, pummeling into her.

Their hips crashed. The pleasure of his body on hers was almost as great as his cock driving sensation deeper, deeper. Until she felt herself begin to clench once more, another climax rippling through her.

"Jesus, girl . . . you are so beautiful. So damn good . . . Ah!"

He shuddered, his mouth latching onto her throat as he came. And she held on, her arms around his neck.

She tried to think of what they'd talked about. About how his command of her affected her, made the sex so intense. But she was too worn out, too spent. She closed her eyes, and with him softening inside her, she drifted off.

four

Dante opened his eyes, peering at the clock on his nightstand. They'd slept for a while. It was early afternoon now. And he was starving.

"Kara."

She didn't stir.

He watched her sleep, as he'd done earlier. Why was he so fascinated with this woman?

She was gorgeous. He loved her lean, toned body, her endlessly long legs. The flawless curve of her ass. Her pale, smooth skin. He loved her long, silky hair, how the light made it look like it was woven with gold and bronze.

Jesus, he was a poet suddenly. What the hell was up with him?

He ran a hand over his beard stubble, thinking. Or trying not to think, maybe. He needed to shut his brain down and enjoy her being there. In his house. In his bed. It was Saturday. Maybe he could keep her there all weekend. Fuck her again. Spank her . . . maybe more.

His cock rose, but he was too hungry to give in to it. Food first. Then sex. If she was up for it.

He'd make sure she was.

"Kara, hey." He touched her cheek, and her lids fluttered, then closed. "Time to wake up."

"Hmm, what?"

She looked up at him, her hazel eyes still half-lidded. Something sweet about her, all sleepy like this. Vulnerable. As vulnerable as she was when he was spanking her.

"I need to eat. You've used up all my reserves," he teased her.

"I'm pretty sure you used most of it yourself." She yawned, stretched her arms over her head, the sheet falling away from her superb breasts. Her nipples were hardening, going dark, he couldn't help but notice.

Food.

"Either way, I'm about ready to pass out," he said. "Up with you."

He rolled her onto her side and smacked her ass, making her laugh.

"If we're going somewhere, I could really use a shower, if that's okay," she said, sitting upright on the edge of the bed.

"I'm cooking."

"Really?" She looked at him over her shoulder.

God, her eyelashes were the longest he'd ever seen.

Stop it. Get yourself under control, buddy.

"Yes, really. What, you don't think I can cook?"

"You do seem awfully used to people waiting on you."

"I am." He crossed his arms over his chest. "But I also make the best pancakes you've ever had."

"That sounds like a challenge."

"Try me."

She grinned at him. He didn't want to think about why that made him so damn happy. Okay, maybe not happy. Cheerful.

Something . . .

Something he was not going to think about right now.

He stood up, facing away from her to distract himself. He got a pair of pajama pants out of his dresser and pulled them on. "We can shower later. Are you hungry?"

Oh yeah, to have her in the shower . . .

He had a thing for the shower. Seeing a woman wet, the water running over her skin. The steam rising around him while he bent her over and slid into her . . . He had a great shower for sex. It was big enough to throw a party in. All smooth, pale granite with a bench seat, three showerheads, a vertical row of body jets. He was getting hard again thinking about Kara in his shower, her wet body . . .

"I'm glad you're planning to feed me," she said, bringing him out of his shower fantasy. "I could eat a horse."

"Pancakes will have to do. Here, this will be more comfortable than your dress."

He handed her the top to his pajamas, which he never wore. She slipped the navy blue flannel over her head. It was enormous on her, the hem brushing her thighs, the front opening in a deep vee between her breasts. She looked a hell of a lot better in it than he did. She looked amazing. Sexy as hell.

"Warm enough?" he asked her, trying to remember that they had to eat.

"Yes. Fine." She came up beside him. She was still tall, even without her heels on. Her bare legs looked especially naked to him from under the hem of the pajama top.

"To the kitchen, wench. You're going to help me."

"Bossy, aren't you?"

He looked down at her, locking his gaze with hers. "Yes. Yes, I am."

She smiled. But he saw her features go a little soft at this small reminder of the nature of their relationship.

Not that it was a *relationship*. No, he just meant the dynamics of the sex. Yes, that was it. That was all it ever was for him. It was better that way.

"I hope you like real Vermont maple syrup. Come on."

He led the way across the apartment, the dark wood floors cool beneath his bare feet. The afternoon light shone through the tall windows that opened up an entire wall to the city, and another to a view of Elliott Bay.

"What an incredible view," Kara said, following him.

"That's why I bought the place. Mostly, anyway." He would show her the shower later, when they were done eating. "I like to see the water during the day. And the city at night."

"You get it all here, it being a corner unit. Wow, your kitchen is amazing."

They moved behind the tall bar, and Kara ran her hand over the black and gray granite counter. The sleek black cabinets and brushed steel appliances were nice, he supposed, but he'd always wanted something a little warmer.

"I've been thinking about remodeling, actually," he told her.

"I don't know why you would. This is gorgeous."

He shrugged, loading up the coffeemaker and switching it on. "It's not really my taste. It's a little cold, don't you think?"

"It's beautiful. But I can see what you mean, I suppose. It's all very slick. What's your dream kitchen, Dante?" she asked while he pulled ingredients from the cupboard and the refrigerator, a big mixing bowl and his hand blender.

"I like wood. Something more organic. I like the modern aesthetic, too, but it has to be balanced."

He measured the flour, broke eggs into the bowl, added vanilla and the last few ingredients. He handed her the bowl. "Here, go ahead and mix this while I heat the griddle."

She took the bowl from him and turned on the mixer. They were quiet while it ran, the kitchen filled with the low hum of the implement and the warm scents of the vanilla and the coffee. With some warm sense of familiarity.

He was so comfortable with her. Not that he was ever really uncomfortable with anyone. That wasn't in him. But there was some extra degree of comfort with her.

He shook his head, pulled the syrup from the cabinet, putting it in a pan of hot water to warm. He got plates out, flatware, mugs, pulled a pair of linen place mats from a drawer. "You can set us up on the counter," he said, trying to get some sense of control back. Trying not to be so damn distracted by her long legs, the way her hair was a little wild, swinging around her high cheekbones as she moved.

He poured the batter onto the griddle and watched them bubble, flipping the pancakes onto a plate when they were ready and pouring coffee into the mugs.

"You really seem to know what you're doing," Kara commented, picking the mug up and sipping.

"I told you I like to cook. And I *always* know what I'm doing."

He looked up at her and she grinned. She was sitting on one of the barstools, her elbows on the counter. She was a little disheveled, her cheeks flushed. He liked her like this. And he liked that she wasn't the kind of woman who got all tongue-tied after sex. Made it more important than it needed to be. She was relaxed with him.

Fucking perfect.

He really had to stop thinking that. No one was perfect. He wasn't looking for perfect.

He wasn't looking for anything. Never had been. His experience with Erin had taught him well years ago. He wasn't capable of being responsible for someone else. Not like that. No, all he wanted was the temporary responsibility that came with the BDSM play. And when the evening or weekend or even a few months was over, everyone would pack up and go home. But he could enjoy this while it was happening. He intended to.

He finished the batch of pancakes and loaded up their plates, sat down next to Kara at the bar. She dug in right away. He liked that, too, that she wasn't one of those girls who ate like a bird—or pretended to. He liked even the lushness of her mouth as she ate.

"This is so good, Dante. I don't know when the last time was I had pancakes. I never had them as a kid, so it doesn't occur to me very often."

"You never had pancakes as a kid?"

She shrugged, taking another bite and chewing for a few moments. "I just . . . My parents weren't very . . . They weren't into being parents. My mom didn't really cook or . . . I had a strange childhood."

"You seemed pretty normal in high school."

"Did I? That's good, I suppose. My parents weren't weirdos or anything. They were just absorbed in their work. Focused. Maybe to the exclusion of anything else. I just think . . . Their minds work at an amazing pace, and they don't know how to slow down. They're brilliant, both of them."

"That's where you get it from, then."

Her cheeks flushed. "No, I didn't. They really are geniuses, my mother and my father. I didn't inherit the genius IQ. A huge disappointment for them." She put her fork down, wiped her mouth very carefully.

"That must have been a difficult environment to grow up in." She looked at him. Looking to see if he pitied her, he thought. He didn't. "Sorry. I didn't mean to hit a sore spot."

"No. It's okay. I don't mind telling. Not like I usually do. I mean, this is not stuff I normally talk about . . . God, I don't know what I mean."

He put down his fork. "Kara, last night was your first experience with pain play. Sometimes that can open a person up. It happens a lot. You might feel more vulnerable today. It can make you connect with old issues. Some people even cry."

She shook her head. "It's not like that for me. I don't feel bad or scared. I just feel . . . relieved. Released. As if I've let something go. That opening up, I guess. It's making me feel lighter. Does that make sense?"

"Yeah. It does. I'm glad you're feeling good about it. Because that means you'll probably want to do it again." He grinned at her, and she smiled back. Gorgeous smile. "But let me know if that changes."

"I will."

Kara still didn't know why she'd started to tell Dante about her parents, her childhood. It wasn't like her. Not with a guy. And especially not after Jake. Opening up with him had chased him away. Of course, the very thing that Jake had judged her for, Dante was obviously into. Still, the emotional stuff was different. That was the kind of thing she'd talk to Lucie—her best friend—about, but not to a man.

"Dante . . . I'm sorry."

He set his coffee mug down. "For what?"

"For going on about my history with my parents. My issues with them. I'm sure it's the last thing you want to hear. I'm sorry I'm being such a girl."

He grinned. His dimples were back, making her want to reach out and touch them. "I like that you're a girl."

"But it's not me. We really don't have to do this post-sex discussion stuff. This getting-to-know-each-other thing. This can be just sex. I'm fine with that."

"Okay." He was looking wary, as if he didn't quite believe her.

"Really, Dante."

He nodded. "Okay. But I'm good with the talking. It's part of being a good dominant, if nothing else. Even if it's just a little spanking, nothing too hard-core. It helps me to know how your head works. How you might respond to different things."

"So this stuff, what we're doing . . ."

"BDSM play," he finished for her.

"Yes. Some of it is psychological? Is that what you're saying?"

"Most of it is psychological." He chewed the last bite of his pancakes. "Think about it. That sense of release. Of relief. I haven't seen you for years, but just talking to you for a few minutes I can see that you're probably very much in control in your everyday life. Confident. Competent. Someone who handles everything. The person others come to for advice, or when something needs to get done. Am I correct?"

"Yes. Absolutely."

"Giving yourself over to me is a natural outlet for you. Not only giving yourself over to me, but to the process. You don't have to make any decisions. You don't have to *do* anything. You just lie back and take it all in. You seemed to get that almost immediately. Which says to me that you've really needed it."

"Maybe." She paused, trying to process all of the information, how it applied to her. "But a big part of it is also that you're so into this stuff. You didn't judge me. Not for one second."

He nodded. "Which goes back to the psychology." He paused, lowered his voice. "Why is it so important that you not be judged, Kara?"

She froze. She didn't want to talk to him about this stuff. About the shame her relationship with Jake had left behind. The shame she'd felt so often growing up with her brilliant, over-achieving parents.

Never good enough.

Except that here, with him, she felt good enough. For the first time.

It was too much to take in. And this was casual sex. She had to stop thinking about it in such serious terms. He'd called it "play." That was all it was.

"Okay," he said after a minute. "You don't have to tell me. I have a tendency to make demands. But I can dial it back."

He grinned at her, and she had the sense he was doing it to make her more comfortable.

"You're a nice man, Dante."

It was true. He was a good man. One of the best she'd ever met. She'd known it in high school. He'd only seemed to have grown more into it.

"Except when I'm being mean," he teased.

"Not mean, really. Just . . . wicked."

"But you like that."

He reached out and brushed his fingers over her wrist, picked it up and laid a soft kiss there. Bit into her flesh, just enough that she could feel the sharp edge of his teeth.

"I do," she said, trying to keep the sudden tremor of lust out of her voice, and not succeeding.

She was burning up inside again already, her sex needy once more. And she could see the desire stark on his face.

"Have you had enough to eat, Kara?"

"For now."

His tone dropped an octave. "Then why don't I put you in the shower?"

He didn't wait for her to answer. He took her hand, slipped his other arm around her waist and led her to the bathroom, one of the few walled rooms, which took up much of the back wall of the loft apartment.

He stripped the pajama top off her and she stood naked, her

nipples hardening with the cool air and excitement as he reached into the enormous shower stall and turned on the water. He stripped his pajama pants off, opened a drawer in the modern maple vanity and pulled out a string of condom packets.

"Oh, I hope you intend to use those," she told him, her sex going damp.

He grinned, all strong white teeth and flashing dimples and desire soft around his lush mouth. She glanced down, found him hard, ready. She shivered.

"I intend to do a lot of things to you in there," he said, pulling her close.

He bent to kiss her, his mouth tasting of hot coffee and maple syrup. Sweet and strong, just like him. And God, the man could kiss. His lips were soft, yet demanding. His tongue slipping in and taking over her mouth. Making her shudder with desire, small ripples running over her body. His chest was a hard plane of muscle against her breasts. His abs were just as solid. And his cock was a rigid shaft pressing against her stomach.

He pulled his mouth from hers long enough to get them into the shower. And then it was all wet heat as water fell, seemingly from everywhere at once. All she knew was that they were soaking wet, their bodies plastered together. Slippery skin and the scent of citrus and something darker . . . the musk he smelled of, she realized. His soap. Even the scent of it was making her body heat, her sex throb with need.

He pulled back then, holding her at arm's length.

"Christ, you're beautiful like this, Kara," he told her. "I love this. To see your wet skin. The water all over you. It's another fetish of mine, the shower. The water itself." He ran a finger between her breasts, down the center of her stomach. "Wet skin. I should have put you in here in one of my white dress shirts. I really love that. To watch the fabric go opaque . . ." He touched the tip of one of her nipples with his fingertip. "But this is good, too. Seeing you harden. Seeing the pink turn darker when you become more excited."

She pulled in a tight breath. She loved to hear him say these things to her.

"Dante . . ."

"What is it?"

"Come on . . ."

He laughed, a low, sexy sound. "Come on, what?"

"Come on and really touch me. I want to feel your hands on me. I want to feel how different it is in the water."

He laughed again, a low chuckle. "Fucking perfect," he murmured as he cupped both her breasts in his hands, sliding them over her skin.

"Oh, that's good . . ." She closed her eyes, giving herself over to the sensation.

It *was* different. Not that she'd never had sex in the shower before. But she'd never focused on the slickness before. On the difference. Not with any other man.

Dante made her see things differently. Feel things in a whole new light. And it was mind-blowing.

"Yeah, I like that," he said. "Keep your eyes closed, Kara. Don't move."

She melted all over at the authority in his voice. At being told what to do.

Maybe he was right about what it did to her head. But she

couldn't think about it. Desire was like a tide, pouring through her in a drenching wave as the water ran over her skin.

"Stand there, yes . . . and spread your thighs for me. Good girl."

A small shiver at that.

Good girl.

She couldn't think now about why she loved hearing those words so much.

Then she couldn't think at all as she felt a spray of water against her cleft.

"Oh . . ."

"Hold still, Kara," he said again, and she schooled herself to stop squirming.

She let her lashes flutter open for one moment, saw him kneeling in front of her, the shining chrome shower wand in one hand, a bar of soap in the other. And as she closed her eyes once more, he began to wash her.

She'd never experienced anything like it. He soaped her up with his hand, his fingers slippery. Lovely. Massaging her pussy lips until she thought she would die of sensation. She had to bite her lip in order to keep still for him. Her breath was a heavy, panting rasp in her chest.

"You like this," he said. "I can feel your flesh swelling under my touch. I can see how plump your clit is. So pretty."

He massaged her clitoris, and she gasped.

"Ah!"

"Shh, Kara. Be still. Be quiet for me. You can do it."

The warm spray of water over her cleft then, and the pleasure was like silk. Sleek, sinuous, shimmering through her body.

She took in a breath, held it as he moved the water away and went back to work with his slippery hand.

"Spread wider," he ordered, and she did it without question.

Her mind was going to some misty place, she realized. Sort of emptying out. Going quiet. Like a soft, white noise in her head.

"Good, Kara," Dante told her. "Hold still now."

Water at the apex of her thighs again, but sharper this time, the hard pummeling of a massage cycle aimed right at her clitoris.

She had to lock her legs, had to hold back her climax.

"Do you need to come?" he asked her.

"Yes . . . now!"

"Not now, Kara. Hold on to it. Hold yourself at that edge. Hold it until I tell you I want you to come."

"God . . ."

But she swallowed, nodded. Steeled herself against the on-slaught of sensation.

"Think about everything you're feeling. Separate it out," he instructed, his voice gone soft. "The water from the shower over-head. My hand on you. My voice. The texture of the soap. Have you ever felt anything so slippery in your life? I don't think I have. The soap and how unbelievably wet your pussy is right now. Incredible."

She tried to do as he said. In her mind, she took a moment to recognize each sensation by itself. It seemed to make it all build, multiply. She took in a deep breath, held it in her lungs.

"Good girl, Kara. That's it. Think about the pleasure build-ing inside you. And hold it back. Hold it together. For *me*, Kara."

"Yes," she whispered. "For you."

"Ah, that's exactly where I want you."

A rise in pleasure at the tone of his voice. Knowing she was doing what he wanted. What he demanded of her.

"I'm going to let you come in a moment," he said.

"Oh, please . . ."

He ran his fingers into her slit, the soap making his touch unbearably slick as he moved his hand up and down. Faster and faster.

"Dante!"

"Hold it, Kara."

"God . . ."

He kept rubbing, his soap-slicked hand sending desire through her, piercing her. Amazing how sharp the pleasure felt against the softness of his soapy fingers. Her climax was like a wall of pleasure, waiting to crash down on her.

"Dante, please. Please," she keened.

"Almost, my beautiful girl."

His fingers slid over the hard, needy nub, over and over. Then he paused. One breath, then two. He pinched it, hard.

"Oh!"

"It hurts, doesn't it, Kara?"

"Yes," she gasped.

"What else?" he asked, command in his tone again.

"It feels . . . so good . . ."

He pinched harder, tugging at the same time.

"Ah, God, Dante. I can't . . ."

"Take a breath, Kara."

She did, pulling the steamy air into her lungs, her body poised, aching.

"Now, Kara. Come for me now."

His fingers started that lovely slide again, and she came almost as soon as he told her she could. It was like white light shimmering through her, arcing into her. Shocking her.

She called out as she fell, and he caught her in his arms. She was still coming. Shivering. His fingers kept working between her thighs.

He whispered into her ear, "Good girl. My beautiful girl. Good, Kara."

When she stopped shaking so hard, she realized she was sitting in his lap on the floor of the shower. Her arms were wound tight around his neck. And his arms were strong around her body.

She was still trembling a little, the last of her climax a series of tiny shudders deep inside. She felt wonderful. Except for the small portion of her brain that was telling her this was far too good. Too good to last. Too good for her.

The sex.

Dante.

Don't think. Don't think.

She barely *could* think. Her mind was too numb to process an idea fully.

"Hey. You okay, Kara? What's going on in there?" Dante asked her.

"Yes. Yes. Fine."

As long as she didn't go to that place, where she wasn't good enough.

"You're more than fine," he told her, his voice low and full of smoke. "You're amazing. You came so damn hard. I loved it. That you just fell apart like that."

God, he said the most perfect thing, exactly what she needed to hear. That approval clear in his tone.

"But I need to fuck you now, Kara." He took her hand and pulled it down between them, wrapped her fingers around his thick shaft. "Do you feel how hard I am for you? Come on, stroke it."

She did, moving her hand up the length of him. He was big, his flesh heavy, swollen. She licked her lips, another spark of desire lighting her up like a series of tiny fireworks going off in her system. She loved touching him. Loved the way he felt in her hand. There was some sort of power there. Dizzying, as she felt him pulse in her palm. The power was in being able to bring him pleasure. In pleasing him with her own.

"Ah, so good," he murmured, his hands moving over her skin. "But I need to be inside you."

He stood, picking her up and taking her with him. He took a condom from the packet he'd set on one of the built-in shelves in the pale granite of the big shower, and, tearing it with his teeth, he pulled out the latex sheath and slid it over his erection.

She could not believe how utterly sensual even this was to her, seeing him handle his cock so deftly. Seeing how hard he was.

"Spread for me, Kara. Yes, just like that."

She moved her thighs apart, and he grabbed one of her legs and wrapped it around his waist, opening her up. She held on to his strong shoulders, and as the water flowed over her body and his, he pushed right into her.

"Ah, Dante."

"You feel so good. Jesus, Kara."

Pleasure was as liquid as the fall of the shower: that hot, that sinuous. It moved through her body, undulating, then building as he thrust into her, over and over. His mouth was on hers, kissing her, nipping at her lips. And every driving thrust of his hips, every bite of his sharp teeth, was like a small orgasm in itself.

The sensation of him sliding into her, then pulling out, was exquisite. Overwhelming. That and her body still buzzing with her climax. Her head buzzing with the things she had learned about herself, about the power exchange he'd tried to explain to her, but which she was just coming to really understand.

His skin was impossibly soft under her hands and she gripped his shoulders, her nails biting into the skin. She needed it, somehow. It was too intense; she couldn't help it. She couldn't help her rasping breath, the arching of her hips into his, wanting to take him deeper.

As the steam rose around them, enveloping them in its warm embrace, they both came. They called each other's names, their hips clashing together. It was all need and shattering fulfillment. Wet flesh and a pure, startling pleasure. And Kara let it all go— her body, her mind—and sank into it. Into Dante. Let herself, for the first time, become utterly lost.

five

Kara sat behind the desk in her office, sipping from the extra tall, double-shot latte she'd needed that morning. She was tired—exhausted—and a little sore from her weekend with Dante.

Dante . . .

God, the man was insatiable. She had been, too. They'd barely gotten out of bed the entire weekend—or the shower, where they'd had sex at least four times. Dante really did have a thing for the water. She didn't mind. She'd loved it, in fact. Loved the clean scent of his soap, the steamy air. He'd taught her to really tune in to sensation, and the water was incredible on her skin. Even showering at home this morning after he'd dropped her off had had a newly sensual aura to it.

It had been the most amazing weekend, and when they'd woken up early this morning she hadn't wanted it to be over. But it was Monday, and time for work. Not that she'd be able to concentrate on a single thing. She was sleep deprived, worn-out, sore in all the best places. And thinking of Dante.

He hadn't been ready for her to leave, either. That had been clear enough when he'd woken her at five thirty to have sex. Slipping into her while they were both groggy, half-asleep, his hips pumping until they'd both come, gasping their pleasure into the still morning air.

No matter how many times they'd done it over the weekend, he was still hard for her. And there was something she loved about that predawn sex, when they were both still half-asleep. He was irresistible, with his mussed hair, the dark, scratchy stubble on his chin. It made him seem more male. More primal. There was something almost surreal about it. Almost romantic.

Don't go there.

She sipped her coffee, letting the heat relax her a little. She wasn't a romantic kind of girl. The last of that had been killed off with Jake. No matter how hot the sex was with Dante, she would remember that it was just that: sex.

The hottest, most intense sex she'd ever had.

Still, nothing more than sex.

She was fine with that. Just an intense chemical connection. No strings. They'd known each other for so long that it was comfortable, too, even if they hadn't kept in touch over the years. He was familiar enough that it didn't feel as if she were sleeping with a complete stranger. Friendly but casual, nothing more. But she was glad Dante had said he'd call her today, that they'd see each other again.

She sank back in her chair, taking another slug of her coffee, and stared out the window, which overlooked downtown Seattle.

It was raining a little. She didn't mind it. It gave her a sense of being cocooned, somehow. Looking down, she could see umbrellas moving down the sidewalk, the people beneath them hidden away.

Why did this familiar view look different to her today? Why did she feel so different? Was it that psychological fallout Dante had talked to her about? She didn't feel bad. Just . . . changed a little.

She ran her thumbs up the sides of her thick paper cup, enjoying the heat. Remembering the heat of Dante's hands on her skin . . .

Her sex went damp, and she crossed her legs, trying to ease the ache there.

Dante . . .

She could picture his deep brown gaze, his eyes so intense she could barely stand to look into them, sometimes, but compelled to at the same time. His mouth, which was really too lush for a man. She liked the way it softened his angular features, loved the contrast of it. And those authoritative orders issuing from such a soft-looking mouth . . . It was too good.

She remembered the way he used that mouth, too. All over her skin, between her thighs.

She sighed, her body heating. And jumped when her cell phone rang.

She smoothed a hand over her hair, as if someone could see her, before picking it up.

"Hello?"

"Kara."

His voice was deep, rich. Sexy as hell.

"Dante. Good morning."

"Yes, it is. How are you?"

"Tired, but good."

"Sore?"

"Yes, a little."

"But you like it." It was a statement, not a question. She liked that, too.

"Yes." She laughed. "I like it a lot."

"Good, then you're still interested in doing it again?"

"I might be."

"Oh, it's far too late to play coy with me. I watched you come into my hands just this morning."

Her body went blazing hot, simply hearing him say it.

"Dante . . ."

"You're slipping down into that space even now, aren't you, beautiful girl? But I won't take it any further. I know you have to work."

She pulled in a breath, tried to calm herself. "Are you at work now, too?"

"Yes. First day at the new job. Nice office. I think I'm going to like it here. And there are some great places to eat in this neighborhood. Maybe we can meet for lunch this week. Someplace with a long tablecloth. I have this fantasy about getting you off under the table. Someplace just a little public. What do you think of that?"

Oh God, she was soaking wet.

"I think that's . . . very interesting."

He chuckled, sounding pleased.

"How far away do you work?" he asked. "I've just realized I

never asked the name of the firm you work for. We were too busy with other things."

"It's—" Her main line buzzed. "I'm sorry, Dante. There's a call coming in on my work phone. Can you hold on a moment?"

"That's okay. I'll leave you with that thought and call you tonight. I have a meeting in a few minutes."

"Okay."

"Have a good day. And, Kara. Think about that lunch."

"Mmm, I will."

They hung up and she picked up her work line.

"Hi, Ruby. What's up?" she asked her secretary.

"I'm supposed to remind you there's a meeting in about five minutes in the big conference room."

"Ah, I'd forgotten about it. I'm a bit slow this morning. Thanks, Ruby. I'll be right there."

She gulped down a little more of her latte, flipped open the compact mirror she kept in her desk to touch up her lipstick, stood and straightened her charcoal-gray pencil skirt. Time to forget about Dante and focus on work.

She opened her office door and made her way down the hall, her heels clacking on the hardwood floor. The firm of Kelleher, Landers and Tate was in a beautiful, classic brick building with high windows and all the gorgeous old architecture preserved. She appreciated the ornate crown molding, the wide-planked wood floors, and that they always furnished the office in antiques, or at least antique reproductions, making it look like something out of the 1940s, if it weren't for the computers on every desk. It made for a cozier work environment than the too-often sterile offices that were so common everywhere else.

As she walked into the conference room she remembered they were introducing a new junior partner today. She'd been a little annoyed about it last week. She thought it would have been more fair to hire from within the firm. Not that she was eligible herself; she hadn't been there long enough. But there were several people who should be. Theresa Jackson had been there for years, and worked plenty of overtime. And Gary Auerbach, too. Apparently the new guy was some hotshot they'd stolen from another firm, which was why, she supposed, they hadn't told anyone who it was yet.

She nodding a greeting to the other attorneys already present and found a seat at the enormous oak table. Ruby came in right behind her and stood against one wall, a notepad in her hand. She smiled at Ruby, who winked back. Ruby was the youngest of the secretaries and hadn't been with them for long, but she was amazingly efficient. She worked for several of the attorneys in the office, but she was always available when Kara needed anything—one of those incredibly capable people. Kara liked her; they'd taken to having lunch together now and then. She was good company.

Kara took the water pitcher from the center of the table and poured herself a glass, sipped it. And nearly spit it out when the new junior partner walked into the room with her boss, Lyle Kelleher.

Dante.

She took another sip of water, trying not to cough and attract attention to herself.

Holy mother of . . .

She choked, trying too hard to swallow, and Dante caught her eye. He raised an eyebrow, but other than that his face remained calm.

She could not believe this.

Breathe, Kara!

She took in a breath, watching him as he was seated at the other end of the long table.

Next to her Theresa whispered, "You okay, Kara?"

"What? Yes. I'm fine. Thanks."

But inside she was absolutely on fire. Burning with equal amounts of lust and anxiety.

He *couldn't* be the new junior partner. She wasn't supposed to *like* the new junior partner. He was the enemy. The man who'd taken the job away from two people whom she respected and who had deserved this promotion.

She certainly wasn't supposed to be sleeping with the new junior partner.

What the hell was she going to do?

She glanced at Theresa, whose face remained calm. But Theresa always seemed calm; it was one of the things that made her such a good attorney. The only thing betraying her serene expression and neat-as-a-pin appearance was the sharp glitter in her brown eyes and a tiny trembling in her perfect chignon.

Kara was shivering inside. She twisted her hands together in her lap and tried to take a deep breath. Her mind was going a hundred miles an hour.

It couldn't be Dante. But Lyle was guiding him to a seat right next to his, at the head of the table. The older man was smiling, looking pleased, bobbing his gray head as he exchanged a few quiet words with *the new junior partner.*

Shit.

Everyone else filed in and sat, and Lyle rose to his feet. He was close to seventy, but still stood ramrod straight, an elegant, powerful man. "I'd like to introduce you all to Dante De Matteo, the newest junior partner at Kelleher, Landers and Tate."

Everyone applauded as Dante stood and smiled to the staff. Kara tried to smile back, but knew her face was frozen. Dante glanced at her, then quickly away. His expression revealed nothing. Surely he must be as bowled over as she was?

Lyle went on. "Dante has an astonishing track record for a man of his age and experience. We were lucky to convince him to join us here. I'm sure you'll all do your best to welcome him, to help him acclimate to our firm. And I'm sure you'll all be as pleased with his presence among us as I am. We expect great things from this young man. Big things." Lyle smiled indulgently.

Oh yes, big things, where Dante was concerned . . .

God, she shouldn't be thinking this way at work! But she couldn't help herself. Even as the resentment over the position going to someone other than Theresa or Gary filtered through her system, as well as the shock of seeing Dante in her office, desire ran thick in her veins.

He looked wonderful in his dark gray suit. His shirt was a stark white, his tie a rich, glowing amber, making his eyes an almost liquid gold.

The man sure cleaned up good. Better than good.

She crossed her legs, trying to ignore the sudden sharp ache between them.

This was not acceptable. She could not lust over a man she worked with. She certainly couldn't see him anymore. That was a recipe for disaster. And he was a junior partner, which meant, basically, that she was working under him.

Shit again.

She had to calm down. Figure this out. She had to get back to her office and call Lucie to talk it out with her. She wasn't the kind of woman who habitually told her best friend every detail of her sex life, but this was more than she could handle on her own.

A disaster. That was what this was.

Lyle finished his speech; then the other partners, Edward Tate and Charles Landers, each got up and extolled Dante's virtues before the meeting broke up and everyone got up to introduce themselves and shake his hand.

Kara hung back, clenching her fists at her sides to keep from twisting her fingers together like some anxious old woman.

Ruby came up beside her. "I know you're angry Gary or Theresa didn't get this," she said, keeping her voice down, "but you seem really upset, Kara."

"What? I'm fine. It's just . . . Yes, I'm upset. For them."

Ruby nodded sympathetically, her brown spiral curls brushing her cheeks. "Maybe he'll crash and burn and the bosses will see their mistake."

Kara shook her head, her gaze on Dante, who was chatting confidently with the staff. "No. I don't think so."

"Are you okay?" Ruby asked.

"Of course." She turned to look at her. "I guess I'd better go say hello." She smiled wanly and moved toward the small crowd gathered around Dante.

He caught her gaze as she approached, flashed her a brief smile.

So, he was playing it cool. A good idea, she knew. Still, there was a small knot in her stomach. Something in her that wanted him to acknowledge her in some way.

Don't be silly.

She couldn't afford to be. This was work. Her career. One her parents had wanted for her more than she had herself, but she'd sweated through school and the bar exam to achieve it. And she wasn't about to get silly—or risk her job—over a man.

Theresa, standing next to Dante, grabbed Kara's hand. "Dante, this is Kara Crawford."

"It's nice to see you," he said smoothly.

She had to swallow, hard, taking his cue. "And you. It's been a long time. High school was more years ago than I like to think about. I hope you'll like it here."

He grinned, his dimples creasing his cheeks. Gorgeous and charming as ever. "I'm sure I will."

Why the hell did she feel so shaky? Only a few minutes ago they'd been flirting on the phone.

Only a few hours ago they'd been naked together in his bed.

He was just a man. Just another man.

Liar, liar . . .

She had to get out of there.

Pants on fire . . .

"If you'll excuse me, there's a client waiting for my call," she managed to choke out.

She nodded, ducked her head and left the conference room, making her way as quickly as she could back to the privacy of her office. She shut the door behind her, stood leaning against it for a few moments, trying to catch her breath. Then she moved to her desk, picked up her phone and dialed Lucie's number.

She listened to the ringing, her heart hammering, hoping Lucie wasn't busy and could talk. She'd just expanded her catering company, Luscious, and she'd been spending a lot of hours directing the remodeling of the new kitchen she was renting, an enormous undertaking, Kara knew.

"Come on, come on," she muttered, pacing her office, her phone gripped in her fingers.

"Hello?"

"Lucie! Thank God you're there."

"Jesus, Kara, are you all right?"

"Everyone keeps asking me that."

"Well, are you?"

"Yes. I'm fine. At least I think . . ." She paused, blew out a long breath. "I don't know what I am."

"Could you clarify a bit? Is there a hospital involved?"

"What? No, nothing like that. Nothing that serious. I mean, it *is* serious, but no one is dying. Except for me." She moved behind her desk and sat down in her chair, pushing her hair from her face. "I'm sorry. I'm not making sense, am I?"

"Nope. Care to try?" Lucie asked her.

"Okay. Okay." Kara reached for the bottled water she always kept on her desk and took a sip. "You remember the other night at your housewarming party?"

"Well, I did drink a lot of wine. What are we referring to specifically?"

"Dante De Matteo."

Even saying his name made her warm all over.

"Oh yes. You two were out on the porch talking and I came out and . . . I *did* interrupt something!" Lucie sounded triumphant.

"Not really. Not at that point."

"Out with it, Kara. What happened between you two? And don't even try to deny that something did. I can hear it in your voice."

"Oh, I'm not denying it. I'm calling to tell you about it. I just . . . I'm a little breathless."

"That good, huh?"

"Lucie . . ."

"Well, was it?" Lucie pressed her.

Kara groaned. "Yes."

"So, you two got a little wild together? That's not such a big deal. You're no virgin, and neither am I. I'm not going to judge you, sweetie."

"It's not that." Kara took another sip from her water bottle, wishing for some fresh coffee. She picked up her latte cup and shook it, but it was empty. She put it back on the desk with a small sigh. "We spent the entire weekend at his place. And it was . . . amazing. And I'm not saying I'm in love with the guy or anything, just that the sex was incredible. And we'd planned to see each other again. And then this morning . . . Oh God."

Kara closed her eyes, her hand pressing against her aching forehead.

"What? Was he a jerk to you? Because I don't care if we were all friends in high school, I will be perfectly happy to call him and give him a good tongue-lashing."

"He wasn't a jerk. He drove me home this morning. After we had sex at the crack of dawn. For about the hundredth time. But then I got to work . . . and he's *here*."

"At your office? He came to see you at work?"

"No. He was just . . . here. He works here, Lucie. Not only does he work here; he's the new junior partner."

"What?" Lucie had heard Kara complaining for weeks about the firm refusing to promote from within, so she was familiar with what the position meant to her. "You're kidding."

"I wish I was."

"That must have been a shock. And you can't even hate him because he was great in bed. Can you?"

"No." Kara sighed. "Definitely not. But I can't see him again, either. And we have to talk about it. After work tonight, I guess. I'm not looking forward to it. And working with him is going to be really uncomfortable. Especially because . . . I'd really love to keep sleeping with him."

"It was that good? Really?"

"Really."

"Wow."

She could remember even now, through her pounding pulse beat, the feel of his body pressed against hers. The dark, masculine scent of his skin. His hands on her. His mouth . . .

"So you'll talk to him tonight?"

"Hmm? Oh yes. I'll have to. I'd talk to him sooner, but he's the star of the show around here at the moment. The partners are gloating, showing him off like a prize horse. Everyone is fawning over him. And I'm locked in my office so I don't have to face him in front of them all."

"It'll be a lot easier once you've talked to him. Just tell him that since you work together, seeing each other would be a bad idea."

"It is, isn't it, Lucie?" Kara asked quietly.

"Yes. You're not considering—"

"No! Of course not." Even if the man could kiss her breathless. Even if simply being with him felt so good. Wonderful. Safe, for some reason she didn't understand. Her gaze went to the window, and she remembered that sensation of feeling cocooned with him, all weekend in his apartment, the same gray sky outside. Remembered how warm and strong his hands were on her flesh . . . "Definitely not."

"Call me after you talk to him, Kara. And maybe we should have lunch sometime soon."

"Are you free? I know you're deep into the remodel."

"Sure. The guys can get by without me for an hour. I'm mostly getting in the way, anyway. They're probably tired of me micromanaging the job. And the new kitchen's not too far from you."

"That would be great. I just feel . . . a little shaken by all this. I don't know why."

"We'll talk it out when I see you. And, you know, some of these construction guys are pretty cute. Maybe I can set you up with one of them? They say there's no better way to get over one man than with a new one."

"I don't think I'm in the mood, but thanks, Lucie."

She heard her friend clucking her tongue. "You do have it bad."

"I'll see you soon."

"Okay. Hang in there, sweetie. Bye."

They hung up and Kara turned to her computer screen and began clicking through e-mail.

Lucie was right. She'd get over this. It wasn't as if she'd wanted more than some great sex, anyway. It was nicer to be with someone she was familiar with, that was all. It was comfortable.

Not comfortable. Safe. But safe didn't mean he didn't make her pulse race, her heart pound with more than simple lust.

No. It's just chemistry, nothing more. Dante just . . . smells right.

She shook her head. She really had to stop thinking of him like that, and more as a coworker.

One she was going to have to see every single day.

She sighed once more. This was not going to be easy.

She brought her focus back to the monitor and her in-box. Two messages from clients. Several from other attorneys in her office she was working cases with. A number of e-mails from Ruby reminding her of calls she should make, new appointments to put in her calendar. And one from Dante, sent only moments earlier.

Damn it.

She bit her lip and clicked on it.

Meet me for lunch?

It was signed "D."

She started typing about it not being a good idea to let the whole office know they already knew each other after pretending to not have seen each other since high school, and how she was sure the partners would want to have lunch with him to celebrate his first day, anyway, and how they probably shouldn't have lunch together at all, *ever*. Then she hit the delete key and started over. She simply wrote that she didn't think it was a good idea and they should talk later.

Too short? But he was a man; they usually preferred to get right to the point, rather than have a long, drawn-out conversation. And it wasn't as if he'd be hurt. She was certain it had been just sex for him, too. Especially after what he'd told her about his kink lifestyle. He'd probably be relieved to be let off the hook without having to have "the talk" with some weepy female about how things just weren't working out.

She found herself frowning.

She didn't want him to be relieved.

Impossible.

Nothing more was going to happen between herself and Dante. It was for the best. It would have ended sooner or later, anyway.

But she sure as hell was going to miss the sex. The smoking-hot sex that was the fulfillment of every dark fantasy she'd ever had. With the guy she'd fantasized about since high school. And who had turned out to be even better than she'd ever dared to imagine.

She bit her lip and hit send.

six

Dante sat in his new office, staring at the computer screen.

Had she really just said no?

It had taken him by surprise, finding Kara in the office, discovering his new job was at the firm where she worked. But for him, it had been a nice surprise. The only problem had been trying not to let it show that his head was immediately filled with fantasies of her bent over his desk . . .

Okay, working with a woman he was sleeping with could get complicated. But so far she'd struck him as the logical type. Not the kind who got overly involved. Emotional. That didn't mean she was cold. Not at all. But he sensed in her an independence that matched his own. He was certain she could handle keeping things casual between them. He still thought she could.

They'd had sex all weekend long. In the bed, in the shower, on the living room rug . . . He'd spanked her, pinched her, fucked her so hard his pelvis felt bruised. And she had loved it all. She'd never been needy, never asked him for anything more. He'd been the one to suggest they stay in touch, see each other that week. So what was up with her now?

It must be the work situation. But as long as they were both fine with nothing more than a little friendly sex—okay, more than a little—there didn't have to be a problem. They could be discreet. It might even serve to keep things interesting.

Very interesting . . .

He could almost wish she was his secretary, rather than another attorney in the firm. Another little role-playing fantasy of his he'd played out before. But he had to admit there was something attractive, too, about the power of her position. He'd always preferred a woman with a good mind. Someone he felt was his equal in every way. Taking her down into submission in the bedroom was even more satisfying with that kind of woman. Overcoming her strength. That was where the real power play happened for him.

Kara was strong. He'd seen that in her.

Now he wanted to see her in his office, naked, lying across his lap . . .

He smiled to himself as he tapped at the keyboard:

Not acceptable. Nijo Sushi at one. Looking forward to it. —D

He hit send and sat back, pleased with himself.

Kara may be strong, but he'd also seen her submissive side. And he knew how she'd respond to this, even if she didn't want to. Now all he had to do was wait until lunchtime, when he could see her. Talk to her.

It was a little ridiculous that he was making such great effort with this woman. But that kind of sex didn't come along every day. Hot and primal and . . . something *easy* between them.

Don't complicate it, buddy.

He ran a hand over his jaw.

It didn't have to be complicated. So they worked together. So what?

What happens when it's over and you have to see each other every day?

But he didn't want to think about that. He couldn't. All he could think of was seeing Kara, kissing away the stubborn set of her mouth. Maybe right there in the restaurant, over sushi and tea.

He'd deal with the rest as it happened. For now, everything was fine. He had a great new job, new employers who seemed to like him, Kara Crawford only a few doors away. And the scent of her was still all over him, despite his morning shower.

Nice.

Oh yes, he was going to like it here. And Kara was going to like him being there. He'd make damn sure of it.

Dante arrived at Nijo Sushi a few minutes before one. It was just far enough from the office that he was fairly certain they wouldn't be spotted together—too close to the touristy waterfront area for most businesspeople. He'd met his best friend, Alec, there for dinner a few weeks earlier and he'd liked the food and the sleek urban décor.

The hostess seated him at a table in the back of the room and he ordered a pot of green tea from the waiter. He wanted a sake,

but it was a workday. He didn't usually drink while he was working. He wasn't sure why the idea even crossed his mind now. Except he had a vague feeling that he needed to calm down.

She's just a woman, like any other.

That was bullshit. She wasn't like anyone he'd ever known.
Except for the Kara he'd known in high school. Sweet and smart
and beautiful. That part of her hadn't changed. Now she was all
woman. Stronger. More worldly. More beautiful than ever.

And he was being an idiot. What the hell was wrong with him?

When the waiter came back with the tea, he ordered the damn
sake.

He glanced at his watch. It was five after one. Too soon to tell
if she'd show.

He tapped his fingers on the tabletop, his gaze wandering
around the room, taking in the exposed brick walls, the dim
lighting, the other people dining, talking. There was a good
lunch crowd, yet there was something quiet, intimate, about the
place, which was one reason he'd chosen it.

When the sake arrived, he ignored the tea, instead pouring
the cold sake from the white china decanter into the small cup,
took a sip. He looked at his watch once more. Ten after.

Had she outplayed him after all? And if so, what was the next
logical step? This was definitely new ground for him. He was
used to being the one in control. Of everything. He preferred it
that way. Liked—needed, maybe—to be in control of things.
Everything worked better that way. No more sad stories like the
one with Erin in college. No giving that a chance to happen. As
long as he was in control, he could take responsibility for everything. Wasn't that what being a man was all about? Just as his

father had taught him. Drummed into his head, really. But despite the guilt trips his father had used on Dante and his brother, Lorenzo, Dad had been right. Responsibility equaled control. It was all one idea, a way to live his life. A way he'd practiced without fail since Erin had died.

A small, sharp twinge in his chest, thinking of Erin. He took another sip of the sake. That would go away eventually, he figured. Why was he even thinking of all this now? His father's sternness, his college girlfriend, old guilt.

He just had to get a handle on things—on Kara—and he'd be fine. Just fine.

He looked at his watch. Fifteen after.

Damn it.

He emptied his cup of sake and poured another. Looked up to signal the waiter to order. And found her standing on the other side of the small table.

She was a little windblown, her silky brown hair mussed. Her cheeks flushed pink—from the cold, probably. Looking like she had in his bed. Naked and flushed with orgasm.

He went hard, just like that. Simply seeing Kara standing there, her eyes glittering with stark annoyance. Her lush mouth set.

Oh, she was pissed. Which gave him more satisfaction than it should.

What the hell. She'd played right into his hands after all.

Buck up, buddy.

He stood, came around the table and held her chair.

"Won't you have a seat, Kara?"

She glared at him, pulled off her trench coat and handed it to him, sat down hard in the chair. He pushed it in for her, took her coat to his own chair and slung it over the back, sat down.

"I ordered some tea for you. Unless you'd prefer sake?"

"I don't usually drink during work hours," she said, her jaw still tight.

He'd never seen her angry before. There was something about it he found enticing.

"Neither do I. Usually."

"But?" she challenged him.

"But . . ." He shrugged. "I'm celebrating. The first day at my new job. I thought you might want to celebrate with me."

She let out a long sigh. "Jesus, Dante, why would I want to do that? We were perfectly fine until you waltzed into my firm this morning, the new junior partner. And now we have to just . . . stop. And I'm fine with that, I really am. But I can't have you . . . asking me to lunch."

She crossed her arms over her chest.

He leaned forward and poured tea into the small glazed cup, slid it across the table toward her. "Have some tea, Kara. You need to calm down."

"I'm perfectly calm. I'm simply asking you to respect the fact that as coworkers, we can't be carrying on . . . an affair."

"Why not? You seemed pretty happy about it this morning."

Her cheeks blazed, and he loved seeing her light up like that, whether with anger or passion. Maybe a mixture of both. Either way, she was one gorgeous woman.

"Dante, you truly don't see the problem here? We're going to see each other five days a week. Which is one reason why people who work together should not sleep together. When things are over, it'll make the work environment uncomfortable for us both."

"More uncomfortable than it'll be now, ending on this note?"

Kara sat back in her chair, blew out a long breath, some of the anger dissipating.

Was he right?

He looked so damn good, sitting there in his perfectly tailored suit, his pose casual and relaxed. The man had a tendency to drape himself over furniture as if he owned it. He had a tendency to behave as if he owned everything. And got away with it.

And it made him even more attractive.

Kara bit her lip, trying to make sense out of it all.

"Dante, dating a coworker is never a good idea," she tried to protest, but it sounded like a lame excuse, even to her.

He leaned in, took her hand in his, his thumb stroking her wrist. His voice was so low she had to lean in to hear him. "So we won't date. We'll just have the most incredible, hot, kinky sex imaginable. At my place. In my bed. On the Persian rug in my living room. The kitchen counter. Or maybe at the club, which I'd love to take you to. And if you're very good, my beautiful girl, on the desk in my office."

"Dante!" She yanked her hand back, her skin burning. She couldn't lie to herself that the heat was anything other than pure desire.

He grinned, just a small, cocky lift at one corner of his mouth. "Ah, I can see you like that idea. Don't go all prim and proper on me now, Kara."

She shook her head. "You're incorrigible."

The grin spread, making his dimples flash. "But you like that about me."

God, she liked everything about him. But she wasn't going to tell him that. Or that her entire body was melting after seeing those dimples, hearing the low, sexy tone of his voice. And, most of all, the fact that he would not take no for an answer.

She wanted to hate him for that. For making her love his command, even now. For making her *need* it. But it was impossible.

She picked up her teacup and sipped, trying to buy time, to calm her racing pulse. The anger had melted along with her body, fusing into a stark, liquid heat she couldn't deny and wasn't sure how to handle.

Dante leaned in, put his hand on her wrist once more. The move seemed incredibly intimate to her. He said quietly, "I can see it, you know. I can feel it in your pulse. Right here, beneath my fingertips." He pressed at her wrist gently. His tone went even lower. "You're pretty worked up, aren't you, Kara? And you can pretend it's all anger. But it's false bravado, isn't it? You don't have to say it for me to know how this will turn out. There may be some more aggressive banter between us. Or perhaps not, at this point. And then we will pick up right where we left off this morning. Can you believe it was only this morning that you were naked in my bed? Crying out with pleasure? Calling my name? Begging me, Kara."

His eyes were glittering as he spoke. So damn sexy she could hardly stand it. And emanating power. She wanted to resist him. To focus on all the reasons why this wasn't a good idea. But she couldn't tear her gaze from his. It was torture. Wanting him. Feeling she shouldn't be doing this . . .

"Oh yes," he went on. "You begged me to fuck you. To make

you come. And you love the begging as much as I do. Hearing that surrender in your voice."

She yanked her wrist away.

"Dante, we should stop this. You should stop."

He shook his head. "Only if you really want me to. But I don't think that's the case."

"You're a lawyer. You could find a way to argue anything."

"The same can be said for you."

She stared at him, rubbing her wrist where his fingers had rested moments before. She felt as if he was still touching her. As if he'd left a mark on her skin. Branded her.

"So, are we going to continue to argue, Kara? Because as you said, I can do that all day. And so can you. But why waste our energy on argument? We both want the same thing. We have from the start. Maybe even back in high school. But we couldn't admit it then. I can admit it now. How about you?"

She started to shake her head. But there was something about the low, even tone of his voice, the absolute control with which he spoke. It reached down inside her, deep down, and shook her to the core.

He was right. She wanted him. Wanted the things they did together. And that was why she was so mad. Because it felt like a risk to have it. Because they worked together, yes. But there was something more . . . some element of danger with him she didn't want to examine too closely.

"Tell me what you're thinking, Kara," he asked. Demanded.

"I'm thinking that . . . you're right."

She looked up at him, but there was no gloating in his expression. There was nothing but pure pleasure on his face, in his smile.

"I was hoping you'd see the error of your ways."

"You're teasing me now." But she didn't really mind.

"Yes. I can't help myself. It makes you blush so beautifully. It makes me think of that lovely shade your ass turns when I'm spanking you."

"Dante, do you have to do that here?"

"Oh yes." His smile widened. "Definitely."

"You are a wicked man," she told him, smiling a little.

"I try."

She shook her head. "I'm not going to get any lunch, am I?"

"I'll order something. I want you well fed for what I have in mind for you later."

Too dangerous, the way her body lit up with a pure, aching need simply thinking about going home with him, getting back into his bed. Or on his kitchen counter. Or the living room floor . . .

"Maybe we should . . . think about this, Dante."

"Maybe you think too much."

"Hmm, well, yes."

He picked up her hand once more, drew it to his lips and laid a soft kiss on her open palm. "Later, when I have you alone, I'll see what I can do to get that brilliant mind of yours to slow down. To empty out. A good spanking always seems to do that for you. But maybe you're ready for something more."

"Are you trying to scare me?"

"Is it working?"

"Maybe."

He grinned, looking pleased with himself.

"And maybe not," she added. "I'm not afraid of the things I crave."

"Aren't you? Wasn't that what held you back from pursuing your desires all these years?"

"Not anymore."

But that was a lie. She wanted Dante. More than she liked to admit. And that scared the hell out of her.

But she was going to have him. She would think about the rest later.

"Let's feed you." He let her hand go, motioned to the waiter and ordered without looking at the menu.

"Do you always do that?" she asked him.

"Do what?"

"Take charge in any given situation?"

The question seemed to surprise him. "Yes. Do you have an issue with me ordering for you?"

She eased back into her chair, the wood biting a little into the sore spots on her behind, making her feel a strange rush of pleasure. She shrugged helplessly. "I like it. I hate to admit that, but I do."

He smiled at her. "We're going to get along just fine." She rolled her eyes, making him laugh. "It's true. And I'm pretty sure we have a few other things in common."

"Like what?"

He shrugged. "We're both lawyers, so we've both been through the hell that is the bar exam."

It was her turn to laugh. "True enough."

Their food came. He'd ordered eel rolls, some salmon sashimi, a calamari salad. All of the things she liked. They both pulled pieces onto their plates, along with the thin slivers of tangy ginger. Dante mixed a bowl of soy sauce and wasabi and pushed it close to her plate. She didn't think to question it. She was getting used to him taking charge already.

A little scary. But she liked it.

Don't think about it. Just enjoy it. Enjoy him.

"So, what else?" he asked her between bites.

"What do you mean?" She bit into a piece of the sashimi. "Oh, this is good."

"I mean what do you like? Aside from kinky sex." He grinned, his dimples flashing, his whiskey eyes sparkling.

"A lot of things."

"Art?"

"Yes. Always," she answered. "But you already knew that. What about you? I gathered from what I saw at your apartment that you have a good eye. Unless you had a decorator."

"No, it's all my own doing, good or bad. I like a little of everything. I like to mix it together. I don't know if anyone else thinks it works. It doesn't matter to me, though. I like it." He paused to take another bite of his sushi. "I've been getting into modern sculpture recently. Abstract pieces. I don't really understand it. I just know what I like."

"You don't have to understand art, in my opinion. It should be more . . . experiential than that. You only have to know what you like, as you said. Movies are the same, I think."

"I agree. There's something for everyone, and it's not up to anyone else to judge. I like watching movies. Always have. I have a fondness for the old classic film noir, stuff from the forties and fifties."

"Seriously? Those are some of my favorites." Why did it surprise her that they should have so much in common? Surprise and excite her. "*Citizen Kane, The Maltese Falcon.* And so many of the noir films center on women of questionable virtue, which appeals to me, for some reason."

"Absolutely. *Double Indemnity.* Lana Turner in *The Postman Always Rings Twice.* Some people think the pacing is slow. It *is* slower. Film styles have changed. But I feel like I need the slower pace sometimes. I like the starkness of black and white on film as much as I do in still art, photography. When I'm up late at night I'll flip through the channels until I find one of the old classics. Or I'll pop in a DVD from my collection."

"I do the same," she told him. "It's relaxing. Soothing. There's something sort of cozy and lonely at the same time about an old movie at three a.m."

He nodded. "There is. Late at night, or sometimes early in the morning. I don't know why. I like those quiet hours, the mood of it. Sometimes I'll get up really early—like five a.m.—and take my motorcycle out. Just ride . . . anywhere. Usually by myself, but sometimes I can talk Alec into going with me."

"You both have motorcycles?"

"It's one of the things that brought us together. Aside from kink." He grinned. "Except that he has deplorable taste in bikes. I'm a BMW man and he has this odd liking for Ducatis. But otherwise, he's a great guy. We've traveled all over together, done some cross-country rides. He's talked me into doing some crazy stuff. But I like that he brings that out in me. And there aren't too many other people who would go cliff diving with me in Mexico."

"I think it sounds exciting."

"Do you?" he asked.

"Yes, absolutely. I've always wanted to do something like that. Something to really challenge myself. What else?" she asked. "Tell me what else you're interested in."

"Making demands, Kara?" he teased her. She could tell it was just teasing by the sparkle in his eyes, the small grin quirking the corners of his mouth. "Trying to shift the balance of power?"

Why did that make her blush? And laugh. "Would that be such a bad thing?"

"As long as you know it'll always shift back to me."

"Oh, don't worry. I wouldn't doubt that for a moment."

He'd broken into a full smile again, his dimples accenting the masculine lushness of his mouth. She couldn't wait until they were alone, until he would kiss her again. Had it only been that morning? She'd nearly forgotten being angry with him, thinking they couldn't see each other anymore. She couldn't wait. Couldn't imagine never feeling his touch again.

He muttered under his breath as his cell phone went off. "Damn it. Sorry; I have to take this." He put the phone to his ear. "This is Dante . . . Hi, Ruby . . . What? . . . No, I haven't forgotten. I'm on my way back now. Give me fifteen minutes."

He hung up and said to Kara, "I did forget. You're very distracting. Not that I mind, but I have a meeting with Ed Tate to go over the cases he's bringing me in on. And they warned me it'll probably be a late night. Which makes me realize we'll have to wait to get together. And tomorrow night I'm already booked."

"Oh. Of course."

She didn't like the enormous surge of disappointment that filtered through her.

He's just a guy. Just sex.

She knew that was a lie. One she wasn't ready to face.

He reached out, took her hand, brushed his thumb over her palm. Heat rippled over her skin. "Wednesday night, then," he said, another command.

"Wednesday is good."

He smiled at her once more. "Excellent."

He paid and they left, going outside, into the cool January afternoon. The sky was gray and heavy with impending rain, but luckily it hadn't started yet. She'd been in too much of a hurry when she'd left the office to meet Dante to think of taking her umbrella. Too excited, a little annoyed at being summoned by him. The annoyance had disappeared as if it had never existed.

Dante hailed a cab and held the door for her. "I'm assuming you'd like to keep things quiet. I'll get another one."

"Thank you. For lunch. And for being mindful of . . . my reputation." She laughed. "God, I sound like some sort of fifties debutante."

He smiled, leaned in and kissed her cheek, just a brief brush of his lips. She was burning up inside immediately. "You're welcome. I'll see you back at the office. And at my place Wednesday night. Be there at seven."

She nodded, the aching desire in her body muting her.

Dante helped her into the cab and she rode back to work, crossing and uncrossing her legs, trying to ease the sharp, pulsing need between her thighs his kiss had left her with.

It's only two days.

Those two days were going to seem like an eternity.

Back to her friendly vibrator, she supposed. But she knew it was going to do nothing more than take the merest edge off. Nothing was going to help calm the heat raging through her system. Nothing but Dante's touch.

Dante.

She shouldn't want him this much. She certainly shouldn't *need* him. But she did. She was afraid that it was more than his demanding kisses, his clever touch. The way he knew what she needed instinctively. The kinky and amazing sex. But she was more afraid to stop and really think it all through. Because if she did, she'd have to face the fact that Dante De Matteo was a man she could fall for.

She had no intention of falling for anyone. She'd done a very good job of that so far. Even with Jake, it had been more about it being easy. Something they had both sort of slipped into, more than anything. It had been convenient.

There was nothing convenient about Dante. He challenged her.

She loved that about him.

Still, that didn't mean she was going to fall for him. She wasn't that kind of girl. Never had been. Never would be.

Just keep telling yourself that.

seven

Kara didn't know how she'd gotten through the last two days. On Monday Dante had disappeared into Ed Tate's office after her lunch with him and they were still in there when she'd left work.

Yesterday Dante had sent her a text message asking for her private e-mail, and she'd given it to him, but she hadn't heard from him since. Now it was the end of their workday on Wednesday and she was getting ready to leave the office. She clicked into her e-mail one last time, hoping for some sort of message from him, even just a confirmation that they were still on for tonight.

There was nothing new in her in-box.

Damn it.

She blew out a breath and closed her e-mail, shut her computer down.

Why was she acting like some starstruck teenager? She'd never been the kind of woman to wait by the phone—or the

computer—for a man. Even with Jake. One of the reasons why
he'd been so drawn to her, he'd told her early in their relationship,
was her independence. He'd liked that he'd had to pursue her, that
she didn't always have time for him.

Maybe she was making things too easy for Dante. Maybe she
should pull back a bit. Tell him she was busy tonight and couldn't
make it after all.

She knew damn well she wasn't about to do that. She couldn't
wait to see him. She was practically trembling all over with need.
The need to see him. For him to touch her. Simply to be with him
again.

Ridiculous.

But she couldn't stop herself.

With a sigh she pulled on her trench coat, picked up her purse
and walked into the hallway. She couldn't help but peek at Dante's
closed office door on her way to the elevator.

So he was still working. Good to know.

Her cell phone went off and she answered it without looking
at the caller ID. Her gaze was still glued to his door at the end of
the long hall.

"Hello?"

"Kara. Did I catch you before you left the building?"

Dante. Her stomach melted, her legs turning to liquid. The
same need that was instantly warming between her thighs.

"Hi. Yes, I'm still here," she told him. "I was just leaving."

"Don't."

"Um . . . okay. Are you working late?"

"Staying late, maybe. Is anyone else still here?"

"Yes, a few people."

"Ruby?" he asked.

"No, she left about an hour ago. Why?"

"Because I want you to come to my office."

"Now?"

"Yes, Kara. Now."

There was no arguing with that tone. She didn't want to. And she understood he wasn't planning to go over case files with her. She swallowed.

"Okay. I'll be right there."

She glanced around the office. Gary's door was open and she could see him in there, talking with his law clerk.

She took in a breath and moved back down the hall toward Dante's office. And nearly bumped into Theresa, who was coming out of her own office, pulling on her coat.

"Kara, you're working late?"

"Oh no. Well, maybe. I just . . . need to check something."

"Want me to hold the elevator for you?"

"What? No. No, thanks. I don't want to keep you waiting. It may take me a few minutes."

"Okay. See you in the morning."

"Good night."

She walked into her office, counted to thirty, peeked out to make sure Theresa had gone. She felt like a kid sneaking around after school, which was oddly exciting. But the excitement had everything to do with Dante.

Dante.

Another small rush of need washed over her as she moved across the hall to his door, opened it and slipped through, shutting the door quietly behind her.

He was sitting behind his desk, handsome as hell in his black suit, his dark blue shirt striking against the golden brown of his eyes. A slow smile lit his face, and he nodded at her.

"Take your coat off, Kara."

No greeting. Just that simple command.

She loved it.

She slid her coat from her shoulders and laid it down on the brown leather sofa against one wall, set her purse next to it.

"Come here," he said quietly.

He watched her as she crossed the room. She could feel her body heating up beneath his penetrating gaze. She licked her lips, approached his desk.

"You look great in these tight skirts you wear," he told her, his tone all smoke and heat. "That sexy, businesswoman look. It suits you." He stood, moved in closer, making her breath catch. "And it makes your ass look superb. But I want a better look."

He wrapped his hands around her waist, turned her until her back was to him.

"Good," he said, his tone low. "Now bend over and brace your hands on the desk."

She found herself doing it, her mind emptying out at an alarming rate.

Don't think. Can't think now . . .

"Beautiful, Kara. Perfect. The curve of your ass in this skirt is . . . perfect."

He moved in close behind her and slid his hand over her hip, then her bottom. She could feel the heat of him through the soft, fine wool of her skirt. She was going wet already, her sex a dark throbbing between her legs.

He leaned over her until his breath was warm on her cheek. He whispered, "Hold still for me now."

One sharp spank and she gasped.

"Did I surprise you?" he asked her. "You should have known what I was going to do when I bent you over the desk."

"There are still people in the office," she said, her voice sounding small, barely a protest at all.

"Yes. But that only makes it more exciting."

"I didn't lock your office door behind me."

"No one will come in. You have to trust me, Kara. Do you trust me?"

"Yes," she whispered.

She did. She had to. She was helpless already against the on-slaught of desire. Drowning in it.

"Good. Very good."

He smacked her again, the sensation dulled a bit by the fabric between his hand and her ass.

"Oh!"

"Shh, Kara," Dante whispered to her. He moved her hair aside and laid a kiss on the back of her neck, making her shiver. "Jesus, your skin is so hot. I have to touch it. Touch you . . ."

She felt him move back for a moment as he lifted her skirt, sliding it up around her waist.

"Ah, I should have known you'd be wearing a thong under that tight skirt. I love the way it looks with the boots. Someday I'll have to have you in nothing but these boots."

She was shaking even before he touched her. Then he smoothed his palm over her bottom, and she went soaking wet. She had to grip the edge of his desk, forcing herself to hold still.

He kept moving his hand over her bare flesh, the sensation soft and sweet. Yet she yearned for that harder touch.

"Dante, please . . ."

"Eager, beautiful girl? I like that. But you'll have to wait until I'm ready. Take a breath, let it out. And wait."

She moaned quietly. He laughed, a small wicked chuckle. He kept stroking her skin—with his palm, with his fingertips. It was wonderful. It was torture.

"Just sink into my touch," he told her. "Keep breathing. Yes, that's it."

She tried to do as he said. And after a few moments she found herself doing it. Sinking. Drifting. Her eyes closed.

The sharp smack on her bottom made her flinch. Then pleasure flooded her body, her sex. Pleasure and intensity and the dark scent of him surrounding her. She found herself surging back into him.

Another low chuckle from him. "I love that you love this. That you respond this way."

He smacked her again. This time she was braced for it. But it still hurt. Still felt wonderful. Like something she *required*.

He paused to graze her burning flesh with his palm, then smacked again. And again and again. Just hard enough to hurt, for the sting to reverberate through her with small ripples of pleasure.

"God, Dante . . ."

"What is it, Kara?" he asked, one hand going into her hair. He buried his fingers in it, then grasped tightly, right next to her scalp. And even that was purely erotic to her, carrying the sensation deeper into her aching body.

"Please touch me, Dante. Please."

"I love it when you ask like that. So nicely." He smoothed his hand over her hip, sliding it around and cupping her mound.

"Ah, Dante . . ."

His voice was a whisper in her ear, his breath warming her skin. "Is this what you need, my beautiful girl?"

Then he slipped his fingers under the lace and right into her wet heat.

"Oh!"

"You're so damn slick. So wet," he murmured as his fingers moved, up and down her cleft, probing at her opening, then teasing the swollen folds once more. "Do you like it, Kara? Tell me."

God, that commanding tone. His hands on her.

"Yes. Yes."

He found the hard nub of her clitoris and brushed his fingertips over the tip. Her hips moved of their own accord, arching into his touch.

"Ah, that's good, Kara. Give your need to me. Give yourself to me."

He pressed onto her clit, and pleasure shafted into her, making her breath come in hard, ragged pants. When he started to roll her clitoris between his fingers, she could barely breathe.

"Dante . . . I'm going to come."

"Not yet."

He spanked her with his free hand. One hard smack on her ass and she had to bite her lip to keep from crying out. The sharp sting only made her feel the edge of pleasure more keenly, driving it higher.

"Hang on, Kara. Hang on to it. You can come when I tell you," he said, desire thick in his voice.

He really started to spank her then, a volley of quick slaps. Not too hard, not too loudly. But the pace drove the sting deeper into her skin. And all the while he worked her clitoris. Everything seemed to fuse together: his hand on her ass, his fingers on her clit, the small, wicked threat of being caught. It was an overload of pleasure she could barely control. But she wouldn't come until he told her to. She would *not* do it. And that was a different pleasure in itself.

He spanked her harder, and desire took her to a dizzying height. She poised there. Painful. Exquisite.

"Dante . . ."

"Are you ready?"

"God, yes!"

"Come on, then, Kara. Come for me."

He pressed onto her clit, rubbing, rubbing, his other hand striking her naked flesh. Pain and pleasure joined, merged into a pure sensation that dazzled her, blinded her as she came. Hard spasms, over and over. She bit her lip to keep from crying out, to hold back the scream that wanted to fight its way past her clenched jaw. When it was over she trembled, barely holding herself upright, the edge of the desk biting into her palms.

He kissed the back of her neck, stroked her hair with one hand while he held her upright with the other wrapped around her waist. "That was good, Kara. Amazing. I'm so damn hard for you. But I won't fuck you here. You'll have to come home with me. Right now."

"Now?" she asked, still breathless.

He turned her in his arms, sliding the hem of her skirt back down over her thighs. His eyes were dark, glittering brown and gold. He looked dangerous. Gorgeous.

"Ah, you're really shaking, baby. Do you know what that does to me?"

She'd come only moments before, yet hearing him say these things to her made her want him. *Need* him. If only he would turn her around again. Bend her over his desk once more and slide into her . . .

But what he did was almost better. He bent his head and kissed her. Really took her mouth. His lips opened hers, his tongue surging in. Hard and demanding. Slippery and sweet. She thought she could almost come again just from him kissing her. It didn't make sense. It didn't have to.

He pulled her in close, crushing her body to his. His erection pressed into her thigh. God, she wanted him. Wanted to touch him as he'd touched her. Wanted to wrap her hands around his thick cock and stroke until he came. Wanted him inside her.

He pulled away. He was breathing hard. So was she.

"I need to get you out of here now," he told her.

"Yes."

She was thrilled that he was as eager as she was. He was looking at her in that way he had. Searching. Focused. His dark brows drawn.

"Fuck, Kara."

"What . . . what is it?"

Was he going to change his mind? Had he remembered another missed meeting? Her heart hammered.

"I can't believe how badly I need you. This is fucking crazy."

Relief filled her. "It is. I don't care."

"Neither do I."

He pulled her in and kissed her once more. And she swore she could feel the hard hammer of his heart in his chest, pressed so tightly to hers.

"Take me home, Dante. Now."

He simply nodded.

It was the first command she'd given him. And might very well be the last. She didn't care. All she wanted was to feel him inside her. To have him spank her again. To kiss her. Hold her. To do it all without any limits other than those *he* imposed on her to meet his desires, or hers.

It *was* crazy. She was losing her mind, maybe. Losing herself in Dante. But she was far too lost to care.

Dante could barely remember how they'd gotten to his place. He'd driven, of course. Probably far more distracted by the sharp, pulsing need for her than was entirely safe.

It wasn't like him to take risks that involved anyone but himself. Riding his motorcycle. Some of the crazy shit he'd done with Alec on their trips together. Shark diving. Hang gliding. He shouldn't be risking Kara's well-being now. But he was too damn eager to be more careful. To take the time to calm down.

He didn't think he would, anyway. Not until he had her, naked and writhing under his hands, his body. Until he'd made her come, over and over. Until he'd come himself, into her sleek, gorgeous body.

Somehow they were in the elevator in his building and he couldn't keep his hands off her one moment longer. It had taken too damn long already, driving home, getting her out of the car. More than half-hard the whole time.

He pulled her in close, his arm going around her slender waist, pausing just long enough to take in her glossy hazel eyes. They were more silver than gold. Glowing with heat. Her skin was flushed, her cheeks pink. Her lips were red, swollen, as if he'd kissed her already the way he wanted to.

He gripped her tighter, bent his head. And pressed his lips to hers.

Ah, so damn sweet. And something wild about her. The way she returned his kiss, her arms coming around his neck and hanging on. Something different from the usual submissive women he was with. But he couldn't think about anyone else right now.

Only Kara.

Restlessly, he untied the belt of her trench coat and slid his hands under it.

Have to get the damn clothes off.

The elevator came to a smooth stop, the bell ringing, and he pulled away from her. Fucking torture.

Taking her hand, he led her down the hall to his door, turned his key in the lock. Then they were inside, and he flipped on the light in the foyer.

He had a flash of the first time he'd taken her home with him. Going down on her against the door. The ocean taste of her on his lips.

Again.

She was quiet as he tore her coat off, then his. She stood still and silent as he undressed her, revealing that silky, pale skin one piece of clothing at a time: dress, bra, the lacy thong, her high suede boots. He picked her up and carried her to the sofa—the bed was too damn far away—and she twined her arms around his neck once more, hanging on. Her body was so warm in his arms. Sweet against him. Making him hard as steel.

He laid her on the sofa, trying to be gentle when all he really wanted was to throw her down and get his hands all over her. His mouth.

Yes.

"Lie back, Kara," he said, his voice rough. "Let me do everything. Everything . . ."

She did as he asked, her soft brown hair a little wild against the pillows. Her eyes were a metallic gleam from beneath her lowered lids. He could see that she was sinking deeper into subspace, that raw and floating head space a bottom often went into. She was so fucking responsive. So much more submissive than she knew. Yet there was an undeniable strength to her. That she'd even let him do this, take her over in this way.

But he was thinking too much.

Just touch her. Have her.

He put his hands on her thighs and she opened for him. Just spread her legs until he could see the wet pink of her pussy.

Jesus.

He couldn't bother to undress himself. He licked his lips.

Too beautiful.

He knelt on the floor next to the sofa and bent to taste her.

She was sweet and smoky as he drew his tongue in one long stroke up her slit. He heard her sharp intake of breath. The quiet sigh as she released it. Tasted her again.

He pushed deeper between her folds, found her entrance. Moving her thighs wider, he opened her up. Spread the soft folds of her pussy lips. And pushed his tongue inside her.

Her breath was a muffled, ragged pant as he began to fuck her with his tongue. Her hips arched higher, pushing into his face, and he grasped them in both hands. Held her down. And the moment he did, she grew impossibly wetter, tried to grind down onto his mouth. But he held on, kept control of her hips.

Pleasure was searing hot, making him so damn hard he could barely stand it. Except that he *needed* this. To give her pleasure. To make her come.

Soon she was gasping. But he didn't stop. Just kept thrusting with his tongue, tasting her, deep inside. She was shaking. Moaning. He loved it that she didn't speak, even to beg.

When he released one hip to press on the hard nub of her clit, she came apart. He didn't know how else to describe it. Her pussy clenched around his tongue and her hips bucked, no matter how he tried to hold her. She groaned, a primal sound, deep in her throat. And the harder she came, the harder his cock grew. Hard and aching.

But he didn't want to stop. Wanted her to come again. Needed her to. He kept at it, shifting so that his tongue was on her clit and his fingers were pressing inside her, fucking her as he'd just done with his tongue. She was gasping, breathless. He loved it.

And as he plunged inside her with his fingers, drew them out, plunged again, he sucked her clit into his mouth. Swirled his tongue over the tip.

Just need to hear her come again.

He needed to taste that sweet and salty rush on his tongue.

Yes . . .

It was a driving need. Even more driving than his own desire. To feel her drowning in it. Taken under.

Soon she was coming again, calling out this time, yelling until she was hoarse. And it was fucking beautiful.

She was fucking beautiful.

Have to have her. Now.

He pushed back, took in her flushed face, her gorgeous breasts, blushing as pink as her cheeks. He reached out and pinched her nipples—he couldn't help himself—her answering groan going through him like wildfire.

"Stay right here," he told her, getting up to grab a condom from the box on his night table.

He came back to her, stripped down as quickly as he could. She watched him, kept her gaze on his body, watched his cock as he sheathed it. Even her gaze on him was pure sex. So intense, he had to stop and stroke himself for a moment, his fingers running up and down the shaft. Pleasure was sweet and keen, sharp in his cock, his belly. Her lips parted, her tongue flicking out to lick her plush lips. And that was it—it was too much for him.

He lowered himself onto her. Or maybe he fell on her. He didn't know. It happened too fast. Out of control as he drove right into her.

Wet and tight and too fucking good to be believed. Then he stopped thinking altogether. He thrust, over and over, driving deep. And sensation was like a blanket of thunder, pounding into him: his cock, his belly. His mind.

He was vaguely aware of Kara crying out. Of the soft texture of her breasts pressed against his chest. Of the sweetness of her skin as he sank his teeth into the tender flesh of her throat.

There was nothing but pleasure, her skin, their limbs tangled together. And the sensation mounting moment by moment. Thrust by thrust.

His cock was the center point. But it was all over him: skin and muscle and bone. When he came it was like a brilliant light pouring into him. Dazzling him. Making him call out.

"Kara!"

He couldn't stop. He kept pumping his hips. And she rose to meet him, over and over. And then she was crying out, gasping. Sobbing his name.

"Dante . . . God, Dante . . ."

Still he moved, his hips arching, into her, into her, over and over. He was done coming, but he couldn't get deep enough.

Close enough.

He felt as if there was a ripping sensation in his chest, in his head. Something just opening him up. Something unfamiliar and not entirely welcome. Yet sweet. Something that was all about Kara.

His cock was still thrumming. Her body was still pulsing, holding him tight: pussy and arms and legs wrapped around him. And he understood in some distant way that he was wrapped up in her. Body. Mind. He was afraid to ask himself what else.

eight

When Dante woke it was still dark outside. A glance at the clock told him it was five in the morning. Still another hour and a half before he should get up for work.

Kara slept beside him. The light he'd left on in the foyer shone still, the tiniest bit of luminescence reaching the bedroom area of the loft. But it was enough that after a few moments he could make out her features. She was fine-boned, her cheekbones high and curved. Her mouth impossibly lush. Gorgeous. Her silky hair was draped over the pillow. He loved the texture of it. Loved the way it framed her face when she was awake. Loved the abandon in the way it was spread out now. Or during sex.

He moved his gaze lower, could make out the sensual rise and curve of her body beneath the blanket. Remembered what her body felt like under his hands.

She'd always been athletic, with this hard-toned, graceful

body, even in high school. Now she had just a touch of added curves, a little more fullness. Femininity. And her face was so much the same. Prettier now, maybe. But she'd been pretty then. She still had that freshness about her. Her skin was flawless. Baby soft.

He stroked one finger along her jaw, over her cheek, and her eyes fluttered open.

"Hi." Her voice was rough with sleep, and the smallest trace of desire, he thought. Or maybe that was wishful thinking. He was hardening again just looking at her.

Crazy.

"Hey. Sorry to wake you. I just . . . I don't know. Wanted to touch you."

He couldn't believe he'd said that out loud. Maybe he was still foggy with sleep. But she smiled—he could see the gleam of her teeth in the half-dark room.

"It's okay. I like it," she told him. "That you want to touch me. That you woke me up. And there's that early morning quiet I love so much."

"Yeah. But . . ." What did he want to say to her? He didn't know what the hell was going on with him. "I was just looking at you and thinking how much the same you look. Almost like you're still sixteen."

"I'm hardly sixteen anymore."

"I know that. It's weird, though, seeing you after all these years. I don't know much about what's happened with you in be-tween. Only the basics. School. The career stuff."

Why did it feel so important to ask her about her life? Just catching up, maybe. That didn't explain why he *needed* to know.

"Not much else has happened with me." She paused, dragged her fingers through her long hair. "I've just been doing life, I guess, like everyone else. School and work. Friends. Relationships that didn't work out."

"And how do you think that's affected you?"

She was quiet a moment. "My last relationship went so badly. I think it really . . . rocked me. Not that I was so madly in love with him because, looking back, I wasn't. I think maybe . . . I had too much ego tied up in it. He was this great-looking guy, successful. Great on paper. I felt like being with him was what I *should* be doing. My parents were thrilled with him. Or the idea of him, anyway. They never actually made the time to meet him. God, I don't know why I'm telling you this."

"Because I asked," he said quietly. "I tend to get philosophical this early in the morning, when it's still dark out."

He knew it was bullshit. Some lame excuse.

She turned onto her side, facing him. "But is this the sort of thing you were asking about?"

"I want to know whatever you want to tell me."

It was true. He did.

"Okay." She pushed her hair back once more, tucking it behind her ear, baring her shoulder. He smoothed his hand over her skin. He couldn't help himself.

"I really don't know why I'm telling you this, in particular," she said. "Maybe because I'm not quite awake yet. Or because it's dark out, as you said, and it feels . . . safe."

"Do you want to tell me more? You don't have to."

She nodded her head.

"When Jake broke things off with me I was devastated. But

more because it was a blow to my ego. My self-esteem. And I was shocked. Because I have never been one of those girls. Someone who gets her self-image all tied up in a man. At least, I'd never thought of myself that way. But he judged me so harshly. So *instantly*. And I mean, the moment he found out that I wanted to be spanked, to do something that was outside the ordinary realm of sex he was familiar with—comfortable with, I guess—it was over. Just like that. And it took me a little while to realize that my reaction to the breakup wasn't about him, as much as it was . . . It was too reminiscent of my parents. Never measuring up. And the fact that he would leave me over something like that. It made me feel dirty, when that had never seemed dirty to me before. Nothing about sex had ever seemed intrinsically wrong to me before, as long as it was between two consenting adults, you know?"

"I feel the same way. That's exactly it."

He loved that she got it, that they were on the same page when it came to sex. But then, he'd already suspected this about her, had felt it right away.

"I was so angry," she went on. "At him. At myself. But I was also just . . . crushed. And looking back, that was definitely more about the whole thing with my parents, the way they'd always looked at me, and found me wanting. The way that left me feeling about myself beneath the confident exterior I'd constructed and mostly believed in. I don't mean to sound whiny or pathetic. But that was how it was for me growing up. This constant state of being rejected by them."

"I don't think you're whining or being pathetic," he told her.

"I'm twenty-nine years old. I feel like I should be over it by now. Do you ever feel like that, Dante? God, tell me I'm not the only sad story here."

Dante shrugged. "I had plenty of issues with my dad. I still do. I don't have a real connection with him. He's always been so harsh. Demanding. A perfectionist. Totally unforgiving of weakness. You know, my mom's health has never been good, and he judges her for that, I think, even while he's holding it over my head, my brother's head. That man can wield a guilt trip like nobody else. If we didn't do our homework or forgot to mow the lawn, normal kid stuff, he was on us. We had to be responsible. We were letting our mother down. And God forbid we ever showed a chink in our armor. Even when we were five, six years old, we weren't allowed to cry if we got hurt. I broke my arm falling off my bike when I was ten, and I just gritted my teeth while they set the break. The nurses all told me how brave I was, but it wasn't that. I didn't dare cry. Didn't dare complain."

He remembered it so clearly. The starchy, chemical scent of the emergency room. His father's glare. His mother standing behind his father, looking over his shoulder, afraid to say anything. Afraid to comfort her child. A shiver of disgust ran through him. He swallowed it down, as he always did.

Why did he want to tell Kara about this? He couldn't figure it out. All he knew was that he trusted her in a way he hadn't really trusted anyone but his brother, Renzo, in a long time. He'd never even discussed his family issues with Alec in such an in-depth way, and he was Dante's best friend.

His eyes had adjusted to the dim light, and he could see Kara watching him. There was no pity on her face. Just an openness.

"I don't see my parents often because, to tell you the truth, I can hardly stand it," he said. "I feel bad because my mom is so damn . . . faded. Like my father's just sucked the lifeblood out of her. I've always hated that and it's only gotten worse over the years. I hate that I can't protect her from him. But she wouldn't let me any more than he would."

"I'm sorry, Dante," Kara said, her voice soft.

"Christ, I shouldn't have told you that. It doesn't matter." He ran a hand over his jaw, over the spiky stubble there.

"Of course it does. The things that happen to us growing up make us who we are, for bad or good. And obviously it's made you a responsible man."

"Yeah. Maybe. I keep striving to be responsible. But I know my limits."

He wasn't as horrified at having revealed himself as he should be. Something about it being *Kara* he was talking to. That and the layer of dark that was like a protective blanket. A cocoon. But he wasn't used to it.

"Dante . . ."

"What is it?"

"I just felt you go tense all over."

"Hey, that's my job," he tried to joke, but it came out sounding stiff.

"I'm not reading you. Not like that. But . . . what else are you thinking?"

He didn't want to tell her. But he was going to do it.

"I'm thinking about my limits. About . . . this girlfriend I had in college."

"I'd heard something about that," Kara said, her tone soft and low. "That she'd been killed in an accident."

"It was my fault."

"I don't understand."

"It was my fault," he said again. His jaw was so tight it ached. But he was going to tell her the rest. "I should have driven her home that night. There was a party and I'd been studying . . . By the time I got there everyone was drunk but me. I should have taken her. But I didn't want to leave. I let one of her friends drive her, and they were both more than a little buzzed on beer. And she was upset that I didn't want to spend time with her. It was true; I didn't. I wanted to hang out with my friends."

"Dante, you were a college kid. We were all a little foolish in those days."

He sighed. "Now I sound pathetic."

"More than me?" she teased, trying to lighten the mood.

It had hit her while he was talking that maybe they were delving too deep. Even though it felt good, lying here in his bed, with dawn lightening the sky outside in shifting clouds of black and gray. It had felt good, until she'd started thinking about it too much. Until this opening-up-to-each-other thing got too scary for them both. She could sense it in him. Felt her own fear like something astringent in the back of her throat.

If they could only stop this part, just keep things where they'd been—amazing sex between old friends—then she could handle it.

"We don't have to talk about this anymore," he said.

"Okay. Not a problem. Let's change the subject."

He obviously did feel the same way she did, that they'd gone too deep. Which was a good thing. Wasn't it?

He rolled her onto her back and lowered his body over hers.

"There are a few things I can think of that I'd rather do with our time before work today." His voice was full of smoke. Full of need.

Instantly her sex lit up, desire coursing through her at the press of his hard body on hers. The scent of him, as dark as the winter sky. Her mind shut off as if a switch had been flipped. She was grateful for it.

She opened her thighs for him, and in a moment his hard cock was sheathed and sliding into her. His hands were on her breasts, his plush lips on her neck. Sensation took over as he arched his hips, surged into her. Lovely and sharp and sweet all at once.

And she let it all go, let go of the old, bitter memories, her own and his. Let go of the fear that made her heart pound with worry about allowing herself to get too close to him. And she let herself become lost in Dante once more.

Kara's fingers tapped on the edge of her keyboard as she glanced at the clock on her office wall for the tenth time that afternoon. She was waiting for six o'clock. It couldn't come soon enough.

She would see Dante at six. She would meet him in his office, as he'd told her to. He'd given her other instructions, as well.

And, following them, she'd slipped her panties off after lunch. Had spent all day being hyperaware of that nakedness beneath her black sweaterdress.

They'd been doing this for three weeks now. Meeting in Dante's office as everyone else was leaving to go home. The idea of being in a semipublic place was as thrilling as his touch, his command of her. She picked up a pen and let it roll through her fingers, remembering that sensation. The feel of his hands on her. The look he got in his eyes . . .

She started doodling on the notepad next to her phone, drawing an eye. But it wasn't enough. She tore the paper off, crumpled it and began again, outlining his face, his broad shoulders.

How to get the clean angles of his jaw, his cheekbones, just right? And that lush mouth, his expression . . . She was too out of practice. Yet it felt good to draw.

Even better to paint, maybe.

She hadn't thought about it in a long time. But Dante was so beautiful. A man who looked like he did should be painted. His image preserved.

God, he was really getting to her. His dark good looks. His touch. Everything they did together.

She let the pen drop from her fingers. Sighed.

She knew they were taking some small risk with their jobs, even though he'd taken to locking the office door after that first time. And she understood now that it had been meant to challenge her trust in him. He hadn't needed to do it again, take that kind of chance. Still, she knew it was all a little crazy. But she couldn't help herself.

She was getting wet simply thinking about it. The fifteen

minutes she had to wait would be excruciating. She was aching, needing him.

God, she'd turned into some sort of nymphomaniac, but that amused her more than it bothered her. Most of the time, anyway.

He would never fuck her at work. But he'd bend her over his desk, or over his lap in his office chair, and spank her. It was never a hard spanking, never rough enough to make her cry out. He wasn't willing to really take that kind of risk with her, which she appreciated. But it was enough to give her that edge of pain with her pleasure. He'd spank her, pinch her, while he got her off with his hands. She loved it. Loved it when he laid her down on the leather sofa in his office and went down on her, holding her body still, forcing her weight into the cushions. Making her feel completely taken over.

She was still surprised at how much she loved his dominance. How easily she'd given herself over to it. To him. And when he took her back to his place, it was even better. He was harder on her, as she became used to the BDSM play. She could take more. Wanted more. They'd even talked about going to his club, the Pleasure Dome. She was a little nervous about it, but the idea excited her, too. Especially the thought of doing the things they did together with other people watching.

She shivered and looked at the clock again. Five more minutes. She pulled her compact from her desk drawer and checked her reflection. Her hazel eyes were sparkling, her cheeks a little flushed. She ran a brush through her hair, slicked on a little lip gloss. Nothing too dark—he would likely kiss it off, anyway. She smiled at herself before clicking the compact shut and getting out of her chair.

She smoothed her dress down over her hips, her stomach, shook her hair out. Time to go. To him.

Dante.

When she opened the door to his office he was standing right there, barely allowing her room to slip through. He reached out with one hand and closed it behind her. She could smell his scent immediately, that dark, sexy musk.

"You're late," he said.

"What? It's exactly six," she protested.

Dante shook his head, his dark gaze gleaming with desire and a little wicked mischief. "It's almost one minute after. I'll have to find an appropriate punishment."

"Oh, I hope so," she found herself purring.

He'd never played the punishment game with her. She was surprised at how much she liked it. How her body was responding. But she'd probably respond to Dante this way, with desire shimmering over her skin in one long, undulating wave after another, no matter what he said. What he did.

He grabbed her and pulled her into his arms, holding her body hard against his. She loved how strong he was. How he dwarfed her. He held on so tightly she could barely breathe. And the spanking started at once, simply standing there a foot or two inside the door. He gripped her with one arm around her waist, while with his free hand he smacked her ass. A few times, then he slid her dress up and began to pinch her, small pinches that became harder and harder.

She could hear his rasping breath in her ear. Could feel his erect cock against her stomach. And she was absolutely soaked.

He moved his hand down over her ass, pinching, pinching.

"Spread for me," he ordered.

She parted her thighs. Gasped when his fingers pinched the lips of her sex. It was too good. Pleasure and pain battling, taking her under. Her nipples were two hard nubs against the lace of her bra. She wanted to feel them against his chest, wanted his punishing fingers pinching them hard.

"Dante, please . . ."

"I love it when you beg," he told her, giving her another hard twist of his fingers on her flesh.

"Touch me, Dante. I need you. I need to come."

"You think coming is an appropriate punishment?" he asked her. But she heard the teasing tone in his voice.

"Yes."

He laughed, moving with her still clasped tightly to his big body. He pushed her down roughly onto the couch. And she loved it, that he handled her this way. Then he was on her, pressing her down into the sofa cushions, the leather cool against her naked bottom. He spread her thighs and dove right in, using his hands to hold her wide-open while he licked her cleft in long, lovely strokes.

"Ah, God, Dante . . ."

He drove two fingers into her, making her gasp. She arched up off the couch, and he answered by thrusting deeper into her body. By sucking her hard clitoris into his mouth, grazing it with his teeth. And she came in a shiver of pure pleasure. It was brilliant, burning hot. She had to bite her lip to keep from screaming his name.

He sat up and looked at her. *Watched* her, as he so often did.

There was something a little different about the way he was looking at her. Something dark in his eyes, as if he was really *thinking* about something. Considering something. As she looked at him, she could swear she saw something shift, a flash of emotion, but it was gone too quickly for her to be certain. And she was too distracted by the last of her climax humming in her system. By his male beauty.

He was so beautiful she could hardly stand it. But as much as she wanted to reach for him, she knew to keep her arms still at her sides. To let him set the pace. And even that thrilled her.

"You're ready, Kara."

"Yes," she whispered. "I need to feel you inside me, Dante."

"For that, too. But I meant you're ready for more. You're ready for the club. I'm taking you to the Pleasure Dome this weekend."

"Oh."

Her mind churned, full of flashing images of what the club might be like. Naked bodies, the crack of whips, sensual anticipation heavy in the air.

"Do you like that idea? Because your face just flushed. Gorgeously. The same way you blush when I slip my hands between your thighs. Like this."

He did just that, his fingers feathering over her still-pulsing cleft. He smiled. "Christ, I love to see you like this. I could stay here and torture you all night. But I need to eat dinner first. Then I need to fuck you. Spank you again. But right now we'll go to a restaurant. Have some food. And while we have our dinner, you'll think about the club. About the things I'm going to do to you there."

"Yes, Dante." She could barely think. But every thought was about the club, the Pleasure Dome. Being there with Dante. Submitting to him in a way she never had before.

"And, Kara . . ."

"Yes?" she breathed. She was trembling all over. With the last of her climax. With the need to do it again.

"No panties at dinner. I may need you to be naked under that pretty dress." He pulled it down over her hips and stood, holding his hand out to help her up. "Shall we go?"

The restaurant was a big Italian place close to the water. Good food, excellent wine selection. But Dante didn't want to drink tonight. He wanted to stay focused on Kara. On what he had in mind for their evening.

They were seated at the back in a quiet corner, as he'd requested. It was one of those curving, red leatherette booths with a long white tablecloth. Perfect.

Kara was leaning into him a little. Loose from her orgasm still. He loved to see her this way. Devoid of her usual reserve. Relaxed.

He ordered their dinner—a light pasta dish for them both—then pulled her closer.

"How are you, beautiful girl?" he asked her.

"Wonderful."

"You seem a little tense."

"No. Well. I'm just wondering what you have up your sleeve." She smiled at him. Stunning. Gorgeous smile. Gorgeous face.

"Ah. You'll find out soon enough."

"You like to make me wait. For anything and everything."

"There's something about waiting that builds anticipation like nothing else."

"Is everything you do so well thought out?" she asked.

He nodded. "Yes. As a matter of fact, it is."

"You have such control issues, Dante."

"You like that about me."

"I do."

She was really grinning now. So was he. He liked this easy banter between them. That she took the teasing so well. Dished it back once in a while herself.

"So, what's going on in that wicked mind tonight?" she asked him, curling into him a little. Her body was warm next to his, her scent in the air, which was something fresh and floral and in direct contrast to the strength of her persona—the one she showed to the outside world.

He leaned in closer and whispered in her ear, "I'm going to get you off right here at the table. And I want you to come before our dinner arrives."

"Dante!"

"An argument?"

He heard her draw in a long breath. "No."

He pulled back and smiled at her. She didn't return the smile. But he could see the desire glimmering in her eyes. In the red fullness of her mouth. He kept smiling at her as he reached under the tablecloth, beneath the hem of her dress. And found the damp heat between her thighs.

"Ah, perfect," he whispered to her. "Spread for me, Kara. Good."

She opened her thighs, her eyes going wide as he slid his fingers inside her. Then her lashes fluttered, her gaze glazing as he began to pump gently.

"Keep your eyes on mine," he told her quietly. "I don't need to tell you not to let your expression betray what's going on here."

"No, Dante," she answered, arching her hips a little into his hand.

"Not even now," he instructed, pressing her clit with his thumb.

She bit her lip. His smile widened. He was hard as steel for her. But that could wait.

The waiter brought their drinks and Dante paused for a moment, nodded his head. And began again the moment the waiter turned his back.

"Does this excite you, Kara? To be touched this way in front of all these people?"

"Yes. God . . ."

"Can you come here, in front of all these people? Or is it too much for you?"

"I don't know . . . Yes. It's perfect."

He laughed. "*You're* perfect," he told her, thrusting deeper with his fingers, pressing harder and circling with his thumb.

She was trying not to writhe. He felt the tension in her muscles. He felt her sex tightening. Those first pre-climax spasms. He moved a little faster. Kept his head close to hers.

"Keep it quiet, beautiful girl," he commanded. "You can turn your face into my shoulder while you come. Do it now."

Nothing more than a soft gasp from her as she pressed her face into his shoulder, just as he'd instructed. But he could feel it in her body, that hard shiver, that tight clasp of her sex around his fingers as she climaxed.

Christ, he was hard as rock. His cock ached as she came into his hand. He kept working her until he was certain she was finished. Then he withdrew his fingers from her and tilted her chin so he could see her. Her cheeks were blazing, her eyes glossy, her pupils wide. And as she watched, he pressed the tip of his finger to his lips and licked.

"You taste better than anything they could serve here," he told her quietly. "You know how I love the taste of you. I can't get enough."

She smiled, dropped her head onto his shoulder.

It was true. He couldn't get enough of her. Her taste. Her sleek skin. Everything.

Crazy.

He was going crazy. Crazy for this girl. As crazy as he'd ever been for her back in high school. Much worse now that he knew the taste of her. Knew her body. Had felt her tremble in his arms with desire. Shattering with pleasure.

He had to get it under control. Certainly before he took her to the Pleasure Dome. Having her there would be like some wild fantasy come true. So much more than it would be with any other woman. Because it was *Kara*.

Oh yes. He was going crazy. Losing it, with her. He didn't know where it was going to end. He couldn't even think about it now. All he could think of was Kara. Having her. Tonight. This weekend at the club.

He had to pull himself together. And he would do it. He just had to fuck her first . . .

Control was the name of the game for him. Always had been. Always would be.

She tilted her head to look up at him, those metallic eyes—gold and silver and green—glossy and gleaming in the low light. Christ, she was beautiful. Smart. Elegant.

And he was so full of shit. Because for the first time in his life, something was happening that he didn't entirely have control over. And that something was Kara Crawford.

nine

Kara was back at her desk the next day, almost as if her night with Dante had never happened. Except for the welts on her ass and thighs that made her smile. That sense of being well used deep in her sex. She loved it.

Why, then, did she feel so agitated today?

She realized she was tapping her nails on the edge of her keyboard and made herself stop. She'd been at work for only an hour, but she'd gotten nothing done. Hadn't even answered e-mails yet. All she'd done was sit and brood.

She spun her chair to look out the window behind her. The sky was dark, the rain coming down in a gentle sprinkle that promised to get heavier as the day wore on. Usually the clouds and the falling rain made her feel cozy. But today they only made her feel . . . alone. Lonely.

What was going on with her? She'd had another wonderful

night with Dante. In his office, at the restaurant, then at his apartment. They hadn't played too hard—he said he wanted to save her strength for the club Saturday night. And she was excited about going. The idea was thrilling. So why was she so out of sorts?

She'd woken up this way, an hour before Dante's alarm went off. As usual, he'd dropped her off at home so she could get ready for work. And as she often did when they got together during the week, she'd left her car parked in the garage across from the office, then taken a cab in this morning. But, riding through the gray, damp streets, she'd been moody.

If she thought about it, she'd felt moody the moment she'd woken up. Dante had still been asleep beside her, his big body so still and quiet. She'd leaned closer just to hear him breathe. And she'd felt a little sad.

Maybe this was just some extended bottoming out?

She shook her head, moving her chair back around to face her desk. She had to stop thinking, put these strange feelings aside, and get some work done. She'd never been one to sit around brooding about a man, and she wasn't about to start now. If this was some bottoming-out thing, she could handle it, just as she handled everything else life had thrown at her. Being submissive didn't have to mean she was weak. Dante had told her that himself.

Maybe she should call him, ask him about this? She went to reach for the phone, let her hand hover there.

She sighed, and dropped her hand.

Dante. Everything circled back to him these days. And she didn't like it.

She bit her lip and reached for the phone once more. But this time she dialed Lucie's number.

"Luscious."

"Lucie, it's me."

"Kara, hi. What have you been up to? You've been on my mind, but I've been so busy with the kitchen remodel. It's almost done and things are crazy here."

"I've been meaning to call you, too, Lucie. I'm sorry I haven't. I've just been so . . . absorbed."

"Hmm, why am I so certain you're not talking about work?"

"I'm not. I've been seeing Dante. I know I said I wasn't going to, but I've been spending a lot of time with him and it's gotten . . . confusing. Can we meet for lunch?" Kara asked. "I really need to talk to someone."

"Are things going okay with him?"

"Yes. And no. I'm just questioning everything today. And I'm making myself a little nuts. Do you have time to meet?"

"I've got contractors coming to do some finishing work today and I have to be here," Lucie said. "Can you meet me here? I'll get some sandwiches or something."

"That would be great. Is one okay?"

"Perfect. I'll see you then."

"Thanks, Lucie."

Kara hung up. She wasn't sure how she'd go about talking to Lucie about all the things she and Dante had been doing together. The things they planned to do. But she didn't know how else to explain the feelings she was having. Hell, she couldn't explain them to herself. But she was hoping if she put all the information out on the table, Lucie might be able to help her figure out what to do, how to feel. How to toughen up again, get back to her usual self.

Maybe that self is too closed off. Maybe this is healthier.

Why didn't it feel better, then? It felt awful. Scary.

She glanced at the clock. She seemed to be doing a lot of that these days, measuring time. It was four hours until she could see Lucie. With another sigh, she resolved to get her head together and get some work done. There would be plenty of time to brood later.

At twenty to one Kara stood up from her desk, having accomplished very little. She pulled her coat and hat on, grabbed her purse, and headed to Lucie's new catering kitchen. It wasn't far, but she had to fight her way through the downtown traffic.

Finally, she pulled up across the street from the converted brick warehouse Lucie had recently rented. Her new sign hung over the wide, brushed-metal door, the word "Luscious" done in a graceful, dark pink script and outlined in black and gold. Getting out of the car, Kara ran through the rain and pulled the heavy door open, slipping inside.

She pulled her hat off, pushing her hair back from her face, and took off her coat. Looking around, she found Lucie behind a long wood counter painted a pristine white.

"Kara," Lucie greeted her with a smile, "it's so good to see you." The petite blonde slipped from behind the counter and gave her a hug. "So, what do you think?"

Kara took in the vaulted ceilings, the pink and white walls, the pair of antique French armoires in a whitewash finish flanking three low settees done in gold velvet.

"I know this space isn't very large," Lucie interjected, "but the kitchen in the back is huge. I can bake hundreds of cupcakes a day. And I'm set up to do wedding cakes, too, which I think will help really establish the business. It's so much better than trying to do it all out of my house."

"It's gorgeous," Kara told her, moving to the counter and running her hand over the smooth surface. "You've done such a good job here. I love the mix of antiques in the industrial space. And you know I know nothing about kitchens, but I'm sure it's perfect. Your cupcakes are the best in the world; I think this is what you needed for things to really take off."

Lucie beamed, her dark brown eyes shining as she took Kara's coat and slung it over the counter. "I'm just so damn proud of it. I feel like a kindergartner with my first finger painting." She took Kara's hand and led her to the sitting area. "Come on and get comfortable while I bring lunch out. I ordered from this great gourmet deli around the corner since I'm not stocked up here yet. I hope you're hungry."

"I can always eat, no matter what's going on."

"Good. I'll be right back."

Kara's cell phone chimed as she was sitting down, letting her know she had a text message.

Dante.

Lucie came back, carrying a tray with sandwiches and two bottles of their favorite iced green tea. She set it down on the glass coffee table and settled onto one of the settees.

"Is that your beau?"

Kara sighed, nodded. "Yes."

"Why don't you sound happier about it?"

She shrugged. "I honestly don't know. Things have been great between us."

Lucie handed Kara her sandwich on a china plate. "I hope you like it. It's prosciutto and Brie. So, what do you think the problem is? And you don't have to worry about the workmen overhearing. They're out back taking their lunch break."

"I'm hoping you can help me figure it out." Kara took her plate, taking a moment to get her thoughts organized. "It's . . . complicated. And I think a little of it is leftovers from Jake. I know some of it is, anyway. But mostly it's about what's happening now between Dante and me." She stopped, sipped her tea. Lucie was waiting silently, giving her time to think it through. "Okay. I have to tell you something about the . . . dynamic between us. It's not the usual casual dating relationship. Dante is . . . a sexual dominant. And we've been . . . doing some fairly extreme stuff together that's making things a lot more intense."

"Ah."

"That's it? 'Ah'?"

"Kara, honey, neither of us are virgins. And I've delved into a little kink myself, from time to time."

"You've never told me that." Although Kara wasn't completely surprised. Lucie was one of those women who exuded sex.

Her friend shrugged. "It's never come up. I'm telling you now so you'll understand you don't have to worry that I'll judge you."

"That does help. I've been a little worried about sharing this with you. I should have known better."

"I don't blame you for being cautious, even with me. It's okay."

Kara took a bite of her sandwich, trying to figure out where to really begin. So much had happened in just the last few weeks. She swallowed, and put her plate down.

"So . . ." she started, "for the last few weeks things have been great. The sex is amazing. He's shown me things, sides of myself, I never really knew were there. I mean, I've had urges that I've never explored before, and since I've been doing these things with him, it's opened me up in ways I didn't expect. Which is good. But it's also getting a little scary. And I can't quite figure out what it is that's scaring me."

"Is he too demanding? Making you do things you don't want to do?"

"No. He never would. He's completely responsible and conscious of what he's doing. He's always in control. Which has allowed me not to be, for the first time in my life, probably. When we're in those roles, he treats me like I'm . . . precious."

Her cheeks went hot, saying it all out loud. And at the memory of that sense of being cherished. Treasured. Why did she feel like she wanted to cry, suddenly?

"That's the way it should be," Lucie said, her brown eyes going soft. "So what's wrong?"

"Maybe *I'm* wrong," Kara said. Her chest was going tight, and her throat, making it hard to speak. She pulled in some air, let it go. "I never wanted a relationship, Lucie. I'm not looking for that. The mess I made with Jake was enough to last me for a long time. And Dante doesn't want that, either, so we're on the same page. Or, we have been. But things are suddenly feeling so . . . serious. I don't know; maybe it's not so sudden. There's been this slow build between us. I've been getting to know him and he's an amazing person. He's really . . . noble. And kind. Gorgeous. I can't find anything wrong with him, to tell you the truth."

"Do you think that's why you're blaming yourself? Because he's so 'perfect,' for lack of a better word?" Lucie asked. "Because—

and I'm not saying this to be cruel—but you have a tendency to take all the blame for everything, Kara. What happened with Jake. Never getting your parents' approval. In both of those situations, you didn't do anything wrong. And how you're feeling about Dante now isn't necessarily *wrong*."

"It is for me," Kara insisted. "I didn't want to have feelings for him. I don't need it right now. And I can't separate out how much is this . . . vulnerability caused by the things we're doing and how much is valid. True."

"Let me tell you a little of what I know about this kind of kink. It *does* open you up. But it opens you up to the truth inside you. It doesn't make you imagine things that aren't already there."

"Even if that's true, Lucie, I don't *want* it." The tears were threatening again. She bit them back. "I don't want to feel something for yet another man who is ultimately going to reject me."

"Honey, why would he reject you?"

"Because he doesn't want to be in a serious relationship any more than I do."

"Except that some part of you does," Lucie suggested quietly.

"Yes. Shit." Kara pushed her hair from her face, blew out a long breath. "Saying it out loud only makes it worse."

"I think at some point you'll have to decide what you want, Kara. If you want a relationship and Dante doesn't, then you'll need to cut it off. I don't want to see you hurt again."

"Neither do I."

"But," Lucie went on, "I think it may be too soon to know. Is there any chance he's feeling the same way you do?"

"I don't know. I don't think so. He seems pretty decisive. And I'm just the kinky girl to him now. I don't know that he'd ever see me any other way. And it's not like we're really even dating. He doesn't take me to movies or out to eat. Except for this lunch the first day I found out he was working at my firm. But he only wanted to talk to me about that. And . . . he took me to dinner last night, but going to the restaurant was . . . It was a sexual thing. It wasn't about dating. It wasn't romantic." She paused, remembering the things he'd said to her. The way he'd looked at her. She sighed. "Except at the end it *was*. For me. For a few moments. God, I don't know. I'm thinking in circles."

Lucie leaned forward, reaching for her hand across the table. "If you have real feelings for him, Kara, and if there's any chance things could work, then maybe you need to give it that chance. Give it a little longer, anyway. I can't help you make this decision, but it sounds like there could be something here you need to explore. I'm not convinced that he can't see beyond the kink. He'd be a fool not to."

"Thanks, Lucie." Kara squeezed Lucie's hand, let it go. "Thanks for listening. I just need to make a decision."

And it needed to be soon. They were due to go to the Pleasure Dome in a few days. And she had a feeling the play was going to get a lot more serious. Which meant her feelings could get more serious, too.

She wanted to go to the club. Wanted to experience that with Dante. There had never been any question about it. The question was only if she could keep her emotions under control.

It had never been a problem for her before. The thing with Jake had happened because she'd *chosen* to open her heart to him, even if she'd never really opened to him entirely. It had been a mistake, yes, but one she'd made by choice.

Was continuing to see Dante, taking this risk with her heart, going to be worth it, in the end? She didn't know. But she was already in deep enough that she accepted she wasn't going to turn away from him. No matter how afraid she was.

She was going to keep seeing him. She was going to the Pleasure Dome with him. Even though she knew, with him, she was risking everything.

Dante paced in front of the long row of windows in his living room, his gaze on the night sky outside. It wasn't raining, for once, and the stars burned, tiny pinpoints of light against a backdrop of dark velvet.

He was waiting for Kara to arrive for their night at the Pleasure Dome. He'd told her to take a cab to his place. She was due any minute. But he could hardly stand it.

It was more than the usual excitement brought about by the anticipation of a night at the club ahead. It was a tightness in his gut. An eagerness to touch her. *Be* with her.

Stop it. Just calm down, buddy.

He didn't want to think of her like this. Didn't want to think of any woman this way. With such primal *need*.

He'd always managed to keep a comfortable distance from the women he dated. He did it consciously, by choice. He had his reasons why, and he was aware of them. But with Kara, that choice was being taken from him, bit by bit. He was losing control. It was still hard to believe, and even harder to accept.

Could he keep seeing her and maintain any semblance of control, outside of the roles they played in their kink activities? At least there, he knew he was in command.

Mostly.

Damn it.

He forced himself to stop pacing, to look out over Elliott Bay below him. It was too dark to really see the water, but lights from the docked boats glimmered. It was an amazing view. A million-dollar view. On those rare clear days the horizon seemed to stretch forever, the water sparkling, brilliant. And the nighttime view was like a string of jewels—the boats on the water on one side, the city of Seattle spread out in panorama on the other. But he couldn't have cared less at the moment. He turned away, ran a hand over his jaw.

Don't think so damned much.

He needed to keep it together. Especially tonight. Kara's first visit to a BDSM club could be overwhelming. He had to be in total command.

Just focus on the club. On your role as a dominant.

He was fine in that role. Always had been. Focused. Strong. He'd have to be tonight. Because there was something different about taking Kara there, to the Pleasure Dome. About the idea of stripping her down and playing her in front of all those people. Exciting as hell. He had to stop thinking about what else was lurking beneath the surface of the sexual thrill, the thrill of power play.

He took in a deep breath, forcing his mind to calm. His body.

The buzzer went off and he jerked, startled.

She was there.

Kara.

He opened the door.

She was so fucking beautiful. Her long, brown hair, a blend of chocolate and caramel, was loose around her shoulders, which were bared by the white leather corset-style dress she wore. Her lips were painted red, which made him go hard instantly—the vampy mouth in her lovely face that always held some air of innocence.

Jesus.

"Dante?"

"What? Sorry." He hadn't realized he'd kept her standing in the hall while he stared at her. "Come on in."

He took her hand and pulled her into the apartment. He stood there, looking at her once more, taking it all in.

The dress was short, baring a smooth expanse of firm thigh between the hem and the tops of her white stiletto-heeled boots. Her legs were endless when she was wearing heels. Hell, they were endless even in bare feet. But the boots were fantastic on her. Flawless.

She was quiet, standing before him, her hands hanging at her sides. He could see that she was going down already, into subspace, that misty place in her mind where a bottom really began to let go. He'd take her much deeper before the night was over.

A sharp twitch of need in his cock at the thought of it. Better to get to the club as quickly as possible. If they stayed in his apartment any longer, he was going to tear that little dress off her and fuck her right there on the hard floor of the foyer. With those hot, white boots on . . .

He blinked, realizing she was waiting for him to do something. She was holding her trench coat in her hand. He took it from her and slipped it around her shoulders, got his leather jacket and put it on.

"Are you ready, Kara?"

"Yes. Ready. Excited. And a little nervous. I knew I would be, but this is . . . I'm a bit overwhelmed. Not knowing quite what to expect."

"That's all normal." He could say the same for himself to-night. "It'll be fine, I promise. And if anything makes you seriously uncomfortable, if you begin to panic, tell me and we'll go. I would never force the club scene on anyone. But I wouldn't take you there if I wasn't convinced you could handle it. I think you're going to love it."

She nodded, a small smile on her lovely face. "So do I. I really am ready."

"Good girl. Let's go."

Outside, he hailed a cab. He wasn't certain how worked up he'd be himself by the end of the night. Adrenaline. Endorphins. He didn't think it would be a good idea for him to drive.

On the short ride to the club, Kara was quiet beside him. But she was leaning into him, her body warm through the little leather dress, her coat. When he put a hand on her thigh she was burning up.

Too good, that hot, silky flesh. But what was coming later was even better.

They got out in front of the club, an old gray-brick warehouse with a heavy red door. He nodded to the doorman, who, recognizing Dante from his frequent visits there, let them inside. The interior of the club's main floor was dimly lit in red and amber, the walls dark. Around the room were pieces of large equipment: the tall St. Andrew's crosses, the racks and bondage tables, the enormous wooden bondage frames where people wove intricate patterns in rope, holding their bottoms captive. The rope work was beautiful, but it wasn't really his thing. He was more into sensation play.

Keeping an arm around Kara's waist, he moved them toward a row of spanking benches. Yes, this was what he loved. And he knew she would love it, too. That sensual heat of his hand coming down on her skin. He loved the occasional toy: the paddle, the flogger, the clamps. But with her, he simply couldn't get enough of her flesh beneath his hands.

Kara's head was spinning. She'd been sinking into subspace ever since she'd started the ritual of getting dressed, preparing herself for Dante. It was something she'd become used to, something that happened whenever she was getting ready to meet him, even those times when she was going into his office at the end of a workday. But this was different, being at the club. Now that they were really there, in the Pleasure Dome, that soft, sinking sensation threatened to take her over completely.

It was wonderful and frightening at the same time, and she was glad for the solid stability of Dante's big body next to hers. For how tightly he hung on to her. There was command in his grip. It made her feel safer. It made her want to be there that much more.

The club was a lot larger than she'd expected, an enormous warehouse space with vaulted ceilings. There were dozens of people there already, using the equipment or sitting in groups on the sofas and chairs at the edges of the room. Everything was dark: the walls, the furnishings, the lighting. It seemed appropriate for such a place, somehow. Music thumped in the background, a consistent, sensual beat, helping to create an atmosphere of tension, anticipation.

But she noticed all of these things at the edge of her consciousness. What really filled her head, her body, were thoughts of Dante touching her. Spanking her. Commanding her.

He led her to a wall where wide chairs upholstered in dark red velvet punctuated a row of leather-covered spanking benches. She understood what they were, what they were for; she'd looked them up online a long time ago, and again more recently. How had Dante sensed this was exactly what she craved most?

But as he took her to the chair and set down the leather duffel he'd brought with him, nerves filled her, making her tremble. Was she really going to do this?

"Dante . . ."

"Shh, it's going to be okay," he told her, stroking her hair from her face.

He helped her off with her coat, removed his, and laid them both over the back of the chair. Every motion was precise, controlled.

She took a deep breath, tried to calm herself by focusing on his absolute control. By reminding herself that she was in good hands with him, literally.

He put his hands on her shoulders, gazing down at her. His features were so strong, so purely masculine. Beautiful.

"Kara," he said quietly. She could feel the heat of him, desperately wanted him to kiss her. "I'm going to take your clothes off."

"Oh . . ."

She felt shocked, somehow. She wasn't sure why. There were a number of naked people at the club. She'd known to expect it. Still, the idea made her shake with equal measures of nerves and a stark, driving lust.

Need him. Need this.

He leaned in closer, his mouth right next to hers. "Kara, take a deep breath. All you have to do is obey me. Simply do as I say. I will take care of everything else."

She nodded. She knew he'd take care of her at the club. And her mind was going empty, then refilling with a blanket of soft, white noise. She let herself fall into it a little as Dante began to undress her.

He reached behind her and unzipped her dress. She felt the cool brush of the leather as he drew it over her head. All she had on underneath was a white lace thong.

"Pretty," he murmured before he slipped that, too, off her body, down over her high boots. Then he took those off, as well, helping her step out of them.

The air was warm on her naked flesh. She had never felt so naked in her entire life as she did now in this room full of other people. It made her shiver with need. With a strange sort of pride. Her nipples were two hard peaks.

Dante smoothed his palms over her shoulders once more, pausing to press down. Just enough pressure to let her know that he was in command. Her mind emptied a little more, her sex going damp.

"Kara, I want you down on your knees," he told her, his voice still that low, soothing tone. "I know we haven't done this before. But it's a beautiful symbol of your submission. I understand you are not a slave. That's not what I'm interested in. Your submission is about what is happening at this moment. Do you understand?"

"Yes, Dante . . . but it's . . . I don't know if I can do it." There was a tight, inexplicable knot in her chest.

"You can. You'd be surprised at how freeing it can be. Simply turning it all over to me. Do you trust me, Kara?"

"Yes. I trust you."

"Then down you go, beautiful girl."

God, was she actually going to do this? Her mind was really spinning now, reeling at a hundred miles an hour. But as fast as it was going, it was almost entirely blank.

Dante held on to her hand, and after a moment's hesitation, she went down, kneeling on the floor.

Her cheeks were burning, but it wasn't embarrassment. It was a heat emanating from deep inside her body. Desire. Intensity. She couldn't figure it out. All she knew was that she was going loose all over, the knot in her chest unraveling, her body signaling her yielding. To *him*.

Dante.

He had his hands on her shoulders again, standing behind her now, pressing down. Holding her still. Holding her *safe*.

He leaned over and said quietly, "Good girl, Kara. Take in a breath. Exhale. And let it go. The control. The fear. I'm right here. Take another breath now. Good."

He stayed with her, taking her through the breathing, helping her to relax. To trust. Her head was buzzing.

"I'm going to let you go for a few minutes to get things set up. I want you to stay just as you are. Will you be all right?"

"Yes. I'll be okay."

"Very good."

She felt him move away, was dimly aware of the slip of the zipper on his duffel bag, small, muffled sounds as he removed things from it. There was a thrill in wondering about it, what he might do, what implement he might use on her. That combination of desire edged in fear. She pulled in a deep breath, focused on the pulse beat of the music she could feel deep in her belly. The eager anticipation in her aching sex, her breasts.

Dante was back at her side after a minute or two, helping her to her feet.

"Come on, Kara. We're going to the spanking bench now."

She paused, had to clench her jaw not to yank her hand back. Why did she have the urge to pull away when this was the very thing she wanted, had fantasized about?

Maybe *that* was why. But she couldn't think enough to figure it out. She was trembling all over.

"Dante . . . no." She was shaking her head slowly. She couldn't stop herself.

He was quiet a moment, his hand going to the back of her neck and massaging it lightly.

"Are you truly saying no, Kara? Because if it really is no, then we can stop. Tell me what you want."

"I . . . I don't know. I can't stop shaking."

He drew her into his side, his arm tight around her waist. His face was close to hers. He said very quietly, "This is all up to you, Kara. *You* decide. That's where your power is in all this. So tell me. Is it yes? Or is it no?"

She felt as if she were on a precipice. Paused. Waiting to fall into the darkness. The unknown. She wanted this. Badly. She was scared to death.

Yes.

No.

Her mind was spinning so hard she was breathless. She had no idea at that moment what her answer would be.

ten

Dante's hand tightened on the back of her neck. She had once more that instant feeling of safety flooding through her. And intense relief.

"Kara, you're in my hands," he told her, his voice that lovely, low tone that soothed her like a balm on her skin. "You'll be fine. You'll be amazing."

He smoothed his other palm over her stomach, and she felt a shiver of lust in her sex. Pulsing, pulsing. She looked at the bench, frightening and incredibly enticing at the same time.

She wanted Dante to be proud of her. Wanted to be proud of herself.

"Dante . . . I . . . I don't want to let the fear get in the way. I want this. Absolutely. I just need to . . . breathe a minute."

"Okay. Take another breath, then. That's it."

He leaned in and kissed her cheek. And when she turned her face up to his, he tilted her chin and kissed her lips.

She was flooded with heat. With the taste of him, the soft texture of his mouth. When he swept inside with his tongue, the heat and the need surged through her body.

Oh yes. Want this . . .

He pulled back to murmur against her lips, "You are so damn beautiful. This will be so good. I'll make it good for you, Kara."

She nodded, most of the fear swept away in the desire washing over her.

"Are you ready?" he asked.

"Yes. Yes."

"You'll be fine. Just do as I tell you, Kara. Give yourself over to me."

She nodded once more, her shoulders going loose again, and followed him.

The spanking bench was like a wooden sawhorse, except that there were two levels to it, and it was covered in red leather. The top was one long, narrow, padded column with armrests on either side. The lower section was made up of narrow ledges on either side, which she knew were for her to rest her knees and elbows on. Here and there were eyebolts to fasten cuffs or rope to. Or chains.

She shivered.

"Climb on, beautiful girl. I'll help you."

Dante held on to her hand, his other hand at her waist. And even as a part of her couldn't believe she was doing it, she mounted the bench, laying her body down on the top level and steadying herself with her elbows on the armrests before bringing her knees up to the lower ledges.

She realized instantly that in this position her naked ass was raised up. Her mound was pressed against the soft leather. And immediately she had the urge to press harder into it, to ease the ache there. But she sensed she shouldn't do anything unless Dante told her to. She wanted only to do what he told her.

Dante leaned over her. "Since this is your first time, I'm not going to bind you. But you are not to move unless I tell you to. Do you understand?"

"Yes. I understand, Dante."

His hands were on her back then, sweeping over her bare skin: her shoulders, down her spine to that sensitive spot at the small of her back. She closed her eyes. She was acutely aware of every touch, of the rhythm he was using as his palms slipped over her, matching the beat of the music playing. It seemed to go on forever, just his hands on her body. And all the while her sex was going hotter and hotter, until she was soaking wet.

She wanted him to spank her. Wanted to ask for it. But she remained quiet. Reveled in the hot, shimmering desire thrumming through her system, lighting up every nerve ending.

One of Dante's hands moved lower, over her buttocks and the backs of her thighs. The other stayed on her lower back, holding her down with that gentle, commanding pressure she loved. She had some strange sense of him touching her everywhere at once. Except where she most needed it.

It grew harder and harder to hold still, her sex throbbing. *Needing.* Her nipples were stiff against the sleek leather surface of the bench. And just when she thought she couldn't take any more, she felt the first feathering touch of his fingertips slipping between her folds.

"Oh . . ." she moaned, surging back.

"No, Kara. Hold still."

She bit her lip, forced her body to quiet. Held her breath as his fingers moved, slipping in her wetness, up and down the length of her cleft.

Pleasure was liquid, long serpentine strands weaving through her limbs, her muscle, her skin. When he pierced her with his fingers, she gasped. And when he plunged deeper inside her, she groaned, her eyes flying open.

Across from her was a man. Young, with a pretty face. An amazing body. He wore nothing but a pair of dark jeans and a leather collar. When she realized what was happening, that this beautiful man was watching what Dante was doing to her, her sex flooded, heat and wet, need and an intensity she'd never experienced before.

She held his gaze. And as a slow smile slid across his face, Dante's hand came down in a sharp smack across her ass.

"Oh!"

Dante's palm smoothed over the burning skin, soothing her. He spanked her again, then another sweet stroke of his hand, and another. The dual sensations made each more acute. Her fingers gripped the padded armrests. The young man's sharp gaze on hers was nearly overwhelming.

Dante pushed his fingers deeper into her.

"Christ, you are soaked, my girl," he said. "And you love him watching you, don't you? You love to be spanked. To be this vulnerable. I love it, too. Seeing you like this. Having an audience. Sharing with others how beautiful you are in your submission. In your desire."

She shivered at his words, at the pleasure in his tone.

He smacked her again, over and over, creating a sharp, fast pace. He kept his fingers pumping inside her. And she was overcome by desire and pain, all at once. Sensation melded together until it was one thing: *need*. Pure. Primal.

Pleasure built, pleasure upon pain. Her head, her body, were soaring. The hot smacking of Dante's hand blended with his thrusting fingers. Her sex swelled, and she pressed her mound into the leather bench; she couldn't help herself. Pressed until there was just enough pressure on her clitoris. She came, shattering, crying out. He kept at it, the spanking, his fingers driving deep. Her pussy was a clenching glove, needing more, more. And the beautiful young man kept his steady gaze on hers, driving her climax on in some inexplicable way.

"God, Dante!"

She couldn't stop coming. She was trembling, the aftershocks of orgasm seeming to last forever.

Finally, her body began to calm. The stranger gave her one last smile and walked away. She felt Dante's hands in her hair, caressing her cheeks, her lips. He was kneeling in front of her, tilting her face up to meet his eyes. They were gleaming golden in the dim light.

"That was excellent," he told her, his low tone laced with desire. "That was perfect, Kara. Beautiful girl."

He kissed her. And those soft lips on hers, the taste of him, the knowledge that it was Dante, made the desire rise in her once more.

"My girl," he murmured against her mouth.

His.

Yes.

He kissed her again, harder this time. His lips a firm press against hers, his tongue invading, driving into her mouth in the same way his fingers had driven into her body only moments before. She was so loose all over, her skin burning where he had spanked her, like some lovely reminder of what he'd done. How he had *made* her his.

He pulled back.

"Come on, let's get you down from there."

He moved around behind her once more, and she waited for him. He gripped her waist and pulled her up, until she was straddling the bench on her knees. His hands slipped around to cup her breasts, and she sighed, arching into his touch. His body was warm behind her, his palms on her full flesh scorching her. Her nipples were so hard they hurt. He pulled at them, twisting, tugging. Not too hard, just hard enough to send shards of new sensation stabbing into her body. Making her aware of how soaking wet she was, the air cool between her spread thighs.

"You love having an audience, don't you, Kara? No one is watching you specifically right now, but can you feel it? The energy in the air? Their presence?"

"Yes," she breathed. It was true. Simply knowing they weren't alone was a thrill in itself. Not as much as it had been when the stranger watched her come, though. Oh no. That had been the most intense experience of her life.

She wanted to do it again. But she also wanted to be alone with Dante. Needed some kind of reassurance from him. She didn't understand it.

Instantly, she was shivering, shaking.

"Dante . . . ?"

"Yes, I feel it. I've got you, baby."

He pulled her from the bench and into his arms, sat down with her on his lap in the big velvet chair. He pulled a blanket around her shoulders, made her drink some water from a bottle he held to her lips.

"Dante, did I . . ."

He rubbed her arms through the blanket. "Shh, yes. You pleased me very much. You were wonderful. Perfect."

How did he know this was exactly what she needed so desperately to hear?

"Dante, I don't feel like . . . myself."

"No, of course not. It's normal. You're bottoming out a little. You'll be fine. I'll take care of you."

When had anyone else ever said that to her? When had anyone said that and meant it? Tears stung her eyes.

Love him . . .

No. That was just the experience talking. The lightness in her head. The bottoming out.

Why, then, did her entire body surge with the rightness of the idea? Why did she have to bite her lip to keep from telling him?

Oh God, she couldn't tell him. Not *him*.

Not *her*.

She swallowed the tears. Promised herself she would deal with this—look at it—later, when her head was screwed on straight again.

"Kara, you're too tense. Let's do some breathing, try to get you to relax again."

"I can't."

He held her tighter, until she could feel the strong, steady beat of his heart against her rib cage. "You can. Just follow me. Inhale, a nice, deep breath."

With some effort she did as he said. Eventually her racing pulse calmed; her mind stopped spinning. The breathing helped. But what helped more than anything was his solid frame so close to hers. His arms around her. His scent all around her, that dark, elemental *male*.

He ran a hand down her spine, his fingers brushing, stroking. When he got to the small of her back, he made lazy circles on her skin. And just as it had before, his touch began to light her body up with desire.

How could she feel this now, right after what had amounted to a small meltdown? She was so confused. But it was so much easier to simply give in. To his touch. To the pleasure flooding her body once more. To Dante.

He whispered to her, "I need to get you home. To fuck you in my bed. Come on, my beautiful girl."

Another small rush of heat went through her.

Yes, in his bed. His arms.

She wanted whatever he wanted of her. Even more strongly than she had before, when he had her on the spanking bench. She wanted—needed—to be as close to him as possible.

He stood her on her feet and dressed her. Carefully. Gently. And she had once more that sense of being cherished by him.

She knew in the back of her mind that it was all about the dynamics of the power play. His role as a dominant. But she would take what she could get for now. Would hang on to it later, when he'd finished with her, as he inevitably would. She knew in her heart that nothing this good could possibly last.

Dante's head was spinning as they rode in a cab over the wet streets, back to his place.

Having Kara at the club was almost too much for him. He was vaguely ashamed. He'd come too close to losing control with her. To turning her over on that spanking bench and fucking her right there.

She'd been incredibly turned on by that male sub watching them. Hell, so had he. Not that he was into the boys. But he loved the exhibitionism. Was so damn proud of Kara's beauty, her responsiveness.

He'd grown so hard he could barely stand it. It had taken everything he'd had not to press up against her gorgeously pinking ass, to pull himself from his slacks and thrust right into her. But he'd promised himself he wouldn't do that. Not her first time at the club. And something had shifted when she'd started to bottom out. Even when she'd still been straddling the bench and he'd had the erection of his life, pressing against the small of her back. He'd become almost unbearably protective of her. And along with it had come a need to have her all to himself. It was a sense of ownership and a desire he could barely control, each element making the other spiral, soar.

Mine.

He groaned. He was still hard as a rock, his cock aching. And her beautiful body pressed close into his side, still loose from her climax, still deep in subspace. It was too good. They couldn't get back to his place fast enough.

He looked at her. Her eyes were half-closed, just a glimmer of gold and heat from beneath her long lashes. Her mouth was red, swollen-looking. Christ, she was beautiful.

He reached over and pressed one finger to those lush lips. And felt a shock of lust go through him when she sucked one fingertip into her mouth.

Like heat and sleek velvet inside her mouth. He groaned. Her pussy would feel nearly the same. But tighter. Just as wet.

He slipped a hand between her thighs, smiled when her eyes fluttered open, went wide as he ran his fingers over her damp cleft.

Oh yes, she was soaked, as he knew she would be. Ready for him.

"Hold still," he told her, keeping his voice soft. But unable to resist doing this.

The driver was paying them no attention, listening to some staticky music on the radio. Dante looked back to Kara, watched her teeth come down on her bottom lip as he slid his fingers deeper and began to pump.

Her hips arched, but he shook his head. She settled back immediately.

Ah, she was perfect, this girl. Not the first time he'd thought that.

He listened to the harshness of her breath as he worked her with his hand. He grew harder with each moment. Ready to explode.

"Have to fuck you soon, my girl," he told her, his voice a soft whisper in her ear.

She blinked up at him. But she was perhaps too far gone to respond. He didn't mind. He loved it, actually.

The cab pulled up in front of his place and he slipped his hand from her body. She gave a soft, resigned sigh. He paid the driver, giving him far too large a tip. Didn't matter. He just had to get Kara into the apartment.

Once they were upstairs he stripped her down quickly. He had to pause, to look at her, to take it all in: her flushed cheeks, her breasts, which looked full and heavy, the nipples swollen and a gorgeous dark red. Luscious. He couldn't wait to see her wet all over. He started to take his clothes off, unbuttoning his shirt—and paused.

Even better to see her in his shirt, the water coming down over the white fabric. He groaned.

He kicked off his shoes, took everything off but his shirt. Even the hem of the fine cotton on his hard cock was excruciating, sending a small shock of pleasure through him. But it was even better as he pulled his shirt off and helped her into it.

She wasn't under the water yet and his cock was pulsing in anticipation. Ready to come any moment.

He stepped into the shower, taking her with him. He hadn't had her in there enough lately. And why had he not put her in one of his shirts yet? Seen the water plastering the cotton against her skin, as it was doing now.

He groaned.

"Jesus, Kara. You are so damn beautiful, so damn hot like this. I love to see your skin beneath the wet fabric. The silhouette of your body. There's something so incredible about this for me. I can't even tell you what it makes me want to do to you."

She was quiet, pliant, as he ran his hands over her shoulders, her breasts, which were gorgeously outlined under the wet white cotton. It was nearly translucent now, it was so wet, which was exactly the way he liked it.

He ran his hands under the shirt, across her stomach. Shivered when she did. When he leaned in and sucked one stiff nipple into his mouth through the cotton, his cock felt like it was going to go off like a volcano. He had to pull away, to take a few deep breaths, command himself to calm.

"God, Dante. This is . . . I've never felt anything like it."

"Glad it's good for you, baby," he muttered, taking her breasts in his hands once more, cupping them, thumbing the nipples. Listening to her panting breath. To his own.

He pressed up against her, the sensation of the wet cotton and the curve of her stomach nearly sending him over the edge every other moment. He had to stop, pull in a breath once more, grit his teeth to hang on to any sense of control.

Calm down. Need to calm down.

He stepped back. Christ, she was gorgeous like this. But he had to slow the pace down or it was all going to be over too damn soon.

He grabbed the big sponge and his favorite bar of citrus-and-musk soap and lathered her up—just her thighs, her stomach under the hem of the shirt. He loved that it made her smell like him. He didn't know why. But it didn't matter. What mattered was the way her nipples went darker, harder, beneath the wet fabric. Her small sighs. The way she watched him with pure desire on her face as he washed himself, sliding the sponge over his hard cock.

He was rinsing himself off when she said, "Dante, please. Let me. Let me touch you."

He smiled at her, nodded, and she took the shower wand from him, got down on her knees and aimed the water at his belly, then lower.

The hot water was like a thousand gentle needles on his needy flesh. He moaned.

She moved the sprayer between his thighs and he spread them wider. She shifted the wand, so that the water hit his balls.

"Ah, Jesus, that's good," he muttered, pleasure arcing into him in a hard current. He had to clench his jaw, to hold out against it.

She cupped his balls in her hand, massaging gently, and he thought he might die of pleasure. The things she was doing to him, the sight of her in his shirt, the wet cotton pulling against her skin. He braced his hands on her shoulders, her wet hair streaming down her back. He began to pump his hips a little; he couldn't help it. She glanced up at him, her cheeks flushed, her gaze burning. And, holding his gaze with hers, she held his cock in her hand and brushed the tip across her lips.

"Ah, God, Kara . . ."

Pleasure was a keen rush into his system. And when she sucked the head of his cock into her plush, hot mouth, his knees felt as if they might buckle.

He braced himself against the granite walls of the shower, tried to breathe. But it became harder and harder as she swirled her tongue over the tip, dipping it into the small hole, then plunging down to swallow him, taking him deeper, deeper.

"Kara, I'm going to come if you keep this up. I'm going to come right now, baby . . ."

But he'd lost all control of the situation. She sucked harder, drawing him into her throat, then slipping to the very tip, then down again. Her hand held on to his cock at the base, never letting go. And she still held the sprayer on his tight balls.

He was going out of his mind. Pumping into her mouth. Too roughly, probably, but she was taking it.

Perfect . . .

Pleasure rose, sharp and nearly painful. She worked him as mercilessly as he'd ever worked her. And in moments he was on that edge, his hold tenuous. On everything: Control. His orgasm. *Her.*

As he came he called her name, over and over. His hips surged into her mouth. She sucked him so hard it hurt. It felt amazing. He'd never come so damn hard in his life.

After, he was shaking all over. Kara got to her feet and actually helped him to sit on the bench built into the shower. He was panting, trying hard to catch his breath.

And it was Kara soothing him, sitting next to him on the bench while the water fell all around them. While it ran down the cotton shirt plastered to her body, over his naked skin, in soft, warm rivulets.

She was stroking him with her hands, just his shoulders, his cheek. Her touch was . . . tender.

It took him a moment to recognize it. It was so unfamiliar, a woman touching him this way. He didn't usually allow it. It was too intimate, when it was outside the bounds of the roles of dominant and submissive. The bounds of power play. The power play

in which *he* was the dominant one. Not that she was being dominant. But he'd let down his guard, somehow. Because of Kara. She
had taken him there. And it was more than the searing pleasure
he felt at her touch, simply looking at her. It was . . . just *her*.

This had never happened to him before. That a woman had
reduced him to . . . this. A man who had no control over his own
desire. His own pleasure.

Emotion.

He was in a small panic. But even that was like some vague
shadow at the edge of his consciousness, behind the pure pleasure
he still felt shimmering through his system.

He could not believe it. He was too spent to really think about
it. And it felt so fucking good he couldn't find it within himself to
truly care after those first surprising moments.

Nothing had ever felt better than Kara. Nothing. She was all
he could think about. All he wanted. And it was too good for him
to consider that this sort of thought had never crossed his mind
before in his life.

Kara.

For the first time, he didn't want anything—or anyone—else.

eleven

Kara woke up in the dark, her heart pounding. It took her a moment to get her bearings. To remember where she was. And as soon as she did, the reason for her hammering heart came back to her in a flood, filling her with panic.

She loved him.

Impossible. But true.

God damn it.

She sat up, shoved her hands into her hair.

This could not be happening. Not to her. And certainly not with him.

Dante was that unobtainable guy. She should know better. She *did* know better. She'd simply been too far gone last night to have done anything about it.

This was nothing more than fun and games to him. A serious sort of game, but a game nevertheless. He'd been clear with her from the start. And she'd thought she'd been clear herself. No more relationships. No more opening her heart. No more risks with her emotions. And now, her emotions had blown up, reached deeper into her heart than ever before.

How had she thought she could do this—go to this kind of sexual extreme—without her heart getting involved?

She was a fool.

She loved him.

He would know something was going on with her. He was too perceptive. That was part of what made him so good at being a dominant. But it brought her no comfort now.

She dropped her hands into her lap and stared through the tall windows at the night sky. Light was coming up from the streets, a faint glow of amber and silver, lighting up the clouds covering the moon. It felt lonely to her, even thinking of walking down that nighttime street, in the dark and the Seattle damp. Unbearably lonely. Still, she had a terrible urge to leave. Simply to get up, get dressed and slip out. Before Dante woke and realized there was something horribly wrong with her.

That was how it felt. As if she were . . . sick.

She moaned and wrapped her arms around her body.

"Kara?"

Damn it.

His voice was thick with sleep. She didn't want to look at him. She knew it would all be over then. She would feel it too much. She'd either tell him, which would be a complete disaster. Or she'd have to leave. *Have* to. Leave and maybe never come back.

A sharp pain in her chest at the thought.

"Kara," he said again. "What's up? Can't sleep?"

"No," she said simply. She didn't know what else to say. Didn't trust her voice to remain steady.

"Come here," he said, sitting up and reaching for her.

She shrugged him off.

"Kara?" She could hear the confusion in his voice. "What's going on?"

She shook her head. She was blowing it. Had already blown it with Dante by falling in love with him.

She was angry with herself. With him, for reasons she couldn't even comprehend. It was all a dark jumble inside her.

"Come on. Tell me," he insisted.

"So you can do your job?" she asked, bitterness lacing her voice. She couldn't help it. She wouldn't turn around and look at him.

"What? No. I . . . Tell me what's happening here."

"I don't know. That's just it. Shit. Or maybe I do. Maybe I'm too aware that all of this is about you doing your dom role and me being the pliant little subbie girl."

"I've never looked at you like that. You know that. I thought you did."

"Okay. Maybe not. But you do perceive yourself that way. And what I need to know is . . . is there anything beyond that, Dante?"

She swallowed hard. Had she really said these things to him?

He was quiet for so long she began to really be afraid. Maybe she'd pushed him too hard. But what was he going to do? Ask her to leave? A part of her wanted to. The rest of her wanted him to wrap her up in his arms and ask her to stay with him.

Forever.

Don't be an idiot.

Her stomach ached. Her heart ached.

"Jesus, Kara."

Here it came. She threw back the covers and started to get up. But he grabbed her arm, forced her to face him.

"Where are you going? What is really going on here?"

Anger flooded her then, hot and powerful. Anger and fear and loss.

She could not do this.

"I'm leaving, Dante."

Even in the dark she could see his jaw drop as he let her go. He shook his head.

"I won't keep you here against your will," he said, his tone even, careful.

"Of course not. Because the infamous Dante De Matteo would never do anything that violated the safe, sane and consensual credo. But you would never do anything that really let anyone inside, either, would you?"

He stared at her, shock on his face. She was shocked herself. Then his dark brows drew together and he said so quietly she could barely hear him, "No."

She shook her head. "What does that mean?"

"It means you're right." He paused, drew a hand through his hair. "And it's . . . I've never realized before that it's . . . a failing in me. I've only seen it as necessary. And I still think it is. Mostly. Maybe. Christ, I don't know anymore, Kara."

She couldn't help but soften a little at the self-deprecating tone in his voice. The real confusion there.

"I don't know what's happening to me," he admitted. "But it has something to do with you. And I don't like it—I'll tell you that much. I don't get it. Tonight, after we got back here . . . something happened to me." He stopped, shook his head. "It was different. New. I don't know if I want to think about it too much. I'd pretty much decided I didn't by the time we went to sleep. But if the alternative is you walking out of here right now, then I will think about it. I'll do my best to figure it out."

"Dante . . . I'm sorry."

"For what?"

"For being such a bitch to you about this when I feel the same way. Something is changing and it scares me. That's why I wanted to leave."

"Do you still?"

"No. Not now that I know you want me here. Despite all of . . . this, whatever it is."

"Okay. Okay."

He reached out for her once more and she went to him this time. Her heart was a small, aching hammer in her chest. But she was going to simply let it be. It was a little easier, knowing he was just as confounded by what was happening between them as she was.

They sat in silence for so long that she began to wonder if he'd drifted off. But then he shifted, sliding down until he was lying on his back, and taking her with him until she was laid out over him. Her breasts were pressed against the solid wall of his chest, her bare stomach against his. She could feel the muscle there. The small flex of his erection at the juncture of her thighs. And she had to pull in a gasping breath at the desire surging through her, like a tide. That liquid. That powerful.

"Dante . . ."

"Shh. Just kiss me," he said softly.

The way he said it was like a wave of heat fluttering over her skin, spiraling into her heart. He pulled her head to his, his hands on her cheeks. When he kissed her it was surprisingly tender. His lips brushed over hers, gently, barely touching her. A soft shiver of desire trembled through her, making another layer of need beneath that first, sharp wave. This one was different. Just as intense, but in an entirely different way.

Things were different between them. They'd both admitted something. They'd both opened up. But with his mouth on hers, his tongue slipping in to explore, to demand in a new and tender way, she couldn't think about how scary that was. All she could do was give in. To his kiss. To him. To the still-tenuous and fragile connection she felt between them.

She sighed into his mouth, heard his answering rasping breath as his hips arched, pressing his erection against her dampening mound.

She spread her thighs apart, allowing the tip of his cock to slide along her cleft.

Pure pleasure, that slipping sensation. The velvety touch of his cock against her aching clitoris. And knowing it was him.

Dante.

He began to move, arching, retreating, so that his cock was sliding between the wet folds of flesh, over her clit, and down again. He was still holding on to her face as he kissed her, cupping her cheek. And, reaching down with one hand, he smoothed his palm over the side of her breast, his touch bringing new sensation. She shifted so that he could cup it in his hand, and he brushed the nipple with his fingertips. And even as the rest of his motions—hips and cock and mouth—were excruciatingly gentle, he pinched her nipple between his fingertips.

She gasped. Breathed him in. Sank into the pain that wasn't even pain, somehow, but simply a deeper pleasure. A pleasure that mixed with the tenderness of everything that was happening between them. Of his mouth on hers. The soft surging of his hips, pressing his cock against her. Contrasting. Lovely.

She tilted her hips into his, pressing against the hard ridge of his erection. He kept kissing her, kissing her, his tongue dancing against hers. And his exquisite torture of her nipple sent lovely shocks through her. Pleasure built, a tightening in her sex, in her belly, her breasts. She kept moving, her hips writhing against his.

He pulled his mouth from hers long enough to murmur, "Come for me, my beautiful girl."

And she did. Just came apart, shivering all over as her climax poured through her body. Driven by the hard press of his solid shaft against her clit. She same onto him, grinding against his lovely, hard flesh, panting into his mouth.

His hands were all over her then, stroking her back, her buttocks, her thighs. And every touch sent another delicious wave through her. She was still quivering with the aftershocks of her climax when he reached for a condom, slipped it on, somehow, and raised her body over his.

"Come on, Kara," he said, his voice thick with need.

He held her body poised over his with his hands strong on her waist. She looked into his eyes. They were two glittering points of jet in the dark room. She waited for his signal. For his command. And when he gave a small nod of his chin, she melted a little all over as she lowered herself onto him.

"Oh . . ."

She couldn't help but moan as he filled her. Hard, hot flesh inside her, surging deeper, deeper. He held on to her, moving her body up and down with his strong arms. Bringing her down, over and over, onto his cock.

She loved that even on top of him, *he* was still so firmly in control. He set the pace. He gave her pleasure, took his own. And as he pumped his hips, harder and harder, the mood shifted from tender to primal.

"Christ, Kara," he panted, "I just need to be deep inside you."

"Yes, Dante . . ."

"I need to see you come again. Make yourself come for me."

She reached down and pressed her fingers to her hard clitoris, and sensation flooded her.

"Ah, God," she murmured, overcome with sensation: his cock, her fingers, his command.

"Come on, beautiful girl," he gasped, his hips thrusting, his hard shaft pushing inside her, pulling out. "Do it. Make it happen."

She circled with her fingers, angled her hips so that his thrusting cock hit her G-spot. And with a cry, she came once more.

"Dante! Ah!"

She was shaking, grinding onto his cock, into her own hand. Her sex was clenching hard around his thick, driving flesh.

"Ah, Kara . . ." He jerked up into her, over and over, his grip on her hips tightening. "Christ, baby . . ."

He pulled her down on top of him roughly. Held her close.

"So good . . . so damn good," he murmured into her hair.

And suddenly that tenderness was back, stronger than ever, as he held her.

They were both panting hard, slick with sweat. He was still softening inside her. She didn't want to let him go. Didn't want that separateness of their bodies. He kissed her cheek, her throat, his lips a sweet caress on her skin, and she felt his every touch like some sort of confirmation of what was between them. She didn't want to put a name to it. But it was *something*.

They lay together for a long time, and she slept for a while, lying on top of him, their bodies pressed together. It was lovely, to drift for a while, to wake up so close to him.

The sun was just beginning to rise, turning the clouds outside the windows orange and pink and gold, like a watercolor painting of the sky. She sighed, happy, turned back to him and pressed her face into his neck, breathed him in.

He woke, his arms tightening around her, and it was only then she realized that even as they'd slept, he hadn't let go.

Another surge in her chest, her heart beating, fluttering with something beyond pleasure.

"Baby," Dante murmured. "My girl . . ."

And just like that, desire rose in her once more. His cock hardened beneath her, and she opened her thighs for him again.

He shifted only long enough to pull another condom from the lacquer box next to the bed, to sheathe himself. Then he was inside her. And it was all lovely, sleepy sex this time. The gentle, rocking motion of his hips, and hers. His moans, her sighs. Sensation a slow, burning build, and finally, they reached that peak together, cried out, tumbled over once more.

He kissed her: her cheek, her hair, her jaw. Soft, lovely kisses. She inhaled, taking in the scent of his skin. Of sex. Of the two of them together.

She wrapped her arms around his neck, feeling the heat of his body against hers. The steady rhythm of his heart. That sense of *connection*.

A part of her still wanted to be scared. But she felt too good. *This* felt too good, and she couldn't deny herself.

Just let it be for now.

She couldn't do anything else, really. She felt helpless against the sensations in her body, her heart. The warning bells were silenced by what she was feeling. For the time being, anyway. And she was allowing herself to give in. To Dante's command. To the pleasure of being with him. Even to the crushing fear of being in love with him.

It wasn't as if she had to *do* anything about it. She didn't even have to tell him how she felt. No matter how powerful it was. It was a sweet secret she could hold close.

It had been two weeks since Kara realized she was in love with Dante. The secret was getting harder and harder to keep. She hadn't told Lucie, had never said the words out loud, even to herself. She was afraid if she did, it would make it even more real. And even allowing the thought to run through her mind was about as real as she could handle.

That and simply *being* with him.

She'd been drawing him. And drawing the city. The clouds hanging over the view of Elliott Bay she could see from the windows of his apartment. The mountains in the distance. A bowl of fruit on her small kitchen table.

She'd found some of her charcoal pencils and an old drawing

pad. She hadn't dared to dig out her paints. It was too soon. She felt too unsure about it. About giving in to that need. That desire. It felt too . . . indulgent.

But she knew it was because of Dante. Because of the way he was making her feel. About him. About herself. He was beginning to make her question the old ideas—outmoded now, she'd come to realize—about her life and what she should be doing. About some of the choices she'd made. The way she'd held herself back because she was too afraid of what others might think of her.

Her parents, mostly. Which was ridiculous. She was a grown woman. But her relationship with Jake hadn't helped, either. And she'd allowed it. Allowed Jake and his judgment of her to color her thinking.

Maybe she wasn't as strong a woman as she'd thought herself to be.

Or maybe she simply wasn't thinking clearly about any of this. Maybe she should put her charcoals away. Forget about painting . . .

She stood in front of her office windows, looking down on the rainy city, letting it soothe her tangled thoughts. Cars splashed through the street, a few umbrellas dotted the sidewalks. A part of her wanted to be out there, feeling the damp Seattle air, always touched with a little ocean salt from the bay. There was something about the way the city smelled in the rain that felt like home to her. Cozy, even in the middle of a storm. She loved that sensation of being held warm in her coat, with the damp air chilling her feet through her boots.

She shivered. Being outside in the familiar February weather wasn't the only thing she craved. It was Dante, too.

It was always Dante.

She left the window and sat back down in her chair, picking up her cell phone. Maybe there would be a message from him? He often sent her sexy little texts throughout the day when he wasn't in court. Or sometimes even when he was, which seemed particularly wicked. A few words from him could make her hot all over in an instant. Could warm her needy heart.

God, she hated being needy. She was *not* that girl—never had been. But with Dante she couldn't help it.

The last weeks had been wonderful and difficult, all at the same time—a delicious kind of torture she'd never experienced before. They were together almost every night, and on the weekends. On the nights she didn't see him, she tried to stay busy. She'd taken work home with her a few times, had met Lucie for dinner, had browsed through her favorite bookstore. But it was as if every moment she wasn't with Dante happened at a distance. She felt removed from everything but him.

Lucie had known something was up that night at dinner, but she hadn't pushed. And Kara hadn't called her very often. She knew Lucie wouldn't wait forever for her to spit it out, so it seemed better to avoid her for now.

She didn't know how much longer she could hold it inside, though. Every night with Dante she was afraid it would come bursting out. She'd been disappointed and relieved that he hadn't taken her back to the Pleasure Dome yet. It was too intense there; she was certain if they went there, she'd drop too far into subspace to control it, and the words would come tumbling out, her secret revealed.

She couldn't do that. If she told him, they would both have to face it, and it would all be over. And she couldn't help but flash back to the last time she'd revealed a secret to a man, when she'd told Jake about her kinkier desires. That had been the end of everything. Which was fine. He was all wrong for her. But still, it was the idea of giving up the secret, especially one she *knew* she had to keep to herself.

She sighed, set her phone down and brought a brief she was working on up on her computer screen. It was Friday, and she was supposed to turn this in on Monday afternoon. If she didn't get her head together and do some work, Monday would be hell. She forced herself to focus. Eventually, her brain began to shift gears and she immersed herself in work.

It was nearly five o'clock when her cell phone beeped, telling her she had a message. She smoothed back her hair with her palm, her heart beating. She had to calm down. It wasn't necessarily a message from him.

But it was.

My place tonight. Seven o'clock.

She smiled to herself. They hadn't talked about seeing each other tonight; she thought he'd mentioned that he had plans with his friend Alec. But before she could answer, another text popped up.

Never mind. Can't wait. Come to my office at six.

Her smile broadened, her body going warm. Her nipples came up hard beneath her lace bra.

One hour. A whole hour before she would see him. And then, who knew what might happen?

She loved that—that he kept her on her toes. She was amazed she didn't resent him for it. And probably the old Kara would have. But Dante was showing her that giving up her power by choice didn't equal being weak. And it was a revelation to her. Freeing. Just as he'd suggested it could be when they'd first met. She wouldn't have been able to believe it then. But these weeks with him had changed so much for her.

She hadn't expected this thing with Dante to bring about any real self-discovery. Looking back, she didn't know what she had expected. A brief fling with an old crush, maybe. A foray into her darker fantasies. She had never thought she'd fall so hard. That her every waking moment would be consumed by thoughts of him.

Sex with Dante. Dante's big bed. Dante's beautiful body. The velvet of his skin. The command of his hands, his voice.

Dante.

Only one more hour . . .

twelve

Dante glanced at the clock for the tenth time in the last hour. Five of six. Only a few more minutes until Kara was with him.

He'd stopped questioning this constant craving for her. He'd just agreed with himself that he didn't have to understand it to enjoy it. On some deeper level he knew perfectly well he was avoiding something. He simply chose not to look at it any more closely.

And Kara was an amazing woman; why shouldn't he enjoy her? She was sexy as hell. As smart as he was, probably smarter, which was something he didn't come upon often enough. And the sex . . . The kink was always there, the power exchange. Even when they just had sex, without all the edgier stuff, that dynamic was always present.

Of course, it probably always would be, because he was who he was. Had been for most of his adult life. But some of it was

Kara, too. The way she responded. Her need to let go was bone deep. And he loved that about her. Yet it wasn't as important to him as it normally was.

She was right when she'd accused him of using the kink to keep people at a certain distance. He could admit that. He could even admit that he was still doing it with her, to some extent. But she'd broken through the cracks in his armor and found her way in, under his skin. There were too many things that were good between them. The sex, even talking with her. He could talk to her for hours. They often did, staying up late into the night after sex. Or on a lazy Sunday morning. Sometimes they even sat together in companionable silence, which was even stranger.

Scary, if he let himself think about it, so he usually didn't. Not much, anyway. But right now, waiting for her to walk through the door, he couldn't help it.

She would be there any moment. A shiver of anticipation ran through him. Anticipation that was about more than his hardening cock. The thought of bending her over his desk once more.

Just focus on the sex. On the power play.

He ran a hand over his jaw, letting his finger scrape against the end-of-day stubble there. He needed the sharp sensation to ground him.

I am losing it.

Losing it over a woman. Over Kara. It was all he could do to hold it at bay, some days.

A soft knock at his door; then she was slipping through. Gorgeous in one of the tight skirts she often wore that fit her like a glove. This one was a fine red wool. He loved that it wasn't the basic black, or the neutrals most people wore around the office. That she usually wore. It was as if she'd known he was going to ask for her today. As if she'd worn the wickedly sexy skirt just for him.

Maybe she had.

She smiled, and he sat back in his chair, motioning with his chin for her to come to him.

He was hard already.

Keep it under control, buddy.

But as she moved across the room, he was fascinated with the sway of her hips. With the contrast of the sexy, body-hugging skirt and the prim white blouse she wore with it. With how damn long her legs looked in her sheer black tights and high black pumps.

"Dante . . ."

"Kara." He paused to really look her over. Loved the way she squirmed a little under his scrutiny. Loved everything about her.

"Nice," he murmured before reaching out for her and taking her hand.

Just think about the sex. How she feels . . .

He pulled her into his lap. Her bottom was soft across his thighs. There was too much damn fabric in the way, but they were at the office, and he'd made it a policy never to take all her clothes off there. It felt less risky to him, even with the door locked. If anyone knocked, they could pull themselves together in a matter of moments. He'd never stripped her down in his office. Even though all he wanted was to have her naked, to spread her thighs wide so he could go down on her and lick her to orgasm.

A hot surge of need in his cock at the thought of it.

Yes, just focus on that.

He loved to go down on her. Couldn't get enough of the sweet taste of her flesh. Making her come with his mouth. It was one of his favorite things. And it seemed to be one of hers, which made it even hotter.

"How was your day?" he asked her, his arm slipping around her waist and holding on just tight enough that she had some sense of his command. *He* had some sense of his command again, with her hot little body in his lap, making him harder by the moment.

"It was . . . fine."

"Fine?"

"Until you sent me that message."

"Oh? You didn't care for my message?" He reached down with his other hand and gave the inside of her thigh a small pinch.

"Oh! I just . . . couldn't wait to be here with you. I couldn't concentrate on anything else."

He smiled at her. "Good answer. And what was it you wanted from me, Kara?"

She pulled in a soft, sighing breath. "Everything."

Another sharp stab of pleasure deep in his belly, in his cock.

"Ah, you are perfect."

It was true. She *was* perfect.

She surged into him, the curve of her silk-covered breast pressing against his chest. He swore he could feel her sex heating up, even through the layers of her tights, her skirt, his slacks. Fucking torture. He couldn't take it for one more second.

"Stand up for me, Kara."

She did so, no questions asked. If only she knew how submissive she became with him the moment he even hinted that they were in role. It was automatic for her now. He loved it.

"Turn around," he ordered, and she complied. "Kick your shoes off. Good girl."

He reached under her skirt and pulled her tights down, slid her skirt up around her waist and found her naked underneath.

"Ah, nice. Lean over and hold yourself up against the desk. And spread those pretty thighs for me."

She did as he asked, bracing herself on his desk, bending over until he could see her pink pussy lips, glistening with moisture. His mouth watered.

He stroked her naked ass. Felt her shiver. When he slipped a few fingers in between the soft folds of her sex, he found her soaking wet. His cock pulsed.

"Bend over, more—yes, that's it."

Her ass was high in the air, her sex open to him. And he leaned forward in his chair, holding her open with his hand so he could taste her.

Salty sweet, like the sea and the pure nectar of desire. He licked, one long slow stroke along her slit, and she was panting instantly.

He pulled back.

"Keep quiet, Kara."

He moved in and licked again. Her thighs went rigid—he could feel her tensing up—but he also knew it meant she was close to coming already.

He went to work then, licking, licking. Using his thumbs to delve inside her, then sliding them up to press on the hard nub of her clit. She was gasping quietly, pushing back against his face.

"Dante . . ."

He kept licking her, thrusting his tongue deep inside her.

"I'm going to come," she whispered.

He pulled back, pausing to move one hand to her ass. She surged back, knowing what he was going to do, and spread her legs even farther apart. And with his fingers soaked in her juices, he slipped one into her tight anus.

"Ah . . ." She kept her voice low as he pierced her. "So good . . ."

He moved back in, keeping one finger in her ass as he ducked to put his mouth on her again, licking, sucking the soft lips in, one at a time. When he pressed on her clit with his other hand, she exploded, her pussy going drenching wet. Her ass clenched hard around his finger. Her legs shook.

He was so damn hard he could almost come, just feeling her climax. Feeling the velvet texture of her, pussy and ass, all at once.

Christ. Calm down.

But his heart was hammering, going a hundred miles an hour. He was losing his grip on the control he so prided himself on.

If he didn't stop touching her, he was going to come right there, right then, like some adolescent with his first girl.

He pushed away from her, daring to keep just one palm on the small of her back. His breathing was as hard and rasping as hers.

"Get dressed," he told her roughly, standing up and grabbing her tights from the floor.

She turned to look at him, confusion in her hazel eyes, along with the haze of her climax. But he couldn't explain himself.

In moments she had her tights and shoes back on, her skirt smoothed around her hips. Her cheeks were flushed pink.

"Dante, is it . . . Is everything okay?"

"Yeah. No. I need to get you out of here. I can't fucking stand it, Kara. I need to be inside you. I can't wait to get you home." He pulled her in, took her hand and held it for a moment to his aching cock. He muttered against her hot cheek, "I'm going to fuck you in my car. Get your coat."

He heard her swallow. She didn't answer. But when he looked into her eyes, he saw her need there, nearly as powerful as his own. She nodded silently.

It seemed to take forever for them to gather their coats, their briefcases. Then to get downstairs and outside, to the parking structure next door, then up another elevator to get to his car.

He'd parked on the fourth floor. It wasn't entirely empty; there were a few cars leaving the structure, most people on their way out at the end of the day. And it was getting darker by the minute. He didn't care that much. He just had to have her.

He opened the passenger door of his silver BMW and she slid in.

"Push the seat all the way back," he told her, leaning over her to pull a condom packet from the glove box. "And take your tights off again."

She was doing it, everything he asked of her. That made it even better, her compliance. Her submission. Her trust.

Standing next to the car, he took his coat off and tossed it into the backseat, glanced around the garage once more. No one there. Not now, anyway. He was too damn hard to care much. And there was that added thrill of exhibitionism, even though there was no one around at the moment, that he always got when he played at the Pleasure Dome.

He went to the driver's side and got in, pressed a lever and waited for the seat to slide all the way back, then lowered the back until it was fully reclined. He unzipped his slacks and pulled his cock out, sheathing himself quickly. Even his own brief touch was almost too much for him.

"Come here, baby."

He reached for Kara. As she climbed on top of him he saw her eyes, that metallic gaze hazed, glossy. She was deep in subspace. Not letting her talk much always did it to her. Even if he had just bent her over his desk. Taken her over. She was going deeper and deeper every moment. It was beautiful.

But he could barely think of that now. Could barely think at all as she straddled him, her skirt around her hips.

"Just stay right there, Kara. I want to just . . . fuck you." He arched his hips, and slid into her, pleasure shafting into his system. "Ah, Christ, you feel good. Jesus, Kara. Hold still or I'm going to come."

He held his breath, his cock pulsing inside her.

After a few moments and a few long, calming breaths, she asked, "Dante?"

"What is it, baby?"

"I want to . . . Will you let me fuck you?"

Too good, that she would ask him that, even in the bottom head space. She was still there, despite what she'd just asked of him.

"Oh, you are going to kill me, beautiful girl. But yes, fuck me."

She smiled at him, biting her lip as she ground down onto his cock.

"Ah . . ."

Pleasure was like an electric current. Shocking. Sharp. Arcing deep into his belly. He had to bite his own lip not to come.

"Wait," he commanded, holding on to her slim waist while he

pulled in a breath, then another. Tried to calm down again. "Okay," he said, finally.

She started to move, her hips pumping. Her pussy was a hot sheath around him, gripping his cock. Slipping up and down until he was dizzy with sensation, blinded by it.

Pleasure rose so hard it hurt: his cock, his balls, his chest.

"Kara . . ."

She moved faster, riding him hard. And she was so fucking beautiful he could barely stand it. Her flushed face, her red lips. The scent of her female come from earlier.

He held his breath, held his orgasm back, and reached between them to pinch her clit.

"Ah, Dante!"

Then she was coming again. And he was coming with her, her clenching pussy too much for him to take.

"Kara . . . Jesus!"

He was coming so hard he was shaking. His body filled with a keen, cutting pleasure. His chest filled with . . . what?

He couldn't think. He was dazed by sensation. By the feel of Kara collapsing in his arms.

Something had just happened to him. But he didn't know what the hell it was. Something new was always happening with him, when it came to Kara. His experiences with her. His . . . feelings about her.

He wrapped her in his arms and held her close. She was warm against him, her labored breath pushing her soft breasts against his chest. She felt so damn good. Even after he'd come. She felt better than anything had in his life.

There was something about the sex . . . No, it wasn't the sex.

The sex was amazing, and it brought them closer, but it was amazing in part because of what was happening between them *in between* the sex.

His head was reeling. He was trying to get a grip on what was going on inside him. Something new and strange and he was having trouble comprehending it. All he knew was that being with her was right.

For now, buddy.

Yes, for now. And maybe for a while down the road.

Had he ever thought of another woman in these terms? Had he ever been with anyone where his thoughts and plans went beyond that week? That month, maybe?

He'd tried to be in a relationship a few times. But it had never worked. Because he wasn't willing to think about down the road. Not beyond making plans for a weekend getaway a few weeks in advance. Or an evening at the Pleasure Dome.

He was thirty-one years old. Maybe it was time. Even for him.

"Dante?"

"Hmm? Sorry. My mind was wandering. Are you uncomfortable, baby? Do you need to move?"

"A little uncomfortable. But I don't want to move."

Her arms went around his neck and something in his chest surged.

"Hey. Do you want to go have some dinner?" he asked her, not ready to take her home yet.

"Yes. I'm starving, actually."

"Okay. Good. Let's get you put back together."

"Dante?"

"What is it?"

"That was . . . wonderful."

He pulled back to look at her. She had a small, uncertain smile on her face. Her eyes were glowing.

"It was," he told her.

He reached out and stroked her hair from her cheek. It was as soft and sleek as satin. The odd lurching in his chest kicked up a notch.

Kara shivered. He was being so tender with her. He kept stroking her cheek with his fingertips. And she was dazed by it. By his touch. By *him*.

Even within the bounds of another kinky sexual experience, something new and different was going on. *He* felt different. They'd reached yet another new level of some sort. She couldn't figure it all out now. Her head, her body, were still humming with climax. She knew she was still in subspace. It was hard to think, to focus on anything.

But he was asking her to dinner and it felt like a real date. Well, for them, anyway. Maybe most other people didn't start a real date with oral sex at their desk, followed by some rather glorious fucking in the front seat of a car. But Dante was an unusual man. And she was coming to accept that she was an unusual woman. She even liked that idea.

She climbed off his lap, settling into the soft leather of the passenger seat, and they straightened themselves.

"Thai okay with you?" he asked.

"Yes, sure. But, Dante, weren't you supposed to meet Alec tonight?"

"Shit. Yes. Hang on, let me send him a text. It was just a movie. He won't mind if I cancel."

That was different—Dante canceling other plans to be with her. And it made her even more aware that something had shifted.

Impossible that it had happened while they were having sex. It was just sex. What was going on with him?

Dante finished his text, started the engine and pulled out of the parking garage. Wild Ginger wasn't far away and soon they were there, being led to a cozy booth in the back of the restaurant. Kara was surprised when Dante slid in next to her, rather than across from her.

Maybe he wanted to get her off under the table, as he had at the Italian place?

Her heart raced. That would be fine with her. But it seemed . . . unimportant.

But instead of laying his hand on her thigh, he looped his arm across her shoulders, pulling her in close to him.

"You doing okay?" he asked.

"Yes, I'm fine. Why?"

"Just checking in. That's what I'm supposed to do after I've put you in subspace."

She shrugged. "I definitely hit subspace. Even before I got to your office."

"I love that about you."

He was smiling at her, his dimples flashing.

"But . . . there was more to it than that tonight."

His smile faded, his shoulders going a little tense beneath the crisp cotton of his light blue shirt. But he nodded in agreement. "Yeah. There was. There *is* something different happening with us."

"Dante . . . I like what's happening between us. It's changing. And maybe that's good, but . . . when I let myself think about it too much, I get . . . confused. God, I shouldn't have even brought this up. I'm being a girl again."

"No, it's fine. I've been thinking about it, too."

She bit her lip, thinking. "You know I'm not looking for a relationship. Not after my last one."

"Yes . . ."

"And I know you're not, either. I just want you to know I get that."

"Okay." But there was still a question in his voice, as if he wasn't quite sure where she was going with this. Maybe she wasn't, either.

"I guess what I'm asking is, are you okay with us just . . . coasting along like this? Because I think it's good. Really good, just as it is."

"It is. And yes, I'm okay with things as they are. It's good to know we're on the same page. On every level."

"Okay. Good."

She smiled at him, but inside, her pulse was racing. Because the conversation felt like a lie. She was telling Dante what he wanted to hear, rather than the truth. But was she more afraid that he couldn't deal with it, or that she couldn't handle it herself?

As Dante ordered their drinks she realized she needed to switch tracks to something less serious. This was too much to figure out at the moment.

"So, what movie were you and Alec going to see?"

"An action film. A total guy thing." He grinned, his dimples creasing his cheeks once more. "His girlfriend, Dylan, calls it a man-date."

Kara laughed. "That's funny."

"We don't hang out as much as we used to. It's been strange getting used to Alec having a girlfriend. But they're good together. She's been good for him. And Alec is one of those guys I thought I'd never say that about. Or, he was, anyway." He paused, running his fingers over the linen napkin on the table, staring at it for a moment. "He was . . . like me."

He turned to look at her again, and his eyes were going dark, his brows drawn together. Her heart was thumping in her chest.

It doesn't mean anything. He's not implying that he could change, too.

"Ah, here are our drinks. Cheers." He lifted his scotch on the rocks and sipped. "So, I take it you're not a big action film fan?"

She was right—it hadn't meant anything. She sighed inwardly. Did she really want it to?

"Dante, you bastard."

They both looked up to find a hulk of a man with a dark goatee—almost as handsome as Dante—with his hand on the waist of a slender woman with glorious red curls.

"Alec. What are you doing here?"

"When you texted that you couldn't make the movie, we decided to go to dinner."

"Ah. I got . . . waylaid." Dante turned to grin at Kara.

"Are you going to introduce us?" Alec asked, reaching to take Kara's hand in his.

She felt dwarfed by him. A little startled.

"Yes, of course. Kara, Alec and his girlfriend, Dylan. This is Kara Crawford."

So this was Alec. Dante's best friend. And Dante had never thought to mention her to him, apparently. Her heart sank a little. But she tried not to show it as she shook hands with Alec, then Dylan.

"It's nice to meet you." Dylan smiled. She was a beautiful woman, with delicate features and translucent, pale skin.

"You two should join us." Dante motioned at the empty booth seat across from them.

Alec nodded. "Sounds good."

He helped Dylan off with her coat and handed her into the booth. The waitress came immediately and took their drink orders, as well as their coats. Kara couldn't help but notice that Alec ordered for Dylan, just as Dante did for her. Dylan never batted her calm, gray eyes.

"Kara, what do you do?" Dylan asked.

"I'm an attorney. Dante and I work together at Kelleher, Landers and Tate."

"You should never date a woman who's as smart as you are," Alec told Dante with a wink. "It can get you into all kinds of trouble."

Dylan turned to grin at him. "You're really in trouble now," she told him, a teasing note in her voice.

"Ha!"

She raised an eyebrow at him, and he leaned in and kissed her cheek, making her beam.

The waitress brought the drinks and took their orders from the men. Something about it seemed oddly natural for them both, and again, Dylan didn't react at all. But then, Dante had mentioned he and Alec had met at the Pleasure Dome. Which probably meant that Dylan was into the kinky stuff, too. BDSM. Kara's cheeks heated a little. Did that mean Alec and Dylan would know that about her, too? But Dante hadn't even mentioned her to them. She could be just another woman he was seeing.

Doesn't matter. Just act as you normally would.

"What about you, Dylan?" Kara asked. "And Alec?"

"We're both authors," the other woman answered. "I write erotica and Alec writes thrillers."

"Oh! You're Dylan Ivory. I've read your books. I loved *The Art of Desire*."

Dylan blushed. "Thank you. That's so lovely of you to say."

"It's true."

Dylan smiled warmly. Kara had a feeling she'd like this woman, given the chance to know her.

Except that these were Dante's friends. It was unlikely she'd have the opportunity. That would be much too relationship-y for them.

Hadn't she just told him moments earlier that she wasn't interested in a relationship, that she wanted to keep things status quo?

Her stomach began to knot, her pulse to race. She sipped at her drink—a cup of cold sake—but it did nothing to calm her. Why was she so panicky?

"Will you all excuse me? I'll be right back." Dante let her out of the booth and she stood up, feeling foolish.

"I'll go with you," Dylan announced, getting up as well, and Kara had no option but to wait for her.

They made their way to the ladies' room at the back of the restaurant. Once inside, Dylan put a hand on her arm.

"Are you okay, Kara?"

"What? Yes, sure."

"I hope you don't mind me saying so, since we've just met, but you seem a little pale. And flustered."

"Oh, I'm just . . ." She shook her head. "I can't even come up with an excuse," she finished with a small laugh. "And now I'm horribly embarrassed."

"Is it Dante?"

Kara shook her head, miserable. Then she had to nod. It *was* Dante. But she didn't even know this woman. This woman who was the girlfriend of Dante's best friend.

"Kara, I probably shouldn't be sticking my nose in here, but I have to tell you, I have never seen Dante look at anyone the way he's looking at you."

"What do you mean?"

Dylan bit her lip. "Not that I've seen him with too many women, but we've run into him a few times. And he's usually pretty reserved. But you . . . He looks at you with those big puppy dog eyes."

"He does not."

"He does." Dylan's gray eyes sparkled as a slow grin lit her face. "The guy is smitten."

"What? Oh no, I'm sure he's not . . . smitten." Kara pushed a hand through her hair. "We're just . . . dating. Sort of."

"That *is* his usual style. But I'm sure you already know that. You . . . do know that?"

"Yes, of course. Dante has been completely open about his views on dating and relationships."

"God, I'm sorry. I've said too much. It's none of my business."

"No, it's fine," Kara told her, and it was. She was being so nice to her.

Dylan smiled, leaning over the sink to wash her hands. "I have a nosy streak. I really do apologize, Kara."

"It's okay. And it was nice of you to come in here with me. To make sure I was okay."

Dylan dried her hands. "I'll get back to the table, give you a moment to yourself."

Kara smiled at her, relieved that Dylan seemed to know instinctively that she needed to gather herself.

"Thanks."

Dylan nodded and left.

Kara looked at her reflection in the mirror. Her eyes were huge, her cheeks a little pale, still. What was wrong with her?

You're in love with a man who will not love you back.

Her heart hammered, a hard, aching thunder in her chest.

But Dylan said he was smitten . . .

Don't get your hopes up.

No, the higher her hopes went, the more thoroughly they'd be crushed in the end. She was not willing to risk that.

Too bad it was too late.

thirteen

Dante downshifted as he pulled over in front of Kara's building. He didn't know why he'd decided not to take her home with him. It wasn't that they'd already had sex. He could never get enough of that, not with her. He could never get enough of *her*. Just being with her . . .

Maybe that was why.

He was too fascinated with her. Too obsessed. And it had really hit home sitting with Alec and Dylan, the two of them all over each other. The way they looked at each other. The way he felt watching them. Their happiness.

The way a small part of him craved that for the first time.

Time to shake it off.

"Thanks for dinner," Kara said, gathering her coat, her brief-case.

"Sure, you're welcome."

"It was great meeting Alec and Dylan. They seem like nice people."

He nodded. "They are."

Kara sat for a moment, watching him. She bit her lip.

"Dante? Is . . . is everything all right?"

"Yes, of course. Why do you ask?" He hadn't meant to sound so casual. So cool. Cold. But he could feel his walls going up, as if made out of solid concrete.

"I know we hadn't planned to see each other tonight, but it's . . ." She paused, shrugged. "Well, we usually spend the weekend together and . . . Never mind. It's not important." She shook her head, then turned away and reached out to open the car door.

He grabbed her hand. "Kara."

She turned back to him. Her eyes were gleaming in the pale light from the streetlamp, a muted silver and gold. Those long eyelashes framing her wide gaze. There was confusion there. He didn't blame her. He hadn't given her a reason why he was dropping her off at her place on a Friday night. He wasn't so sure himself.

"Don't go," he said quietly.

"What do you mean? You . . . you took me home, and I figured—"

"I know," he interrupted. "I was . . . I don't know what I was thinking. Come back to my place with me."

She was biting her lip again, her teeth coming down on that plush, pink flesh. "I think . . . maybe I should stay here tonight. Maybe it was a good idea. Yes. I think it was. I could use the time to catch up on some work. I have a Monday deadline that I sort of ignored today."

"Ah. Okay. I didn't realize you had work to do."

Why did he feel like an asshole?

"Okay, then."

She sat and looked at him for another moment. He pulled her hand to his lips, kissed the back of it, making her smile. But only a little.

"I'll call you, Kara."

Oh yeah. He *was* an asshole.

He could see the hurt on her face. And he hated himself a little. She nodded, got out of the car.

He watched her until she'd gotten safely into her building, then sat there for a little longer.

He'd never been concerned before when he'd wanted space from a woman he was seeing. It had never been an issue. Not for him, anyway. Why now? Why Kara?

He thought back to his conversation with Alec during dinner tonight, when the women had left the table. Alec had accused him of being a goner. Dante had argued the point, of course. And, Alec being Alec, he had let it go at that, with nothing more than a raised eyebrow to drive his point home.

Alec was right.

God damn it.

He turned the engine over and pulled onto the street, gunned it a little too hard as he swung around the corner.

This could not be happening. Not to him. He was not the relationship guy. He was not responsible enough. Obviously. Look what had happened the last time he'd let a woman down. Erin had been *killed*, for God's sake.

He didn't know how to do this stuff. He'd even let his own mother down. Hell, he'd spent his *life* letting his mother down.

First because he hadn't known what to do, then because he'd given up hope of ever being able to do anything.

He was a coward.

He hit the gas harder, the BMW flying over the Seattle streets.

He would not drag Kara down with him.

He got onto the 5 and drove north, heading out of the city. He needed some open country around him. Needed to think. There was a quiet little inn up by Warm Beach. How long would it take him to drive there? He could rent a room, stay for the weekend.

And do what? Brood?

He blew out a long breath.

He was being ridiculous. He was being a coward all over again.

He'd have to face Kara sooner or later. And even more, he'd have to face the fact that he had feelings for her. He wasn't ready to give them a name. Maybe he didn't have to. But he couldn't run from them. Because whether Kara was with him or not, how he felt about her was still going to be there, like a warm weight in his chest that never went away.

God damn it.

He got off at the next exit and turned around, headed back into the city. He was driving too fast. It didn't seem to matter. All that mattered was getting back to her.

He could not believe he was going through this. It wasn't like him. He didn't want it.

He couldn't help it.

He cared about her. He wanted to be with her, damn it. And why shouldn't he be? Just . . . be with her.

By the time he pulled onto her street again he was pretty worked up. He found parking right across from her building and looked up.

The lights were on in her place, so she was still awake. He tried to picture her, warm and safe inside her apartment, but realized he'd never been inside. He had no idea what her place looked like.

He always preferred to take a woman back to his place. Always. To be in control of everything, including the environment. Maybe it was time to give some of that up. A little, anyway.

And he had to see her. *Had* to.

He got out of the car just as the sky opened up. Rain pelted him as he ran across the street. Her door was next to the entrance to the deli in the old brick building. He pressed the buzzer. Silence. He rang again. Where was she?

The wooden door rattled as it swung open.

"Dante? What are you doing here?"

She looked surprised. Shocked, really. And so damn pretty. Innocent, somehow. Maybe it was because her hair was pulled back from her freshly washed face. She had no makeup on. Wore a pair of low-slung cotton pajama bottoms and a thin camisole, both in a soft green that, even in the pale light, made her eyes glow greener than he'd ever seen them. Oddly, she looked sexier than ever.

He leaned a hand in the doorway.

"Can I come in, Kara?"

"I . . . Okay."

She stood back and he moved past her, waited for her to lead him up the narrow staircase. He watched the sensual swing of her ass as she moved up the stairs. He couldn't help himself. But that wasn't why he was here. Not entirely.

Why, then, was he here? He knew Kara would want an answer to that. Deserved an answer.

At the top of the stairs she led him through another door and into her apartment.

The place was purely *her*, for some reason. It just seemed to fit, a combination of old and new, traditional and modern. Just like his place, actually, but combined in a more feminine way. Heavily carved antiques on the old, dark wood floors, a sleek, modern sofa done in white and scattered with plush, brocade pillows. The coffee table was an old steamer trunk topped in glass. A collection of black-and-white photographs on the walls, mostly architectural pieces of old buildings. European, probably. But he was distracting himself. From what was going on in his head. His body.

It was then he noticed the two paintings hanging over an antique sideboard. He moved a few steps toward them. They were both still lifes, done in the heavy oils he remembered her using in high school, but the technique had obviously been refined since then. He saw her initials in the lower right-hand corner: "KC," done in a graceful script.

He reached out, almost touching one of them. "Jesus. These are yours. They're good. Really great. You should be painting, Kara."

She sighed, but didn't say anything.

He turned to look at her, feeling too large for the cozy living room. Awkward, as if he was a giant who would knock everything over, break it all, if he moved too quickly.

"Kara . . ."

She just stood there, watching him, her arms crossed beneath her breasts. He could make out the outline of their taut fullness, the nipples, which had gone a little hard in the cool night air. He shouldn't be noticing these things now. But it was unavoidable. Kara was pure sex to him. When she wasn't being . . . everything else.

He swallowed. Tried to get his thoughts organized.

Say something, buddy. Don't be such a jerk.

He cleared his throat. His head was buzzing. Where to start?

Kara spoke before he could. "Is that why you came here? To tell me what I should be doing, Dante? You're very good at that, I'll admit. But is that why you're really here?" She let out a short, barking laugh. "Do you realize you've never even been here, inside my apartment?"

There was anger in her voice. He didn't blame her.

She went on with a helpless shrug that hurt to see. "You just . . . drop me off at the door like I'm some cheap one-night stand. Why is that, Dante? Does it bring you too close, to be in my home? Do you not want to get to know me that well? It's . . . insulting. Or maybe it's that your escape route is easier if it all happens at your place. You can decide when it's time for me to leave. When you've had enough of me."

"That's the problem, Kara." He took a step toward her, but when her shoulders tensed, her features hardening, he stopped where he was. He said quietly, "I can never get enough of you. And it scares the shit out of me."

His breath was hitching in his lungs. Painful, to say it out loud. To admit it to anyone, even himself.

Her eyes were glossy with emotion and she was biting her lip, hugging her body tighter. But some of the tension in her shoulders had melted away. Still, he stayed where he was. He didn't want to startle her.

"I'm scared, too," she said finally. "I'm more scared than I've ever been in my life. And this is not me, this woman who is . . . made weak by how I feel."

"The same thing is happening to me," he admitted, hating that he had to do it. But he *had* to. "And I don't know what the hell to do with it. I can't . . . care about someone this way. Not me."

"Why not?" she challenged him, anger surging in her voice once more.

Outside, thunder rumbled, low and powerful.

He scrubbed at his jaw. "Because I will fuck it up. Just like I did with Erin. That was devastating. And I didn't even love her. How much worse would it have been if I had? I can't take on that much responsibility for anyone."

"You take on responsibility for people every day. At work. As a dominant."

"I can detach in those situations. I can't . . ." He stopped, shook his head. "I can't detach where you're concerned, Kara. How the mighty have fallen, eh?"

She almost smiled then. "Yes. Me, too."

That made it a little easier. Knowing she was in the same place. That it was hard for her, too. His body relaxed and he smiled back at her.

"So, what the hell do we do here?" he asked, truly lost. Maybe for the first time in his life since Erin had died.

"I don't know. I think . . . I need you to tell me. And that's not about you being the dom. It's just that . . . well, frankly, Dante, I think when it comes to this stuff you're in even worse shape than I am. More shut down. I don't mean to be insulting."

"No. You're right. It's true. I can admit that. I just don't know how two people like us—and yes, like me in particular—do this stuff. We've talked about it before . . ."

"In some pretty limited fashion," she said.

He rubbed a hand over his jaw again, recognized it as something he did when he was stressed or thinking too hard, and forced his hand to drop. "I don't know how to have a more thorough discussion about it. About where we stand. We've been just letting things happen, but that hasn't worked out very well."

"So what are you asking me, Dante?"

"I'm asking . . . Christ, Kara, I can't have this conversation from six feet away." He moved toward her, watching to see if she would bolt. But she stood her ground.

In a moment she was in his arms. She smelled like flowers, that unique Kara scent. Her skin was warm under his hands. He pulled her in, held her close. Inhaled.

"Tell me what you want, Dante," she demanded, her voice gone soft, yet insistent.

"I want you to be my girl," he told her.

His.

Kara's heart was beating a hundred miles an hour.

"Yours . . . how?"

She pulled back enough to look up at him. His brown eyes were dark, burning with a fire she wasn't sure she understood.

"I don't want us to see anyone else," he said fiercely. "Date anyone else. Sleep with anyone else. Play with anyone but each other at the club."

Her heart was pounding, making her a little breathless. "Okay. Anything else?"

"I don't know. I don't know what else this is going to mean. I haven't asked this of any woman before. Can we start there? Can you be okay with that?"

Could she? The idea was almost a relief. As much as she understood she wanted more—wanted it all—she wasn't so certain she would handle things any better than Dante. It was the blind leading the blind, and she couldn't see much more clearly than he could. Maybe taking it one step at a time was for the best.

She nodded, letting out the long breath she hadn't realized she'd been holding almost since Dante had shown up at her door. "I can do that."

He pulled her in tighter then, holding her in his arms in that way that was both comforting and ridiculously sexy at the same time. His command was both of those things to her. And even though he'd come there with uncertainty in his face for the first time, it was back already—that air of surety. Absolute confidence.

"Kara," he said, his voice low. "I need to get you in bed."

Her body lit up immediately, her sex going damp, simply hearing the words from him. That was one thing they never had to question.

She pressed into him, silently letting him know she needed the same thing: to be naked together. To feel him inside her, his hands on her flesh.

He groaned as he bent to kiss her, crushing her lips with his. His tongue slipped inside, and she could taste the scotch he'd had at dinner very faintly, sweet and acrid and *male*. Or maybe that was just him.

His hands were everywhere, pulling her pajamas off, and in moments she was naked. She pressed into his body, her nipples scraping against his shirt. She felt the rain there, smelled the scent of it mixed with his citrus-and-musk soap.

Had she ever met a man who smelled as good as he did?

Thunder roared outside, rattling the windows, followed by a sharp crack of lightning. The scent of ozone made its way into the apartment, mixing with his scent. It was the scent of power. And it was perfect for him.

He pulled away to murmur, "Come on, my beautiful girl. Where's your bed?"

His hands snaked around her, sliding under her bottom, and he picked her up. She wrapped her legs around his waist and he kissed her mouth, her neck, as he moved down the hallway to her bedroom, which was dimly lit by a small lamp on the side table.

He laid her down on the bed. She'd been just getting in when he'd rung her doorbell, and the lavender and white toile-print spread was pulled back, the sheets exposed. They were cool against her skin. He leaned over to flick on the other bedside lamp.

"I need to see you," he told her, his voice gruff with desire.

She wanted to see him, too. She watched as he pulled his shirt off, kicked his way out of his shoes, his slacks. His body was all lean, hard muscle. Washboard abs and broad shoulders. His impressive erection strained against the fabric of his dark boxer briefs. Her sex gave a hard squeeze. She was soaking wet already, simply looking at him, all raw male beauty. As soaking wet as the streets outside as the rain came down in a torrent, rapping against the windows.

He was watching her, his features perfectly still. But he was hard as stone—his cock, his nipples, stiff and dark against his golden skin. She licked her lips and saw his cock twitch. Her sex answered, clenching.

Need him inside me . . .

She parted her thighs, reached for him, and he smiled, paused for a breath, then two. Then he was on her, covering her body with his, his hands going into her hair and holding tight. He kissed her, hard, his tongue sliding in, swirling against hers, tasting, demanding. She wrapped her legs around his waist and hung on.

He rocked his hips, his cock between her thighs, pressing against her entrance. Sliding in her juices. They were gasping their need into each other's mouths immediately.

God, she could come just from this—this lovely slide of flesh against flesh. She angled her hip, until his cock was slipping up her cleft and over her clitoris, down, then up again. Pleasure coiled, a tight pulse beat inside her. A few more thrusting motions of his hips and she was coming, crying out into his mouth. Shivering all over.

When she was done he pulled back to mutter, "Condom."

She gestured toward her night table, and he shifted to reach into the top drawer, finding the condoms in there and pulling one out. He tore the packet open with his teeth, and together they slipped it onto his rigid cock.

He held himself over her, staring down at her. And as he slid into her, she watched the exquisite agony on his face, the pure pleasure as he filled her and she gripped him inside her body.

"Baby, you feel so good. So damn good. I've never felt anything better than you."

He pumped, driving deeper, deeper, still holding himself over her. She kept her gaze on his, his dark, dark eyes glittering with gold in their depths. And an expression she couldn't quite understand. Pleasure and something else . . .

Doesn't matter . . .

No, all that mattered was that he was there with her, the desire building once more, taking her higher and higher. His thrusting cock filling her, driving pleasure ever deeper. His beautiful face as he came, crying her name.

"Kara!"

Then her own climax, pleasure roaring through her like a white light. Brilliant. Dazzling.

He pulled her up then, until they were both sitting upright, her legs draped over his thighs as he knelt on the bed. He held her close, the solid wall of his chest pressed against her breasts. His breathing was a ragged pant in her ear.

"Christ, Kara," he muttered.

Her body was still trembling with her climax, with emotion, when he turned her over with his strong hands, laying her across his lap.

He began to spank her, hard and fast. Her mind went blank so fast she didn't have time to think about it. Just the pain following so closely on the heels of pleasure that it was all one thing. One sensation. Heat and need and love for him, all melded together.

Love him . . .

She bit her lip. She would not say it. Would not even let herself do more than moan wordlessly.

He reached around her, under her, and thrust one hand between her thighs, pressing onto her clitoris. And inexplicably, she was coming again. Writhing in his lap, pleasure thundering through her like the storm outside.

He held her there with one hand on the small of her back, letting her ride out the last waves. Finally the shuddering stopped and she went quiet. She could hear the rain coming down, that and the still-rasping pant of her own breath.

Silently, Dante pulled her up and into his arms. She laid her head on his shoulder. Breathed him in once more.

She was his. He had just shown her that, in a way perhaps no one else might understand. But they knew it. And that was all that mattered.

She pulled in a long breath, let it go. At least, that was what she would tell herself for now.

Dante felt Kara's body go lax in his arms. She was so damn beautiful like this he could hardly stand to look at her: her cheeks flushed, hair everywhere, her cherry-pink lips parted. Her eyelashes rested against her cheeks like long spikes of dark silk.

Jesus. When had he ever thought of a woman in such poetic terms? But that was what she did to him.

That, and completely fuck with his head.

But in a good way. In a way he wanted. Craved.

She moaned softly and shifted, turning her face into his chest, so that he felt her cheek there, smooth and warm.

He wanted her. All the damn time. In his arms. He wanted to be in her body. To command her and see her response. It was amazing. The most amazing thrill he'd ever experienced, all of his motorcycles and cliff diving aside. His other BDSM scenes, with a myriad of women. All faceless now. Maybe they always had been. But Kara he *saw*. Which made the power play a new experience for him.

"Kara."

"Hmm?" She lifted her head, her eyes a sleepy gleam from beneath her half-closed lids. Green and gold and silver. Gorgeous.

"You are fucking beautiful."

She smiled lazily. "Is that what you wanted to tell me?"

"Yes." He smiled back. "And smart. Creative."

She couldn't help but smile self-consciously. "I'm already sleeping with you, Dante. You don't have to try and convince me."

He laughed, pulling her down onto the bed so that they were lying on their sides, facing each other. "If I did, I'd find other ways. And whatever I did before worked, apparently. But I mean it, Kara."

"Thank you." She was quiet a moment. "I'm afraid I'm not very creative anymore."

He brushed her hair from her cheek, enjoying the texture of it, soft and sleek. Like her. "Why do you say that? What about your art?" he asked her, really wanting to know.

"What? I don't paint anymore. Not really."

"Why not?"

She shrugged, but he could see her cheeks flushing. "I gave it up for more . . . mature things. Like my law degree."

"I understand you need to make a living. That it's difficult to do that with art. But, Kara, you can really paint. You have some real talent. You're not some hack doing paint-by-numbers and calling yourself an artist."

"I don't call myself an artist at all," she said quietly.

"Why not?" He wasn't certain why he was questioning her so closely about this. Maybe because he truly believed in her talent. Because he wanted her to be happy.

"I've never seen any reason to," she said. "And it's not relevant anymore, Dante. I've pretty much stopped."

"Pretty much. But not entirely."

"Well, no. Not entirely."

"Doesn't that tell you something?"

"Yes. It tells me that I have a nice hobby once in a while. That doesn't make me an artist."

"Not if you don't try. Have you really tried, Kara?"

She sighed. "No, I haven't. Getting my law degree was no easy task. Building a career."

He shrugged. "I've found time to ride my motorcycle. Go on trips."

She looked away. "Can we change the subject, please?"

"Okay. For now," he agreed. "I just hate to see that kind of talent go to waste. Being able to paint like that is something I'm envious of. To have that kind of passion for something."

"You're passionate about your motorcycle. It sounds like it, anyway."

"It's not the same."

"Isn't it?" she asked him. "And anyway, I don't have that passion anymore. That fire. And it takes fire to pursue art, Dante. I had to give it up when I went to law school. When I decided to take my life more seriously."

"Art can be serious. Who gave you the idea it wasn't?"

She stared at him. Blinked, a range of emotions passing over her features. "Dante, I thought we were going to change the subject?"

"Okay. Sure." He lifted her hand, brushed a kiss across her knuckles. "How about this . . . I've had something on my mind this week. I want to take you back to the Pleasure Dome."

"I'd like that."

"Would you?" Why did he feel like some insecure puppy, asking for her consent? *Needing* her to say yes.

"I've been thinking about it," she said, "wanting to go back. I liked it there. What goes on there. The energy."

"The energy is pretty incredible. All those people in one place. Of one mind."

"There's a certain sensuality to it. No matter how . . . graphic the activity is."

He nodded. She got it. "Yes, exactly."

"I want to go back," she said again. "With you. Only with you, Dante."

His stomach knotted, but it was an oddly pleasant sensation. Just an exquisite sort of tension. Anticipation, he realized.

"Good. We'll go tomorrow night."

He wanted to go to the club, not to distance himself from her, he now recognized, but to be closer. That was new for him, too.

So much was new with Kara. It made him dizzy. It was that

same sort of sensation he'd had when he first jumped off the cliff in Mexico, flying through the air toward the water. Wondering if he'd survive. If he might drown.

He was drowning now. And flying. Either way, he was going to crash at some point. But whether with a soft thud into the water, or the crushing impact of hitting solid ground, he didn't know. But for the first time, he was willing to take that chance.

fourteen

The Pleasure Dome was more crowded than the last time Dante had taken her there, which frightened and thrilled her at the same time. There was the same red and purple lighting, the shadowed corners. Quiet moans, the hiss of a whip, the clinking, metallic slide of chains against the background of resonant music. She loved it immediately, as she had the first time. But being there again, she *knew* the thrill. *Knew* the fear. Had a better idea of what to expect, which made it both better and more difficult. As they moved through the main room and toward the stairs, Kara's heart began to race, a small, thundering hammer in her chest.

She glanced at Dante, and he seemed to sense what she was feeling. His arm tightened around her waist.

"It's okay." His tone was low, soothing. He leaned his head in a little. "They love you already, Kara. And we haven't even started yet. They're watching you cross the room with me. Waiting. Do you see how many heads you turn? This hot little black dress helps, but really, it's you. They can't keep their eyes off you any more than I can."

She looked around her as they passed the different staging areas. Men and women in various states of undress, or in leather. She caught a gaze here and there, and it caused a surge of excitement in her veins, sharp and hot. She had to look away.

Better to keep her eyes on Dante, who was gorgeous and solid next to her in his leather pants, his black shirt that strained against his broad shoulders. Reassuring, simply by his presence.

She turned to him. "I can't look, Dante. I . . . I like knowing it. But right now looking is too much. It's a little overwhelming."

"Then glory in the knowing, beautiful girl."

He gave her waist a squeeze, and she let herself melt into him. Let herself go all soft and girlish in the way only submitting to him had ever allowed her to do.

The walls were coming down; they had been ever since they'd stepped into the club. Before then, actually, while she was at home getting dressed. Preparing herself for the evening ahead. What was it about that small ritual—showering, lotioning and perfuming herself, dressing for him—that brought her down into the first edge of subspace?

But she couldn't really think about it now. They were walking up the stairs, crossing the first room with the dance floor and the stripper poles. She looked at them a bit longingly. She would love to dance for him. To move her body in time with the heavy beat of the music that played everywhere in the club.

There was a woman on one of the poles now, and Dante, again instinctively, seemed to know she wanted to pause and watch.

The woman was all gorgeous ebony skin and dark, wavy hair, dressed in nothing but a few scraps of sleek purple bondage tape made into a bandeau top and a short skirt that hugged her like a second skin. She wore towering stiletto heels in the same purple. Clinging to the pole with both hands, she swung her hips, her head back, her hair hanging like a curtain of jet. As the music moved, so did she, her hips undulating in a figure eight. She turned, resting her back against the pole, and slid down it, her arms in a graceful arch over her head, her hands joined. She looked up, looked right at Kara, and smiled, a slow, sensual parting of her full red lips.

Kara had never been interested in women sexually. And she wasn't now, necessarily. But this elegant creature exuded sexuality. And she couldn't help but respond in some primal way, her pulse heating, her breath quickening as she watched the woman's sensual dance.

"Dante . . ."

"What is it, baby?"

"I've just realized . . . that what goes on here is all . . . hypersensualized. Hypersexualized, maybe, but not in any bad way." She could hardly believe that she was able to put two sentences together when she was already partially in subspace. With all of this going on around her, taking her down deeper. "Isn't that it? Isn't that what happens here? I'm watching this woman and seeing what others might see when they watch *me*. And it's . . . a turn-on. Knowing it from this perspective. Does that make sense to you at all?"

"Absolutely."

He smiled down at her, and she focused on him. His dark,

whiskey eyes, the sharp slant of his cheekbones. The lush curve of his mouth that was generous and wicked at the same time.

She smiled back, and he kept his gaze on hers. Riveting. Commanding. And even though he was doing nothing more than staring at her, his smile slowly fading, his features full of the same desire building inside her, she felt his absolute authority to her core.

She shivered.

"Do you want to be on that pole, Kara?" he asked, his voice quiet. Intimate. "To perform for me? For the others here?"

It was a moment before she could answer. "I love the idea of being watched. *Seen*. But this isn't quite what I want."

"Ah." He paused, watching her, still. "I think I know just the thing."

He led her to one of the big, plush chairs that were positioned here and there around the edges of the room, set his toy bag on the floor beside one of them. He sat down on the large ottoman that was a foot or two in front of the chair. Reaching for her, he pulled her in, until she was standing between him and the chair. She could feel the smooth leather on the back of her knees.

Dante held both her hands in his. "I want you to do something for me, Kara. For me. The others will see you, will be watching. But this is for *me*. Understood?"

"Always for you, Dante. It's always for you."

Why did saying it to him make it feel more true?

"Good girl. Stand right where you are."

He reached and pulled on the zipper holding the front of her black leather corset-style dress, sliding it upward so that it parted to reveal the tops of her thighs. Desire shimmered over her body, making her go a little dizzy.

She loved that she wasn't quite sure what he would have her do. What he would do to her. The mystery in it. The sense that he was the one in control.

His hand slid under the edge of the dress, pushing the zipper up higher, revealing more of her body until it was open to her waist. Her thighs, her stomach, felt wonderfully naked. And he began to stroke her with his hand, brushing it over her skin.

"Spread a little for me, beautiful girl," he told her.

She did as he asked. His palm smoothed over the insides of her thighs, making her sex go damp. He traced the edge of her black lace thong with his fingertips and she shivered. When he slipped his hand underneath the lace, finding her wet cleft, she moaned softly.

"Ah, you like that. Tell me, Kara."

"Yes. I like it. I love it when you touch me."

He smiled, his gaze focused on the apex of her thighs. He leaned in, pressed his lips to the quickly dampening lace, and she groaned.

"You really do like it, don't you? But do you know what I'd like? I'd like to see you do this yourself. Touch yourself. Make yourself come."

"Here?"

A low chuckle from him. "Yes, here. For me, Kara. For *me*."

He looked up at her, his dark gaze boring into her. Making her body heat with the need to please him.

"God . . ." It came out on a small, breathless sigh.

He chuckled again. "I know you're nervous. But you'll do it, won't you?"

"Yes," she said, the word sticking in her throat, which was tight with nerves and a pure, pulsing desire.

"Let's just get rid of this." He pulled the lace thong down in one swift motion, leaving her naked to his sharp gaze, her dress open from the waist down. "Sit, Kara," he told her, pushing her down gently but firmly into the chair behind her.

He was watching her closely as she leaned back in the chair. He nodded his chin, and she knew exactly what he wanted. She parted her thighs.

He smiled. "Perfect, my girl. Beautiful. I can see how wet you are." He reached out, stroked her cleft with his fingertips, brought them to his lips, his tongue flicking out to lick them. "You taste so damn good. I love the taste of you. But I want to watch you now. Come on, Kara. Show me how you like it. Show me your pleasure."

He sat back, watching her, still. It was as if his gaze compelled her, making her move her hands down to caress the insides of her thighs, opening them wider. She watched his face, watched the pleasure soften his features as she touched her hard clitoris with one fingertip.

"Ah, that's it," he said quietly.

She moved her finger lower, over the folds of her pussy lips, and he groaned softly. The sound went through her like a shot of pure heat.

More.

She used both hands to part those plump folds, and, holding herself open to him with one hand, she pressed two fingers inside her.

Pleasure was instant, hot and sharp. Lovely. Even lovelier was Dante's gaze on her, the concentration there. She glanced down and saw the bulge of his erection straining against the black leather pants he wore.

Oh yes . . .

She paused there, holding perfectly still, letting her body absorb the shock of need. Then she slipped her fingers out and began to stroke, running them up and down her slit, sliding in her juices. She was teasing herself by not touching her clit, not dipping inside. Teasing him. Her hips began to pump of their own accord as she arched against her hand.

"Look at them, Kara," he said, his voice a low, guttural tone. "The people watching you. They're as turned on by what you're doing as I am. I can feel it."

She glanced up, and found several men and women watching her from different points around the room. A dozen pairs of glittering eyes. She could sense their pleasure, nearly as heavy in her body as her own.

"For *me*, Kara."

Dante's hand shot out and he gripped her wrist, made her stroke herself faster, controlling the motion of her hand.

"Ah, God, Dante . . ."

"Are you going to come?"

"Yes."

"Not yet," he ordered, pulling his hand away and cupping her face. "Don't stop, Kara. But look at me. Only at me, now."

"Yes," she whispered, the need to please him more powerful than the sensation swarming her system as she continued to stroke her aching flesh.

His gaze was burning hot on hers. "It's just us, Kara. Just you and me. Nothing else matters."

"Yes, Dante."

He let her cheek go and reached between her thighs once more, thrust his fingers inside her.

"Oh!"

He pulled them out, thrust again.

"This is what I want you to do, my girl."

He sat back, moving his hand away.

She pushed two fingers inside herself once more, bit her lip as sensation stabbed deep.

"Deeper," he ordered.

She pressed harder, slid her fingers out, drove them in again. Her breath was a halting pant. Pleasure was liquid running hot in her veins. Dante's gaze was even hotter, making her soft and weak all over.

"Come on, Kara. Make yourself come for me, baby. Do it."

She thrust her fingers deep into her aching sex, and with the other hand, she pressed her clit, circled. Her climax was fast and hard, making her cry out, her hips pump wildly.

"Ah, so beautiful, baby," Dante murmured as she shivered with wave after wave.

She was barely done when he pulled her into his arms and began to kiss her, his tongue sliding into her mouth. He pressed his own fingers into her still-clenching sex, curving them to hit her G-spot. And another climax came thundering down, a powerful wave of pure, stark pleasure.

"Ah God!"

Dante held her tight in his arms as she shook with the force of it.

"Baby . . . that's it . . . so good," he whispered against her mouth.

"Dante . . ."

"What is it, beautiful girl?"

"Just you and me here . . ." She gasped.

"Yes. Just you and me."

She wasn't even sure what she was asking for. But he was giving it to her. Saying exactly what she needed to hear.

His arms tightened around her.

"That was perfect, Kara. Perfect," he said, his voice full of smoke and need. "But I need more from you now."

"Yes. Anything."

He shifted her in his lap until she was straddling him on the wide ottoman, one thigh draped over either side of his long, leather-clad legs, her arms clasped around his neck.

"Lean into me. Good girl. I'm going to spank you now."

All she could do was groan quietly as he pulled her dress up. One sharp smack on her bare flesh and she was writhing. His erection pressed against her naked mound and she ground into him.

He smacked her again, then again, a sharp volley of slaps on her burning flesh. It was so good, the pleasure and the pain building so quickly she was breathless again in moments.

She was writhing, wanton, needing to come again. She needed the thick length of his cock inside her. Needed his hands on her. His mouth. Everything at once.

She was wild with need, with pleasure denied, with the lovely, torturing slaps on her ass.

"Come again, baby. Come for me. You can do it."

He kept spanking her with one hand. With the other he reached between them and into her dress, pinching her nipple hard.

"Oh!"

She ground her mound into the hard bulge in his lap, riding that rock-hard ridge, needing more. And as he twisted her nipple in his fingers, the pain burned into her, branding her. And she came once more in a hard frenzy.

"Dante!"

Again, before it was over, he shifted her, lifting her to her feet this time, then lifting her in his arms.

She was trembling. Weak in his arms.

"Have to fuck you now, my girl. Have to be inside you."

In moments they were in one of the curtained alcoves that were in every corner of the club, and he was setting her down on a high, padded table. He reached blindly for a condom from a bowl on a high shelf, unzipped his leather pants. His cock was a hard, golden shaft of beautiful flesh, darker at the head. She couldn't wait to feel him inside her.

He pulled her roughly to the edge of the table, parted her thighs. And in one hard stroke, he was buried deep in her soaking wet sex.

"Jesus, Kara. Baby . . ."

He held her arms over her head with one hand clasped around both her wrists. He was watching her, his chest heaving with each panting breath. Then he started to move, his hips driving hard into hers. So hard it hurt, but she needed it, needed him.

"Dante . . . please."

Tears pooled in her eyes. She didn't understand. All she knew was the exquisite pleasure of his body inside hers. The aching need for more, somehow.

"Dante," she said again on a sob.

He pulled her body upright, held her tight in his arms as he pounded into her. And as he tensed, finally, shouting her name, as her body shook with yet another sharp, ravaging climax, she cried into his shoulder, cried out.

"Dante, God! Please, please . . . Dante . . ."

She was clinging to him. And he was clinging just as tightly. Her world spun, out of control. And all she knew was his body, and hers. Together. Just the two of them. The rest of the world disappeared.

She didn't remember very clearly the ride back to his place—it was a blur of streetlights and a light rain coming down, making the colors run together on the windshield. The scent of the leather seats in Dante's car. The lovely, dark scent of *him*, mixed with the sharp smell of spent pleasure. But as Dante got her out of the car, then half carried her to the elevator, she had a wild surge of growing panic.

It didn't make any sense to her that it was happening now. But she was full of need. Full of a hard, trembling fear.

"Dante . . . please don't go."

"What? I'm not going anywhere, baby. I'm just taking you inside. Here, one second while I get the front door open."

She sagged against him as he closed the door of his apartment behind them. Just went weak all over. With relief, maybe.

He held on to her, his arms solid around her.

"It's okay," he told her, his tone soothing, calm. "You're just having another chemical rush from the play tonight. Endorphins. Maybe a little overload. You'll be fine. I'm going to undress you, and get us both into bed. All right?"

She nodded mutely. She couldn't think straight. All she could think about, all she knew at that moment, was that she loved him. That after their evening at the club she felt closer to him than ever. And she didn't know how much longer she could hold it in.

She felt dizzy with it. With love. Her need for him—a stark, absolute need she had never felt before in her life.

In moments, it seemed, she was undressed and in his bed, the sheets cool and soft against her naked skin.

"Dante?"

"Shh, baby, I'm right here."

And he was, sliding in next to her, slipping his arm under her neck. She rolled onto her side, pressing into his big body. It wasn't about sex. She just needed to *feel* him.

He stroked her hair from her face, kissed her cheek, her lips, briefly. And she melted into it. The lovely sensation of Dante cherishing her.

It was the most wonderful thing she'd ever felt. She wanted to think about it, what it might mean. To revel in it. But her eyes were so impossibly heavy.

"Dante," she whispered, "I have to tell you something."

Don't do it.

"What is it?"

Have to say it . . .

"It's important . . ."

He was quiet. Waiting for her to speak, she realized. But she couldn't hold her eyes open. Couldn't get her mouth to work. It was as though her body weighed a thousand pounds.

"Mmm . . ."

"Kara?"

She struggled to stay awake, to tell him what she so desperately needed to. But in moments, she faded away.

Dante watched her. Watched over her, like some sort of guardian of her sleep. He could barely make out the silhouette of her cheekbones, her jaw, in the dark. But he knew how beautiful she was, all the same.

A part of him wished she was awake. He didn't even know why. He was too worn-out to perform sexually at that moment. Or maybe not. His desire was endless when it came to Kara. But there was more to it than that.

On the other hand, he needed some time to think. To sort out all the strange ideas sifting through his mind. The weird things he'd been feeling all evening, that had been building over the last few weeks.

The scene with her at the Pleasure Dome had been intense tonight. Beyond intense. There hadn't been any heavy pain play—no more than the usual spanking, which was as far as he'd taken her. He didn't need to go further, to play harder, with Kara. It wasn't about that anymore. Although he'd always love the power exchange, the sensation play, watching her response, he simply didn't feel the need for anything harder. More extreme. But something else had happened tonight . . .

Something new was always happening when he was with her. There was a steady progression to things. Too much to think about.

But maybe it was time he did.

Was it possible he loved this woman?

The thought went through his head, his heart, like a brilliant flash of light. Dazzling. Pure.

His heartbeat accelerated, a tight and racing thump in his chest.

No.

But was that anything more than force of habit, to deny it?

He scrubbed at the stubble on his jaw. Tried to get his head in order. But he couldn't seem to calm down.

He slipped his hand down over his chest, pressing there, as if that alone could slow his erratic heartbeat, soothe him.

Christ. He could not believe it. He wasn't ready to believe it.

He'd known he was feeling something for her. Something new. Special. But this?

Impossible.

Apparently not.

He pulled her sleeping form closer.

He just had to calm down. It was late; he was tired. He didn't have to actually *do* anything about this. He could take some time to really figure out where his head was in regard to all this. All of this . . . love.

He was an idiot. Behaving as if he were some stupid teenager. Which happened all too often with Kara.

He fucking loved her.

Christ.

His pulse sped up, and without really thinking about it, he turned his face to inhale the scent of her hair. It was comforting.

He was losing it.

Had lost it.

Gone.

He didn't know how the hell it had happened. But he had fallen in love, finally. Despite himself. Despite everything he knew about what he was—and wasn't—capable of. And he didn't know what the hell he was going to do about it.

He lay there, her head pillowed on his chest, listening to her breathe. To the sound of the rain against the windows. The occasional distant rumble of thunder. He wanted to stay awake. To figure it all out. But finally, the gentle rhythm of her breathing soothed him. That and the falling rain, making some sort of cocoon around them. His body relaxed, his mind buzzing with sensory overload. At some point, with the moon setting behind a bank of clouds and the stars beginning to fade, he slept.

It was only a few hours later, when, in the first rays of dawn, they both woke. Silently, she went into his arms. He rolled her over, her body all soft curves against him: her breasts, her belly, her sweet thighs. She spread for him and he pushed into her, easy as silk. That fluid, that smooth.

He kissed her as he arched his hips, and she sighed quietly into his mouth. So damn sweet. He couldn't get enough of her.

Kara.

She moved with him, every motion of their bodies like liquid, a perfect rhythm that took no thought. No effort. They slipped into pleasure. Or it flowed over them. He didn't know. But soon she went tight around him, her sex hot and warm. Incredible. She panted, her climax as soft as the early morning light.

Then he was coming, shivering inside her. He held her tighter, his arms around her body. He didn't want to let her go.

Eventually, it occurred to him that he might be crushing her. He rolled off her and she curled into him. His hand went into her hair. His breathing slowed as he flexed his fingers, the fine strands like silk.

"Kara," he whispered. "Baby . . ."

What did he mean to say? But he was so sleepy . . .

He drifted off once more.

fifteen

It was late when Kara woke. She could tell by the angle of the sun outside the windows. She was still half-numb all over, her body buzzing. Her brain.

She turned to find Dante watching her.

"Hey." His voice was low, smoky.

"Hey."

She wasn't sure how she should feel. About what had happened the night before. About how it had left her feeling. Something had happened between them. Again. Things had gone to a whole new level. Not only at the club, but there, in his bed, in the middle of the night. She remembered it like some sort of lovely dream. Except that it had really happened. She had felt it. Had felt the deeper shift in him. In the way he had touched her.

He'd been so, so gentle. So tender. There had been real emotion there, and she knew she wasn't the only one feeling it. He'd felt . . . wide-open to her, for the first time. But now, mostly she was . . . uncertain. About how he truly felt. If she could believe what she'd sensed in him. If she could trust it.

"Kara, you okay?" he asked.

"Oh, I'm . . . Yes, I'm fine."

He propped himself up on one elbow. She couldn't help but notice how mussed his dark hair was. It made him look a little boyish.

"You don't seem fine."

She shrugged, pulling the sheet up higher over her chest. "I'm . . ." She stopped, bit her lip, then looked into his eyes. "Dante, I feel like something has changed again."

"Yes," he said quietly.

"Yes?"

"For me, too."

"So, what does this mean?"

He was quiet for several long moments during which she held her breath. She didn't feel as if she could breathe until he told her. Even while a part of her was afraid to know.

He pushed out a long breath. "It means, for me, anyway, that I'm . . . having feelings I don't know what to do with. And I think you are, too."

She bit her lip harder. "I . . ." Why was her heart pounding so hard? She wanted to tell him exactly how she felt. But she could not do it. "I'm having some of the same thoughts. And having a hard time dealing with it."

"So, we're on the same page again," he said, his dark brows drawn together in question, even though he'd said the words so definitively.

He was waiting for assurance from her, she realized with a

small shock. But to say it to him—it still felt far too risky. She was not going to be the one to tell him first that she loved him.

Then where did that leave them, if he wouldn't tell her? Or if he couldn't recognize it? If perhaps that wasn't what he was feeling at all?

Her heart was a hammer in her chest, knocking painfully against her ribs. She could feel the fear seeping over her, like some sort of venom. Poison. Turning the fear into panic.

She had to get out.

She sat up in bed, so fast she was dizzy for a moment. Then she threw the covers back and swung her legs over the side.

"Kara? What are you doing?"

"I need to go."

"What? You can't go now."

"Yes, I can. I have to, Dante." She stood up, the winter air chilling her bare skin. The dizziness hit her again, and she had to pause, her hand going to her cover her eyes. The light coming through the windows seemed too bright. Too illuminating. She could feel the blood pounding too hard in her veins.

He was beside her in an instant. "What's going on here?"

"I don't know," she said without turning to face him, without acknowledging his hold on her arm. "And maybe that's the problem. I don't know what's happening, what to do. How you feel about anything. You're so vague, Dante. And I'm not asking you for explanations, because I don't have any myself. But I don't think . . . that I can take it anymore. Not right now, anyway. I need to think. I need . . . some time to myself."

"Don't do this, Kara. You're crashing. You need to be where I can keep an eye on you, make sure you're okay."

She whipped around to face him then. Anger surged through her, a fiery hot flow through her system.

He was too damn beautiful, the late-morning light catching his dark hair, edging it in gold. But she wasn't going to allow herself to be distracted.

"Is that all you have to say to me, Dante? Because if it is, then I'm done here. I'm going. I don't care about all of this crashing stuff. And I don't think that's what it is. Not at the core."

"What is it, then?"

He looked truly confused. But she couldn't explain any more to him without revealing far more than she was willing to.

She shook her head. "I am going, Dante. Don't try to stop me. Not now."

She started to get dressed, feeling more vulnerable in her leather club dress than she had standing there naked with him. He held perfectly still, his features shutting down, naked and so beautiful it made her ache to look at him.

He was still watching her as she slipped into her shoes, moved toward the front door where her coat was slung over a console table. She slid her arms into it, feeling colder than ever.

Dante hadn't moved, hadn't said a word. It made her angry. More confused than ever. More certain that she had to leave.

She gave him one more moment, waiting with her hand on the doorknob. But he stood, silent and beautiful as a statue, his mouth a tight, grim line.

She shook her head once more. And left.

Downstairs, she flagged a cab quickly, gave the driver her address and sank back into the hard seat. Her jaw was set, biting back the tears that wanted to come. But she wouldn't allow them.

She hated that being female too often meant the reaction to anger was tears. It made her feel weak.

She hated feeling weak.

She balled her hands into fists, until her nails bit into her palms. The pain grounded her, helped her hold it together.

It wasn't long before the cab arrived at her place. She pulled some cash from her coat pocket to pay the driver, got out, let herself into the building. The stairs seemed endless.

Just get inside, where it's safe.

She opened her front door, slipped inside, shut it behind her. And fell against the door, her back pressed up tight against the wood, as the tears began to fall.

Damn it.

She did not want to do this. To cry over a man. She hadn't cried over Jake. She'd just been mired in a well of self-pity, self-judgment. But she wasn't judging herself this time. Being with Dante had never made her feel she had to.

"God damn it," she muttered.

She pushed off the door, flung her coat off. It landed on the floor. She didn't care. She kept moving, into her bedroom, where she got undressed and, naked, climbed into bed.

Her own bed. Her safe haven.

Except that nothing felt safe to her right now. Nothing felt familiar enough. Not as familiar as Dante's bed. His body.

But he would not love her. So how safe would she ever be with him? She would have to leave all of this love stuff behind. Just get over it. The situation was impossible.

She reached for a tissue from the box on her nightstand, blew her nose, wiped her eyes. But it was useless; the tears kept coming. Pouring down her face. And soon she was sobbing, long, drawn-out sobs, a terrible keening that came from deep in her chest, her body.

She wrapped her arms around herself, held on tight. But it was only Dante's arms that would comfort her. She was lost without him. And she would never have him. Never. Not really. Not in the true and permanent way she wanted, for the first time in her life.

The old feelings of not being good enough, deserving enough, for love came flooding back. All of the old issues created by her cold and distant parents. She'd never been able to please them. To get them to notice her, unless they were being disapproving. And no matter what she did, even choosing to go to law school because they wanted her to, giving up her art—other than the one or two paintings she allowed herself each year—it wasn't enough.

She obviously wasn't enough for Dante, either.

But no, that was her old self talking. Anger flooded her again.

He wasn't enough for *her*. Not if he refused to acknowledge his feelings for her. Not if he couldn't love her. Didn't she deserve that, damn it?

Still, pain poured through her system like a heavy weight she felt in her lungs, her arms and legs. She couldn't move. Couldn't think straight. All she could think of was Dante's face, his dark eyes shuttered, his features taut, as she waited for him to speak. To stop her from leaving, even though she'd told him not to. All she could feel was loss and anger, and the terrible, sharp aching in her heart.

She'd never experienced a broken heart before. She hadn't ever allowed anyone to get close enough to really hurt her. She'd had no idea it would hurt so much. That it would feel as if her heart were made of glass, and had shattered into a thousand pieces, each one piercing her, burrowing deep.

The tears turned to sobs once more. They wrenched their way out of her, twisting in her chest before they tore from her open mouth. Unbelievable pain. Unbelievable sadness.

The sun was lowering outside her window when she blinked her way back to awareness. Late afternoon. She'd been there for hours. She felt worn-out. Drained. Sick to her stomach. She knew she had to get out of bed, drink some water. Wash her face.

Her eyes, her cheeks, felt swollen, tender to the touch. She inhaled on a sigh. How had she let this happen to her?

She would never let this happen again. She didn't know how she was going to survive this. But this would be the last time.

The tears started once more. Unbearable, the hard heat of them on her cheeks, the small sobs that wracked her aching chest. How could one person have so many tears inside them? But even that thought came as if from a great distance, her mind blurred with pain.

She tried to swallow the tears down, to fight them. But she couldn't do it. She rolled into a ball, letting them fall, mindless in her misery. Eventually, she slept.

She dreamed of Dante. His apartment. It was filled with sunlight that seemed to come from everywhere, golden and sweet. He came up behind her, and she sensed rather than saw him. She knew the feel of his arms around her waist, knew the lovely strength of him as he pulled her into his body.

"This is what you should be doing, Kara," he said.

Yes, she thought. Being with him . . .

Before her was an easel, with a half-done painting on it, and she held a brush in her hand. It was the view of Elliott Bay from his window, blues and greens, sunlight piercing the fog. The view from *their* window.

Lovely.

But she wasn't painting anymore. Not really. And she wasn't with Dante, either, was she?

Everything went dark, empty. It was as though she was falling, into an empty space, containing . . . nothing.

The dark, the nothingness, drew around her, closing in. Seeping inside her. She called out for him, "Dante!"

But he wasn't there.

He never would be.

"No," she muttered past the pain.

"No!"

She woke in the dark, shivering from the dampness on her skin, knowing it bone deep.

It was over.

Dante stood staring out the long bank of windows, his gaze on the tiny, twinkling lights that were the boats docked in Elliott Bay below his apartment. He was mostly numb. He had been since Kara left that morning.

Okay, that was a lie. Maybe a part of him was numb. The other part was torn apart, as if he'd been through a paper shredder. Raw and hurting like hell. That part of him was fucking desperate.

He ran his fingers over the sharp stubble on his chin, around the back of his stiff neck.

He was stiff all over. He'd tried to lie down on the couch, exhausted, but he was too edgy to hold still for long. He hadn't slept for one moment after she'd left, and had had only a few hours of sleep before then. But it wasn't the lack of sleep that was the worst of it, that made him hurt all over. It was the lack of *Kara*. Knowing she was gone.

He was . . . bereft. Angry. Angry that she'd left. Angry that he cared so fucking much. Angry at the bitter sense of helplessness that moved through him like a dark sludge in his veins. He was helpless to change things for Kara. To change that basic part of himself the way he'd need to in order to give her what she deserved. He was helpless in loving her. There wasn't a damn thing he could do about that. Fucking helpless.

He hated that more than anything. Always had. He'd hated it when he'd been powerless to do anything to make his mother's life better. Hated when he'd been left feeling it so completely after Erin had died.

He'd figured out long ago that the way to avoid feeling this horrible fucking lack of power was to *always* be in control. Responsible. It made him feel some sense of his own personal power. As if what he did mattered in the world, even if it was only at work, or in the realm of BDSM. As if nothing he didn't expect could happen because he had his life all neatly pinned down.

But somewhere in the back of his mind, he'd known it was a convenient half lie. That all the control in the world, the lie itself, was never going to make him feel whole. And, not knowing what else to do about it, he'd let it be. Let himself live the lie.

Kara had exposed him. To himself, anyway. He hadn't been able to expose his truth to her. The truth that he loved her. That the only thing that would ever make him whole was loving her.

The idea was simply too much to handle. Especially now that she'd made it so clear she didn't want to be with him. That he'd fucked it up. Exactly as he knew he would.

He started to pace, the dark sky, the glow of the streetlights, moving past the edge of his vision in a blur.

He felt . . . overwhelmed by this. For the first time in his adult life, he wasn't sure he could handle this by himself.

The only person he really wanted to talk to about it was Kara. But that was impossible. He knew she wouldn't see him, that he was the last person she wanted to see right now, and he couldn't blame her.

Time to turn to his closest friend. He and Alec didn't discuss emotional stuff very often. They'd never gotten too deep. The closest they'd come was when Alec had been losing his mind over Dylan. But that had been all about Alec revealing himself. Dante never had. He wasn't certain he knew how.

But hell, it had to be better than this endless pacing, this endless cycle of one thought after another racing through his head, only to leave him in the same sorry place.

Maybe Alec could give him some perspective. Help him put his head back together again.

He moved to the console table in the foyer, where his cell phone was plugged into the charger. He pulled the cord out and dialed Alec's number.

"Hello."

"Alec, it's Dante."

"Hey, what's up? I've hardly heard from you lately. I figured you'd check in eventually after we ran into you the other night."

"Yeah, about that . . ."

Christ, where to start? How did people do this?

"What's going on, Dante?" Alec asked. "And don't tell me it's nothing because I can hear it in your voice."

"Ever the intuitive dom."

"Yep. So spill."

He sighed, started pacing again. "Look, can you meet me for a drink?"

"Now? Dylan and I are just finishing dinner."

"Yes, now. Please. I'm sorry about dinner, but I . . . Fuck, can you just do it?"

"Yes. Sure. Of course. Tell me where you want to meet."

"The Back Room? Do you know where it is?" It was a small dive bar close to his building. He knew it would be quiet. That he'd be unlikely to run into anyone from work there, anyone they knew from the club scene.

"I'll find it. Give me about forty-five minutes."

"Okay. Okay."

They hung up and Dante went to take a quick shower, something he'd been avoiding all day. There were too many memories of Kara in there, her sleek body surrounded by steam. Kara in his white dress shirt, her skin nearly as pale as the shirt, but her cheeks pink, her eyes glittering silver and gold with desire. Beautiful. Stunning. He'd had plenty of other women in there. But Kara was the only one who really mattered.

He wasn't sure what that said about him. He didn't exactly like what it implied.

It wasn't long before he was out the door. He decided to walk the six blocks to the bar. He needed to cool off, to stretch his legs. To work off some of this unbearable tension.

It had rained again. The streets were damp, reflecting watery images of the streetlights, the neon from some of the restaurants and storefronts.

He felt like that. Blurred. Distorted. He didn't like it one bit.

Alec was already at the bar when he arrived, and Dante was grateful not to have to sit there, nursing a drink and his own thoughts. He couldn't stand to be in his own head one more fucking minute.

"Alec, hey."

"Hi. I ordered you a shot of Chivas on the rocks. I figured we'd save the good stuff for when you're more yourself."

Dante slid onto the stool next to Alec. "That obvious, huh?"

"Glaringly. To me, anyway."

Dante wrapped his hands around the glass, took a sip, set it back on the bar. Stared at it.

Alec was quiet next to him, sipping at his drink. Dante knew Alec well enough to know he'd sit there all night if that was what it took.

He swallowed another slug of the cold whiskey, tried to savor the burn as it went down his throat. But Alec was right; he couldn't really enjoy it. Not tonight.

"So . . ." Dante started. "Christ, I don't know how to do this. Talk. Really talk."

"It's a little weird, but you get used to it," Alec said, a small teasing note in his voice.

"I'd rather not."

Alec shrugged. "I thought so, too. Before Dylan."

"How is she?" Dante asked.

"She's great. Amazing. But you're changing the subject."

Dante nodded, smiling grimly. "Yeah."

He belted down the last of his drink, the ice cubes hitting his teeth. He waved the bartender over and ordered another.

"This must be serious," Alec said quietly.

"It is." He paused. "So . . . I think I'm in love with Kara."

"That *is* serious."

Dante took a breath, held it in his lungs for several moments, still staring at his glass. "Yes, it is. And that's bullshit. I don't *think* I'm in love with her. I am. So, what the hell do I do, Alec?"

He looked up at his friend, wanting—needing—an answer.

"What do you want to do?"

"Be with her. Even if it scares the shit out of me. Even if I'm convinced I can't do a relationship justice."

"I used to think the same thing."

"I don't know if you had as much reason as I do," Dante said.

"Maybe. Maybe not." Alec took a sip of his drink, set it down on the bar, looked back at Dante. His gaze was direct. But then, Alec was always direct. One of the things Dante had been count-ing on. "Do you think maybe you came to me tonight to be talked into going after her?"

His gut was tightening up. "It's possible."

"I'm not going to tell you to do that."

"You're not."

"No. And I'll tell you why. I know you, Dante. And I think you need to give this some time. Calm down. Give yourself some time to accept how you feel about her. Because I can tell you don't quite believe it yet. And you're going to need to before you see her."

"If she'll see me."

"Ah. Well. Even more reason to give it some time. She probably needs it to cool off from whatever happened between you two."

Dante nodded. "You're right."

"I hope so. Lord knows I fucked up with Dylan. But I'm learning. She tells me I am, anyway."

That made Dante smile. A little. He couldn't help it. Alec Walker was not a man who let anyone tell him anything. Not until Dylan.

Dante was the same way. But he wanted to give this thing with Kara a try. He'd give it a few days, as Alec suggested. And if it meant he had to hear a good ration of shit about his behavior, he knew he deserved it. He would take it. And meanwhile, he'd try to breathe a little. To let Kara breathe.

"Sounds like a good plan," he told Alec. "Thanks."

"Sure. Want me to hang out, maybe watch the sports wrap-up with you?"

"That's all right. I can tell you want to get back to Dylan."

"You can tell?" Alec looked a little shocked.

"It's clear as day, Alec."

"Well, hell."

"No, it's a good thing. I'm glad to see you happy."

Alec nodded, smiled. "I'd like to see you happy, too."

"I wouldn't mind that."

Alec stood, tossed a few twenties on the bar. "Stay and drink some more if you like."

"I might do that."

"And let me know how it goes."

"I will. And, Alec. Thanks."

"Sure."

Alec left before anything more needed to be said.

sixteen

It was Thursday morning, which meant it was donut day at the office—her employers' idea of keeping up company morale toward the end of each week. Not that Kara could imagine swallowing anything more than the tea she'd been living on all week long.

She'd called in sick on Monday, too worn and weepy still to come in. By Tuesday she'd pulled herself together enough to get to the office, and was glad to find that Dante was in court all day. The same on Wednesday. Maybe today she'd be as lucky. She wasn't up to facing him yet. She wasn't sure she ever would be.

That's what you get for becoming involved with someone at work . . .

She sighed quietly as the elevator pinged and she stepped off, into the main lobby of her firm. The receptionist greeted her, and she nodded a greeting to several of her coworkers as she made her way warily down the hall to her office. Ruby, the secretary she shared with several other attorneys—including Dante—followed her in as Kara was pulling off her coat.

"Hey, Kara, the big three have called a meeting this morning. Everyone who's not in court today has to show up."

"Oh. How long do I have?" She glanced at her watch, wondering if she could find some excuse to skip it.

Would Dante be there? Would he be in court again? Didn't she have something urgent to do?

"They've called it for a quarter after eight, so about fifteen minutes. Want a donut? I saved one of the maple bars you like."

Her stomach churned. "Thanks, Ruby. That's so sweet of you, but I'm . . . trying to cut down on sugar."

"I should do the same, but I've already had two jelly donuts." Ruby flashed her a grin. "See you in the conference room in a few minutes."

"Thanks, Ruby."

God, would he be there? She didn't think she could stand it.

She pulled in a deep breath, let it out slowly, trying to remember the calming breathing routines she'd learned in her yoga classes. But her pulse was racing. There was nothing she could do about it; she had to go to the meeting. She would simply have to deal with it.

Where had all her strength gone? She used to be so strong, so together.

She shook her head as she pushed her purse and her briefcase under her desk, turned her computer on and waited for it to boot up. And sighed as she realized she was hoping to find a message from Dante in her in-box.

He hadn't tried to reach her since she'd left his house last Sunday. She knew he'd had a heavy court schedule all week, but surely he would have called or e-mailed her—texted, even—if he'd wanted to talk to her?

Which meant he didn't.

Not that she wanted to talk to him. She was still angry. Still torn apart. Wanting—*needing*—to see him so badly it made her *skin* hurt. She hated that.

Get it together.

She glanced at her watch once more. Time to go to the meeting. She took a few more long breaths, which did little to calm her, and stood up. Feeling chilled, she pulled on the sweater she'd taken to leaving on the back of her office chair this week. She was always cold lately. She had been ever since she'd left Dante, looking shocked and tight-lipped at his place last Sunday.

Naked and beautiful and something lurking in his eyes that could have been pain . . .

Don't think of it now. Just get through the day.

She came into the hall and Ruby was there, smiling at her at first. Then her smile faded.

"Jeez, Kara, you're as white as a sheet. Are you okay?"

"Maybe I haven't completely recovered from the bug I had on Monday."

"Maybe . . ." Ruby said, one eyebrow raised.

"What?" Kara asked defensively.

Ruby stared straight ahead as they moved down the hall. "Nothing. Maybe. Except that Dante De Matteo has had that same look on his face every morning before he leaves for court. And I know it's not his case he's concerned about."

"Ruby . . ."

"It's okay, Kara. I won't say a word to anyone. But I work for both of you, so I see things . . ."

Kara sighed. "And?"

"Well, it's obvious something is going on. I know it's none of my business." She stopped, shook her head. "I'm sorry. I should have just kept my mouth shut. It's just that I really like you. I admire you. And I hate to see you looking so . . . tired. So beat down."

Kara had to swallow hard against the tears burning behind her eyes. She sniffed. "It's okay, Ruby."

"Oh, hell, now I've done it. I really am sorry." Ruby laid a hand on Kara's arm.

"It's okay. Really it is. It's just . . . having anyone show any sympathy kind of brings it to the surface. I haven't even talked to my best friend about it for that reason."

"I'll zip my mouth now, I promise. But . . . let me know if you need anything, okay?"

Kara nodded.

"Why don't you take a moment in the ladies' room before the meeting? I'll cover for you."

"Thanks, Ruby. I might do that. And, Ruby . . . do you know if Dante is here today, or if he's back in court?"

"I'm not sure. I didn't have a chance to look at the schedule before I got the memo from Mr. Kelleher, and I've been running around ever since. Do you want me to find out and let you know before you get to the meeting?"

"No, I don't think there's time. Anyway, either he'll be there or he won't. And I just need to . . . handle things, don't I?"

"Okay. See you in there."

Ruby gave her arm another squeeze before she left her in the hall.

Kara made her way quickly to the restroom, where she washed her hands, letting the warm water soothe her. She knew she couldn't stay for long, but she was glad to have a moment to catch her breath.

She looked at her reflection in the mirror. She *was* a little pale. She patted her cheeks, hoping to bring some color into them, then shrugged. There wasn't much she could do. She had to go.

The meeting room was crowded, most of the firm's staff packed in there, shoulder to shoulder around the big conference table, the administrative staff and clerks standing around the perimeter. The table was full, so Kara went to stand next to Ruby, who gave her a small, encouraging smile.

Charles Landers was standing at the front of the room, nodding and smiling. After a moment he was joined by Lyle Kelleher, then by Edward Tate. They were all three, as always, perfectly put together, elegant and cool, with their dark suits and colorful power ties, their varying shades of silver hair.

Lyle Kelleher cleared his throat, and Kara looked around with some relief. Dante wasn't there.

"We have an announcement today that is both happy and sad," Mr. Kelleher said. He gestured to one of the attorneys who was seated at the big table. "Julie Dillard is leaving us next month, I'm afraid. But she leaves us for good reason. Julie will be moving to Washington, DC. She's been a hard worker, and it has been our pleasure to have had her with us since she graduated law school, first as a law clerk, then as a practicing attorney. We'd like to thank you, Julie, for everything you've given to this firm, and to wish you well in your endeavors."

Everyone applauded and Julie, a petite brunette, nodded and smiled.

"Julie, are you going to practice in DC?" someone asked.

"Actually, I'm going there to get married. And . . . I'm going to open an antiques store, something I've dreamed about for years. I've already found my store space."

There was another round of applause.

"Don't everyone get so excited about the prospect of her giving up the noble practice of law," Charles Landers protested, his blue eyes twinkling with mock indignation.

Kara's heart surged. She was happy for Julie, she truly was. But she was also filled with envy. Julie was going off to find her happiness: marriage, her own business. She was pursuing her dreams.

She was daring to.

At that moment Dante slipped into the crowded room. Kara caught his eye. She hadn't meant to. But as always, she was instantly drawn to him. He started to smile, stopped himself. And she was shocked at how much it hurt, simply being in the same room with him. That he couldn't even smile at her. That she was physically unable to smile at him.

Ruby gave her wrist a quick squeeze, and she was grateful for that small show of support.

The rest of the brief meeting went by in a blur as Kara tried not to look at him. But she *knew* he was there. Felt it down in her bones.

Dante.

Just keep breathing. Get through this.

Finally it was over, and everyone shuffled out the door. Unfortunately, one of the other attorneys needed Ruby for something, so Kara was on her own, praying Dante would leave the room before she had to face him.

She watched as he slipped out the door, and was relieved. She followed her coworkers into the hallway, where everyone split off, going to their own offices. She'd just made it to her office door when Dante appeared beside her.

"Kara, can we talk?"

She felt like she'd been sucker punched. Even hearing his voice was too much for her. She couldn't stand the heat of his body beside her, the scent of him.

"I'd rather not," she answered tightly.

"I understand," he said, keeping his tone low. "But we work in the same building, so it's going to happen sooner or later."

She took in a long breath. "I know that."

He was quiet a moment. She turned to look at him.

Oh, that was a mistake. He was too damned handsome in his silvery-gray suit, his darker gray shirt and charcoal tie. Sophisticated. She remembered how she'd felt the first moment she'd seen him. Just . . . bowled over. She was no less bowled over now.

She had to remember her anger. The hurt that went with it.

"Can we go into your office?" he asked.

"You can say whatever you need to say concerning work right here."

"Come on, Kara. This is not concerning work. Not really."

God, she did not want to do this. Did not want to talk to him.

"Dante, I can't talk with you here. I can't do it. I don't think it's a good idea and . . . I just can't."

"Where, then?"

She shook her head, keeping her eyes glued to the floor. "No-where, Dante. Because that's where the conversation will go. That's where we're going, isn't it?"

"That's something we need to discuss. We need to talk about why you left the way you did."

She raised her chin, looking up at him then. Anger burned in her, hot and fierce. "Really, Dante? If you were so concerned about that, why have you waited all week to tell me?"

He rubbed at his jaw, blew out a breath. "Because . . . I don't know why. Jesus, Kara."

"Great answer, Dante." She ducked her head and opened her office door, shut it behind her, making an effort not to slam it.

Her heart was thundering. Her blood boiling. And the hurt was a raw wound, freshly reopened.

He didn't know? That was the best he could do?

She stalked across the room, sat down hard in her chair, smoothing her hands over the neat chignon she'd pulled her hair into that morning. She could not believe she was doing it, but she was going to plead sick and go home. She picked up her phone, dialed Ruby's extension.

"Ruby, it's Kara. I'm not feeling well. I need you to cancel everything on my calendar today."

"Are you okay?"

"I . . . Not really. I just need to go. Can you take care of it for me?"

"Yes, of course. I'll handle things here. I don't want you to worry about anything. Do what you need to do, Kara."

"Thanks, Ruby. For everything."

She hung up and bent down to drag her purse and her brief-case from under the desk. Got up and pulled her coat back on. She paused for a moment, her hand on the doorknob, hoping Dante was nowhere in sight. She opened the door.

The hall was empty, and she was grateful for it. And angry that Dante hadn't tried any harder to talk with her.

She'd been the one who had told him to go away. That she wasn't going to talk to him.

Maybe she was an idiot. But it had felt like pure survival. It still did.

She sighed, moved down the hall to the elevator, stepped in. And caught sight of Dante coming out of Charles Landers's office. He was staring at her, his face tight, as the elevator doors slid shut.

She kept breathing, pulling air into her lungs as she reached the ground floor, made her way to her car, drove home. By the time she reached her apartment, her chest was aching, the pain so heavy she had to force herself to breathe. And the tears burned behind her eyelids, in her throat.

She shook off her coat, dropped it and her purse, her briefcase, on the floor. On autopilot, she went to the kitchen and put the kettle on for tea. She didn't know what else to do. Tea was an old, familiar comfort, and she needed comfort now.

She needed Dante.

No.

She gripped the edge of the counter, the old white tile cool beneath her fingers. Grounding her. She stared at the tiles, the box of tea on the counter. It was all running together, blurred by the tears pooling in her eyes.

Don't do it.

She couldn't cry anymore. She could not do it. If she gave herself up to the tears again, she was afraid she'd never stop.

The kettle whistled and she gave herself a mental shake, poured the boiling water into one of her cobalt-blue mugs, dipped a bag of Earl Grey tea for several moments before taking the mug between her chilled hands and carrying it into the bedroom.

There, she stepped out of her tailored skirt, pulled her turtleneck sweater over her head. She shivered in the winter air.

She needed to be warm. To climb under the covers with her tea and curl up. Maybe sleep the pain away.

She yanked the covers down, then took off her bra, stepped out of her underwear, and was taking her white cotton knit robe from the hook in her bathroom when she heard a knock at the front door.

She pulled the robe on, tying the sash around her waist as she moved through the apartment. Her pulse was racing. She knew it would be him, somehow.

How had he gotten in past the door downstairs? Had she left it open in her hurry to get home? But she couldn't think about it, could barely think at all.

When she opened the door her heart filled with pain. Need. Dread.

Dante.

"What are you doing here?" she demanded with as much force as she could manage.

She was breathless. Stunned. By the fact that he'd come after her. By the emotion trembling through her system like a series of small shocks. And, underneath it all, she was still mad as hell.

"I had to talk to you, Kara. I realized it wasn't appropriate to talk with you at work."

"But bending me over your desk to spank me was?"

He ran a hand over his dark hair. "That was . . . different."

She let out a short, barking laugh. "Yes, it was."

"I don't blame you for being angry with me. But just . . . let me in." She started to shake her head, to close the door, but he put a hand out, stopping her. "Please, Kara."

His voice had gone soft. She couldn't resist. The anger in her wanted to. Wanted to slam the door in his face, scream at him to go away and leave her alone.

Her heart never wanted him to go.

She took a step back, let him move past her into the apartment. She closed the front door, pulling her robe tighter around her as she turned to face him.

His eyes were glittering with emotion, but she couldn't tell what it was, exactly. And under his eyes were dark circles she'd never seen there before.

It could be his court case. Maybe he was worried, staying up late to work.

She didn't want to hope that it was *her*. That he actually cared in the same way she did. She couldn't believe it was true. She didn't dare.

"Okay," she said finally. "You're here. What do you need to say to me so badly that you had to follow me home in the middle of a workday?"

"Christ, Kara. Screw work. This is important."

"Is it? Why, Dante? You couldn't tell me when we were at the office."

He scrubbed at his jaw. "I don't blame you for being so closed off to me right now. I shouldn't have approached you at work. And I think I know why you left my place on Sunday. I *think* I do. But I need to hear it from you." He took a step toward her. "The truth is, I don't trust myself when it comes to you. My head is all fucked-up. My instincts are fucked-up. So I'm probably way off base."

She couldn't help but challenge him. There was enough anger in her still. "Why do you think I left, Dante?"

"Because I haven't . . . I haven't opened myself to you. Not the way I've asked you to do with me. And it's not fair. I haven't been honest with you. And I'm sorry."

His features had gone soft. She was shivering all over. "I've shut myself off to you, too, Dante."

"You've been totally open with me."

She shook her head. "I haven't."

It was true. She hadn't given him the one crucial piece of the puzzle that was their relationship. A relationship built on the secrets they'd kept from each other, as much as it was on the things they'd revealed. If she was going to be fair about this, she had to tell him the one truth she'd held so close.

"Dante . . ." She looked at him, her gaze catching his, holding it. His eyes were that gleaming whiskey brown she'd come to love. She loved so many things about him. It was time to let him know. To be honest. To reveal her truth.

Remembering her feelings for him made her soften, go loose all over, the anger melting away, along with the fear. Things were so fractured between them already, maybe she had nothing left to lose.

"Dante, the one thing I've been keeping from you is . . . that I love you." She shrugged helplessly. "I do. I love you."

Shock in his eyes. Her heart filled with dread. Had this been a mistake?

"Jesus, Kara."

"And, Dante, there's more," she said, realizing only then by the absolutely torn expression on his face that it was true. "You love me, too." She was shaking, a hard trembling making her legs weak, but she stepped closer to him, until she was only inches away. Close enough to breathe him in.

She waited for him to respond. When he didn't, she tried again through clenched teeth. "You love me, God damn it. I can see it. Feel it. And I love you, despite myself. So I know just how you're feeling. But I'm putting it out here on the table. I am taking that chance, which feels enormous to me. Because I have loved people before. And I've lost out. I've been rejected. By my own parents. By my ex. And I've hated how weak that makes me feel. How powerless. So you reject me, too, if you have to. But I'm not walking away again until you do. Because that would really be where the weakness is. And I refuse to be that person. I refuse."

He shook his head. His face was so dark, his expression so raw, she had no idea what might come next. Her heart was thundering in her chest, her pulse going a million miles an hour. But it felt good that she'd said it, finally. That she'd let the truth out. She felt stronger for it, for being honest. True to herself.

Finally, he shook his head, and said so softly she had to strain to hear him, "You are a hell of a lot braver than I am, Kara."

She waited for more. But he was standing there, his arms hanging at his sides. He was watching her, as he'd done so often before. And after several moments had passed, the anger was coming back, surging through her veins.

"God damn it, Dante! Say something. How do you feel about this? About what I've told you. About *me*? Tell me you love me, or tell me you don't. But I'm not letting you walk away from your feelings. Or mine. *Especially* mine. I deserve better than that."

"Yes, you do. You deserve more than I can give you, Kara."

"That's such bullshit." He looked shocked again, his mouth opening as if he was going to speak, but she wouldn't let him. "That is the same old crap you've been telling yourself for how long? Since you lost your college girlfriend? I don't mean to be less than sympathetic, because I can imagine how awful that must have been for you, whether you loved her or not. But how long are you going to use that as an excuse?"

That seemed to stop him cold. His mouth opened, but nothing came out. He closed it, blinked. And as she watched him, his features shifted, smoothed, the shadows in his eyes clearing.

"Not ever again," he said, grabbing her and holding her arms in his hands, his grip tight. "I'm done with that. Because you're right. It's an old, worn-out excuse. It *is* bullshit. I've used what happened with Erin my entire adult life. My own experiences with my family. My guilt over never being able to help my mother. But the truth is that she didn't want my help. Even when . . ."

He paused, and she could feel him shaking a little through his grip on her arms. And in his eyes was that raw vulnerability she'd seen in him before. Years ago, when he'd hit Brady. And a few times during sex. She had no idea what was coming next.

"Kara, I've never said this to another person, aside from my brother, Lorenzo. But I need to tell you now . . . when I was ten years old I saw my father hit my mother. He slapped her. I don't remember why, what they were arguing about. It only happened that one time, that I know of."

Kara shook her head. She didn't know what to say. And he wasn't finished.

"I guess they worked things out, my parents. And as an adult, there have been so many times when I wanted to tell my mom I'd protect her. But I haven't ever done it. I talked to Lorenzo about it a few years ago and he said he thinks they're fine. And maybe they are. I understand my mother's always wanted my dad to make all the decisions. There must have been . . . I don't know, some sense of safety in that for her. Or maybe her own excuse to be weak. I don't know," he said again. "But I remember that feeling of powerlessness. That fear. I hated it. I still do. It's become a driving force in my life. And my father . . . all the crap he fed my brother and me about how we had to be men. Be responsible. Even when were nine, ten years old. That's too much to put on a kid, for God's sake. And maybe I've always known that. But parents tend to have this . . . sort of weird stranglehold on us. And it's all made me—I've let it make me—into this hyper-responsible guy. It's not that witnessing that one slap has led me into being a dominant so I can sexualize it. But it has been a way for me to work through that . . . absolute helplessness to *help* her. My mother. Erin. But even that I've used to hide behind. And I've known it, too, all along. I haven't wanted to think about it. But being with you, Kara . . . that's changed everything. Made me look deeper."

She was staring at him, hardly able to believe the things he was saying to her. Wanting more from him. But she had to acknowledge what he was giving her, that look inside. "It all makes sense to me, Dante. I've been thinking a lot of these same things recently. I've realized how much of my own self-image has always been related to my parents. And how badly I've needed to move beyond their opinion of me. What I'd gotten from them growing up, what I needed but never got." She paused, biting her lip, trying to think it through. "I have to stop feeling so damn sorry for myself about it. It is what it is. I can't go back, can't change them. All I can change is myself. My relationship with Jake emphasized those same feelings of being judged and coming up short, but you know . . . fuck him. He doesn't deserve that much energy from me, and I'm done feeding into it."

Dante smiled at her then. "Good. Good for you, Kara. Because if he's judging you for who you are, for the things you desire, then his opinion is worth nothing. And if he wasn't able to see you for the amazing woman you are, then his opinions are worth even less. He's an idiot. But I've been an idiot, too. And I don't want to be anymore. You're a lot wiser than I am, Kara. You're right about everything you've said. About you. About me. All of it. Because I love you, Kara. You're right."

Her pulse went into overdrive. "Did you just tell me you love me?"

"I did. I do love you. And I'll tell you again. And again. Until you believe me." His eyes were shining. "I realize I may have to say it a few hundred times to redeem myself. I'm willing to do it."

"God, Dante . . ." Joy flooded her. An absolute flood of emotion that made her legs weak. It was a good thing he had such a tight clasp on her arms. And she needed the contact, the heat of his touch. "Tell me again. I need to hear it."

"I love you, Kara. That's what I came here to tell you." He leaned in and brushed his mouth across hers. She had never felt anything so sweet. "I love you," he whispered again against her lips. "I love you, I love you . . ."

He really kissed her then, his mouth as demanding as it had ever been. But what it was asking of her this time—what he was asking—was for her to love him.

She pulled away. "Tell me again, Dante," she said, laughing through the tears hazing her vision.

He looked into her eyes, his a soft, gleaming brown, like golden smoke. There was more emotion there than she'd ever seen in him. He cupped her cheeks in his warm palms, and she felt his love in that motion alone.

"I love you, Kara. I love you more than I ever thought I could love anyone."

This time when he kissed her, there was more than the heat of desire. There was a passion so deep and true, she could feel it in her soul. He pulled her tighter, their bodies coming together. For the first time, she knew love. And even as it thrilled her, it scared her. She couldn't not be afraid. She didn't know how.

For now, she would melt into him. Just let it be. For the moment, she was done asking questions, demanding answers. Of Dante. Of herself. For once, she was really going to revel in this feeling that made her senses soar in a way they never had before.

He loves me.

She swallowed down the fear. And loved him back.

seventeen

Dante held her close, so close he could feel her heart beating against his. Her mouth was so damn sweet. Knowing she loved him was sweeter than anything he'd ever tasted. Miraculous.

He pulled her closer, needing to crush her against him. To *feel* her . . . He wasn't even sure what he meant by that. All he knew was that he couldn't get close enough.

"Dante," she murmured against his mouth, her tongue moving slowly over his lips, a slow, sensual touch that made his body go wild with need.

Have to have her. Naked. Open.

He lifted her and carried her to her bedroom, setting her down on the bed. Standing there, he simply stared at her for several moments. He was blown away by her beauty. By her porcelain skin. Her long hair lying wild against the pale green sheets that made her metallic gaze gleam with bits of emerald and moss.

There was that innocent seductress about her still, that look in her eyes that told him she needed him as much as he needed her. That her desire burned every bit as bright. Such a contrast against the long lashes.

He could see the fevered, pink flush on her cheeks, between her breasts where her white robe parted.

He leaned over her, one knee on the edge of the bed, and untied the robe. Spread the white cotton with his hand until it fell open, revealing her naked body underneath. Her nipples were hard and dark, impossibly succulent. When she licked her lips, they were just as lush. He didn't know where to start. Where to end.

"Kara," he said, his voice a raw whisper, "Tell me we have all day, all night. Tell me we're not going anywhere. I need to . . . have you all to myself."

"I'm not going anywhere," she told him. "I don't want to be anywhere but here with you."

It made his heart surge to hear her say it. It made him rock-hard.

He bent and brushed a kiss across her lips, then bent lower to kiss her breasts, that gentle rise of soft, fragrant flesh. She sighed, just a soft sound of pleasure, but it went through him like an electric current.

"Jesus, Kara . . ."

She reached up and held his face between her hands, her palms gentle on his cheeks as she held his head to her breasts. He obeyed her silent command, taking one nipple into his mouth to suck.

"Ah, Dante . . ."

He held her rigid flesh in his mouth, swirling his tongue over the tip. She moaned, held him closer, and he sensed her shifting to arch her hips. The idea of her wet, wanting sex was almost too tempting. But he wanted to draw this out. To make it last. To make it good for her.

He lifted his head, looked into her eyes. "Tell me what you want, my baby. Tell me what you need."

"I need you. I just . . . need you to touch me. To be with me. I need . . . everything."

He smiled, his body surging with desire, like heat in his veins.

"I need you, too, my beautiful girl. I had no idea I could need anyone like this."

"Take your clothes off for me, Dante," she demanded quietly.

He smiled as he stood to comply. There was a small grin on her face, and he knew what she was thinking. That this was a small turning of the tables. Yet there was no power play involved right now. It was just them. Love was the equalizer. And that was what this moment was all about. Not that the role play wouldn't happen again. It would. It was in both of them to want it, to need it. But right now, it was about the things they'd just said to each other. The naked selves they had just revealed.

He realized as he took off his jacket, his shirt, his slacks, that this had been happening for weeks. That he hadn't *required* the more extreme sex with Kara that he'd used to distance himself from other women. All he required was *her*.

When he was naked, Kara smiled her approval. And he went even harder, seeing the look in her eyes. Lust. Love. He bent over her once more, taking the other nipple into his mouth, making her gasp. Her fingers were threaded through his hair, hanging on tight. And the scent of her desire was rising, surrounding him, seeping into his system so that it merged with his own. They were one thrumming pulse. His. Hers. Together.

He kept sweeping his tongue over her rigid flesh, his hands cupping the fullness of her breasts, his thumb teasing the other nipple. He stopped now and then to look at her, at her half-closed eyes. Her teeth coming down to bite the lush pink of her lower lip. The darkening red of her nipples. Then he'd go back to his task. He wanted to tease her, excite her, as much as he could simply doing this: sucking her nipples, licking, kneading her breasts.

"God, Dante . . . this is . . . Oh . . ."

He smiled as he kept sucking, licking, stroking. When she arched hard, her hips coming off the bed, her thigh brushing the tip of his cock, he groaned. But he would not give in to his own need. Not until he'd satisfied hers.

He sucked in a breath, taking in her scent, that scent of flowers and female desire. Grew dizzy with it.

Kara.

She was his, finally. Truly his.

Kara was writhing beneath him, out of her head. With the desire burning like molten heat through her body. Centered on her aching breasts as Dante tortured them deliciously with his clever mouth. But sending arcs of pleasure to her sex. Making a strong, rhythmic pulse beat there. Pure desire. *Want* like a humming in her flesh. And all of it about him. Dante.

Hers.

His hair was like silk beneath her palms. His mouth on her

like liquid fire. His love like the wildest aphrodisiac she could ever have imagined.

She wrapped her leg around his, pulling him closer, needing more. And as his thigh settled between hers, it was like a shock of pleasure. And with nothing more than that, his muscular thigh pressed to her wet cleft, his mouth and his hand on her breast, she came, crying out.

"Dante! Ah God . . ."

She bucked against him. She was shivering with wave after wave of pleasure, like fireworks going off behind her closed eyelids.

When Dante groaned and pressed his engorged cock against her belly, it was like coming all over again, to feel his excitement. She spread her thighs, her hands sliding down to his strong buttocks to pull him in.

"Ah, Jesus, my girl, you are going to kill me. Give me a moment."

"Now, Dante. Now."

He laughed. "We need a condom, baby. Hang on."

It would take only a few seconds, but it was too long for her.

"Come on, Dante. I can't wait. Really, I can't."

He was smiling as he held himself over her. His eyes were glowing gold in the afternoon light. So beautiful. And as she watched, his features softened, the smile fading. And his expression turned to one of wonder as he slid inside her.

"Baby," he murmured. "I love you, Kara. Love you, my beautiful girl. You are mine."

Her head was spinning, her body consumed by sensations: pleasure, a need for him that went beyond any physical sensation.

"I love you, too, Dante. I love you."

He wrapped her in his arms. Pulling her almost upright, holding her close as he moved deeper.

"Ah, Kara . . ." He slid out, thrust again, driving pleasure into her in shuddering waves. "You feel so good, baby. Better than anything I've felt in my life."

His hips moved, pressing hard into her, then back. She was filled, over and over, his flesh hard inside her. Heavy. Hot. She ground against him, wanting him deeper. And all the while, pleasure built once more, spiraled, crested.

"Kara," he gasped against her hair. "I need to come. Inside you . . ."

He tensed, surged into her over and over, gasping, crying her name.

"Kara, baby . . . Kara!"

She felt him coming, felt the heat of it inside her, felt his pleasure as though it were her own. And she came with him, a million lights exploding in her body, her mind. Dazzling her. Blinding her.

They held each other close. She was shivering with pleasure, with the wonder of what she was feeling. Of what Dante felt for her. She knew it in every caress, every whispered murmur.

The fear wanted to creep back in, but she wouldn't let it. Not now. Now she let herself glory in the first real sense of safety she'd ever felt with a man—with anyone—in her life. She let herself relax in Dante's embrace, closed her eyes, and slept.

They woke in the afternoon, coming together again. This time there was no preamble, just Dante turning to face her and lifting her leg over his side, sliding inside her. It was a gentle motion, their hips meeting, his rigid flesh clasped inside her. And a slow, aching heat built, a little at a time.

This time sensation was a lovely undulation. The late-afternoon sun slanted through the curtains, casting light and shadow on naked skin. Heat. His body was so beautiful to her, his face as he watched her come once more. Then as he came himself, an expression of exquisite agony making his eyes go dark.

After, he remained inside her, kissed her face, her lips. But she was anxious, suddenly.

"Dante, tell me we don't have to stop."

He chuckled. "I may need a few minutes rest, my eager girl."

"No, I meant this. Being together."

He stared at her, kissed her again. "This is what I want, Kara. *You're* what I want."

His arms went around her, held her close, and she pressed her cheek to his chest, let his heartbeat soothe her.

When she woke again it was dark outside, other than the faint glow from the streetlamps outside her window. Dante still slept beside her; she could feel the gentle rise and fall of his chest.

She stared out at the sky, which was cloudless, filled with stars.

How was it that she could have this? Could she trust it? She'd never really had love before. Never let herself feel it. She didn't know what to expect.

"Hey." His voice was rough, sleepy. "I can hear you thinking."

She was quiet a moment. She didn't know how to share this with him, if it was something they could talk out.

"Can I just . . . think about it for a bit?"

"Hmm . . . only if you feed me. I'm starved."

"Me, too." It was the first time she'd been hungry in days. But suddenly she was ravenous.

"Do you have eggs?" Dante asked. "I can make us an omelet."

"Really?"

"I'm the cook here, remember?"

"Yes, I remember. And I knew it wasn't me. I think I do have eggs. And maybe some cheese."

"That's all I need. Come on."

He got up and lifted her from the bed, and she smiled as she pulled her discarded robe back on, as he slipped back into his slacks. The air was a little cool, but he didn't bother with his shirt, leaving his torso bare. Leaving her to admire, as she had so often before, his broad shoulders, his muscular chest and arms, the tight six-pack of his stomach.

They went into her small kitchen, and she pulled out the ingredients while he rummaged in her cupboards until he found a pan. It took him only a few minutes to whip the omelet up; then they sat at her kitchen table to eat, talking, or chewing quietly together. It was companionable. Comfortable.

Again she had to ask herself if she could really have this. This easy companionship. And the thrilling flutter beneath it that made her cheeks heat to even look at him. It was the strangest combination. Wonderful. Amazing.

Frightening.

She put her fork down, drew in a long breath.

"What's up, baby? You done eating?" Dante asked her.

She said quietly, "I'm still . . . a little afraid. Aren't you afraid, Dante?"

He set his fork down, caught her gaze with his. The honesty

she found there was as dazzling as the sex was, making her breath catch.

"I'm scared to death," he admitted. "But I don't want to let fear control me. I can't let it win. I won't do it. That's why I'm here with you. What are we doing here if we're not willing to be afraid and do it anyway?"

Tears stung her eyes. "And you said I was the strong one. It's not true."

"It is. I see it in you, Kara. I always have. Being afraid doesn't mean you're not strong. It just means you're human. Maybe we won't be great at this relationship thing. I probably won't be. You know that, right?"

She had to laugh. "Yes. But I probably won't be, either."

"Okay. So we're two fallible human beings. Coming together because we love each other." He moved closer. "I love you, Kara. That's enough for me. I hope it is for you, too."

She reached across the table, and he met her halfway, taking her hand in his. His grasp was warm. Reassuring.

"It is, Dante. I love you, and it *is* enough. I have to trust it. But I'm still learning."

"Me, too. We can learn together. I can't imagine doing it any other way."

"Neither can I. I don't want to be alone anymore. I don't want to let my fears dictate what I do, either. How I allow myself to feel. I just want to feel it. And . . . I want to paint again. I'm not giving up law. But I've started to draw recently and I think it's time for me to paint."

"That's great." He was smiling at her, pride shining through his whiskey gaze, his big, warm hand grasping hers.

"The painting is part of it. This transformation. And another part is work . . . I think we need to go to the partners and tell them we're together."

"Yes, absolutely, we'll tell them. And they'll deal with it. There's nothing we need to hide anymore. This is the real thing, not some scandalous affair. All that's changed."

"It has. Us. Me. So much has changed in my head. The painting is only a symptom of that. A good one." She smiled. "But it all started with you. I've had enough of the fear. It might still be there, but I want to be the one in charge of my life. And I want to be with you, Dante. I love you," she told him again. She wasn't sure she could ever tell him enough.

"My beautiful girl," he murmured, pulling her closer.

He kissed her, and in that kiss she felt his love, deep down in her soul. She knew he would help her through this. That they would help each other. That *this* was how it was supposed to be.

She melted into his kiss, the heat and the urgency returning with a force she couldn't deny, couldn't fight. She didn't want to anymore. That last instinct to flee was gone. Dissolved in love.

He moaned, pulling on her hands until he had her in his lap. He kissed her harder. His tongue, the press of his erection underneath her making her heat all over, that lovely, seeping heat that was desire and love all mixed together.

Dante pulled back. "Baby, I need to be with you in the shower. You know how I love that. And with you . . . it has to be with you."

Somehow they moved through her apartment and into her small bathroom. He let her go long enough to turn the hot water on.

"Don't move," he told her. "I'll be right back."

He returned a few moments later with a string of condoms in his hand and a small smile on his face. He moved in and kissed her again, softly, as he slipped her robe from her shoulders, stepped out of his slacks.

The steam was building around them, like some gentle blanket as they stepped into the shower.

He wrapped his hands around her waist, moving her under the water. Kissed her throat as the warm water ran over her hair, her body. And then he took her bottle of liquid soap and carefully washed her all over. His hands were slick, impossibly gentle, as they slipped over her skin. They moved to her breasts, and the hunger was like the steam surrounding them: that gentle, that lovely. His fingers drew circles around her nipples, and they went hard, harder. But the need was a whispering ache, urgent, yet sweet.

She couldn't take her eyes off his hands as he moved them lower, over her thighs, then between them.

"Oh, Dante . . ."

His soap-slicked finger slipped over her cleft, caressing the swollen lips of her sex, and she parted her thighs for him. He massaged her there, sliding up over her clitoris, then back down. Over and over until she was on the edge of climax.

He stopped. Reached behind her for the shower wand and rinsed her off as carefully as he'd soaped her. At last, he moved the spray of hot water between her thighs. The gentle beat of it hit her clit, and he held it there with one hand, while with the other he pulled her body in close. His mouth closed over hers, and as she came she moaned her pleasure against his lips.

She was still shivering with it when he sheathed himself and, wrapping one of her legs around his waist, slid into her.

"Dante," she panted, his thick cock moving inside her, taking her up to that peak once more. Pleasure was dizzying. Blissful. Transcendent, having him inside her body, and knowing he loved her. Feeling it so keenly she couldn't doubt it. Feeling it to her core. "I've never felt this before . . . this . . . God . . ."

He arched his hips, driving deeper. "I know, baby. I know exactly what you mean. It's so good, loving you like this. You're so good for me, Kara." He kissed her, pressing his lips to hers over and over. "We're good together, baby. My beautiful girl."

It was true. She knew it. And every moment with him, the fear grew smaller and smaller, until it faded away. As the sheer pleasure of being with the man she loved, who loved her back, grew inside her, spiraled, she realized that it was truly gone.

"I love you, Dante," she whispered to him as her body began that lovely explosion, like all the stars in the night sky lighting up deep inside her. Lighting her up with pleasure. With love.

"I love you, my girl. *My* girl."

She belonged to him. Truly. Completely. Finally, she knew love. She knew what it was to let it cradle her, keeping her heart safe. Safe at last, with Dante.

Turn over for a sneak peek at the wickedly enticing

Temptation's Edge

the next installment in
the Edge Trilogy

Coming soon from Black Lace

one

Mischa Kennon was a perfectionist. In her work as a tattoo artist. As an author of the short erotic stories she'd had published. In the maintenance of her platinum blonde hair, which she wore in long, polished waves around her shoulders, and her red-lacquered nails, which she kept short to accommodate her work. Her San Francisco apartment was as immaculate as the tattoo shop she owned, Thirteen Roses. She worked hard, played harder. And she was never, ever late. Which made the delay in her flight to Seattle for her best friend's engagement party particularly frustrating.

Finally she was there. The cab pulled up in front of the restaurant—she'd already dropped her luggage at Dylan's apartment, where she would be staying—and she paid the driver and stepped onto the rainy sidewalk in front of Wild Ginger. She swung open the door and moved into the warm interior. She'd been there before when she'd visited Dylan and met her fiancé,

Alec. It was their favorite restaurant and the perfect place for the party to celebrate their upcoming wedding in only a few weeks. Mischa took in a breath as she nodded at the hostess and moved through the busy Thai fusion restaurant toward the back room, where they held private parties.

She was happy for her friend, although the whole marriage thing wasn't for her, personally. She was the independent type. Well, so was Dylan, but she and Alec had something special.

"Honey, you made it!" Dylan's smile was brilliant as she rose from the long table and came to wrap her arms around Mischa in a cloud of the spicy vanilla scent she always wore.

"I'm so sorry I'm late, honey," Mischa apologized. "The damn weather."

"I know. It's our fault for wanting to get married this fall, but we just couldn't wait, and we really want to be married by Thanksgiving."

"Look at you—you have that bridal glow," she told Dylan, holding her friend at arm's length. It was true. Her gray eyes shone as lustrous as her long, curly red hair. "Or maybe you and Alec had some alone time before the party?" she teased with a wink.

Dylan grinned as her fi ancé came up behind them. Alec Walker was a wall of a man, well over six feet tall, with the breadth of a linebacker.

"Maybe we did," he said, laughing as he leaned in to kiss Mischa's cheek. "But a gentleman never kisses and tells. How are you?"

"Fine, thanks. Just glad to be here."

"Dylan mentioned you have a possible business proposal to investigate while you're here?" Alec helped her off with her rain-spattered coat.

Mischa nodded, patted her hair into place. "Thanks, Alec.

Yes, another tattoo artist I know may want to open a new shop in Seattle and is hoping I'll be interested in a partnership, so I thought I'd look into it while I'm here to help with the wedding plans."

Dylan squeezed her hand. "I can't believe I get to have you for two whole weeks. You're sure it's not an inconvenience? Your shop will be all right?"

"I wouldn't dream of letting you do this whole wedding alone. And Billy is the best shop manager I could ask for. Which is why I can even consider expanding here. I figure I can work half time in both places. Which means I'll get to see more of you. But we can talk about that later—tonight is all about you two."

"And we've left you standing here after your long trip. Come on and say hi to everyone."

Dylan grabbed her hand and they moved toward the table where Dylan's friend Kara, whom Mischa had met on previous visits, was just getting out of her chair. Kara reached to give her a quick hug.

"So nice to see you. Do you remember Dante?"

Kara's boyfriend shook her hand. Dante was as tall as Alec, but leaner, with dark hair and eyes that were a sparkling golden brown. He hovered over Kara as protectively as Alec did with Dylan.

Mischa wondered if that unusual protective thing was something that was a natural part of the fact that both men were dominants. She'd played with that a bit herself—the domination and submission dynamic. She'd even been to a few BDSM clubs. Not that she required kink. But it was fun when she was with a guy who was into it. She'd never been able to give herself over to it completely, though. Certainly not the way Dylan and Kara must have, to be in relationships with dominant men. Not that *she'd* be in a relationship, period. But it was lovely to see people who were so happy. The glow these two pairs were giving off was almost enough to make her think about it . . . for a moment or two, anyway.

"Mischa, you have to meet our fabulous baker."

She turned—and caught herself pulling in a long breath as her eyes met a stunning gaze that was a shimmering sea green shot through with amber. He was looking at her, staring at her from beneath dark brows. He had a rugged face. A generous mouth that looked stern until he smiled at her. Then it was all flawless white teeth and frank sensuality. It took her a moment to realize she had to tilt her head back to really see him—he stood taller than even Alec, had shoulders just as broad. She felt a small stirring in her veins, a fluttering in her stomach.

"You're their baker?"

He laughed, a rich, booming sound. "Lord, no. I'm Connor."

His deep tone was laced with a distinctly Irish accent.

God, she loved a man with an accent. It really made her swoon. Hell, she'd been swooning since the moment she'd laid eyes on him.

"Connor Galloway, Mischa Kennon. Connor is a friend of Alec's. He'll be in the wedding party. And I seriously doubt Connor can boil water, never mind bake. He burned the hot dogs the last time the guys went camping."

"Hey, I learned to microwave mac and cheese at my mother's knee," he protested, his brogue a low, rolling thunder that made her belly stir with need.

Down, girl.

Dylan laughed, putting Mischa's hand into that of a petite, smiling blonde woman. "*This* is our baker—and friend—Lucie."

"Hi, Mischa. I've heard so much about you."

"Mischa?" Dylan gave her a nudge with her elbow, making her realize she was still focused on Connor.

Get it together.

She turned and smiled. "It's great to meet you, Lucie. Do we know what kind of cake they want yet?"

The blonde's smile widened into a grin. "We're doing cupcakes. Wait until you see what I have in mind. We're having a tasting session on Wednesday."

"I'll look forward to it."

Sugar was one of her favorite things. She wasn't a dieting girl—she loved food too much—and she was comfortable with her curves. But even the idea of a cupcake tasting couldn't distract her from the towering presence of Connor Galloway as Dylan led her around the table, introducing her to their friends.

He wasn't exactly following them, yet she had the sense that he was watching her from under those dark brows. Whenever she'd glance up for a moment—which she did more often than she'd like to admit—she found his gaze on her. No matter where he was in the room, leaning over the table, talking to various people. That gaze was dark. Penetrating. She wasn't sure what it was he wanted, but it was clear he wanted *something*. It was more than desire—that she recognized easily enough. She was no wallflower. She welcomed desire, from the right man. Knew exactly how to deal with it. She felt his desire. But there was something else . . . some sort of deeper curiosity that *commanded* her attention.

Ah, that must be it. He must be another dominant. But where that air of command elicited a bantering response from her when it came to most of the toppy men she'd come into contact with, Connor's direct searching gaze made her feel . . . warm all over. A sort of odd, melting sensation. As though her knees were actually weak.

Don't be silly.

He was just a man. A dominant man. But many a dominant

man had met his match in her. She wasn't about to be taken down by the admittedly scorchingly sexy Connor Galloway.

Lord, he was sexy.

She sighed, tucked her blonde hair behind her ear as Alec held a chair for her. She thanked him as she seated herself at the long banquet table. And had to pull in a breath as Connor sat down next to her.

"We're to be dinner partners," he said.

A simple remark, yet it felt loaded. As if he meant more than that they would sit next to each other through the meal.

She was reading far too much into things with this man. She must be tired from the long trip up from San Francisco. Either that or it had been too long since she'd been laid.

Was two months too long?

"Shall I order you a drink?" he asked. "I see you don't have one yet."

"Oh . . . yes, a drink would be good." Maybe that was exactly what she needed to relax and pull herself together. "I'll have some cold sake. They have a good selection here."

He raised a brow. "Nothing stronger?"

"Why would you think I'd need something stronger?"

He leaned in and she caught a whiff of his scent, a blend of the rain outside and something dark and earthy. "You strike me as a strong woman. Who may require a stronger drink after your long journey." He grinned, a warm grin she found infectious.

She couldn't help but laugh. "You're right, I could use something stronger. How about a vodka on ice?"

"Grey Goose?"

"Why not?"

The man knew his vodka. She couldn't help but wonder what else he might know. What those large hands had experienced . . .

Okay, this really had to stop. She was sitting at her best friend's engagement party and her panties were going damper by the minute. Over a guy she'd just met. Of course, that was how it usually worked with her. She knew the moment she met a man if she wanted him. There was no dancing around it, the way it often seemed to go for other women. No doubts. She always knew she *wanted* someone. But rarely to this ridiculous degree.

Maybe never.

Even more ridiculous how utterly girly she found herself feeling when he ordered her drink for her, saying to the waiter, "A Grey Goose over ice for the lady. Add two olives, if you will."

That accent . . . the tone of authority in his voice, no matter how polite he'd been. It made her shiver. Distracted her. From the fact that this was Dylan and Alec's party, not some personal meat market for *her*. Although the shopping was quite nice.

Their drinks came and Connor took them from the waiter with an almost imperial nod of his head that was still somehow charming. She noted he drank whiskey straight up. She could smell the perfumy fragrance after he sipped and leaned in close to her.

"How's yours?" he asked.

She lifted her glass, sipped. "Perfect."

"Ah, I may not be able to bake, but I have other talents."

She laughed. "You say that as though you made the drinks yourself."

"That wasn't necessarily what I was referring to."

She lowered her voice, batted her lashes. "Are you flirting with me, Connor Galloway?"

"Why? Are you opposed to the idea?"

"On the contrary."

He grinned, those brilliant white teeth contrasting with his plush red lips. So damn kissable she could feel her own lips twitch.

He took her hand, pulled it to his mouth, and brushed a quick kiss over her knuckles that sent desire spiraling through her in sharp, fluttering arcs.

"You have long fingers," he said, keeping his tone low. "The hands of an artist."

"Do you think so?"

He was still grinning at her. Still making her feel like a teenager with a mad crush. "Well, I admit Alec and Dylan may have mentioned that you are indeed an artist, but yes, you have beautiful hands."

Why was his little compliment making her blush? That and his heavy Irish brogue. She felt a surge of disappointment when he released her hand.

"Thank you."

"You have your own tattoo shop down in San Francisco, they tell me. That's a hard road, running your own business."

"Hard, but wonderful. After years of apprenticing in other people's shops, then renting chair space, I love being my own boss."

"I'll bet you do." His green eyes were twinkling. He was teasing her, and she liked it.

"I do, as a matter of fact. I like being in charge of my life. Doing my art my way."

He nodded. "That I understand. I'm an artist myself, though of a different sort."

She took another sip of her vodka, leaned toward him, intrigued. "What do you do?"

"I'm a concept artist. I design for video games, some for film and television. Spaceships, robots, that sort of thing."

She laughed. "That's like every kid's dream come true."

"It is. Except that it gives me little time to do my own work."

"And what is your own work?"

"I like to sketch in charcoal."

"But not spaceships and robots?"

He shrugged, his massive shoulders rippling with muscle beneath his dark button-down shirt. "I've been more interested in the human form the last couple of years. I've started to do some erotic pieces."

She smiled at him. "Every young *boy's* dream come true."

He nodded. "When I have the time. Which I'm just now beginning to have. I'm at a point where I can start to pick and choose which contracts I want to accept. You're lucky to be your own boss, in charge of your schedule, although I imagine running the show is a lot of work."

"It is, but I have a great team, which helps. And I love it."

Being able to open her own shop was one of her biggest achievements, bigger, even, than getting her art degree. Her business was everything, the one thing in her life she *knew* she'd done right.

"What does your family think of you doing tattoos for a living?" Connor asked.

"My younger sister, Raine, is . . . different from me. She's an English professor, married to a professor of mathematics. She's been supportive, in her way, even though I think she finds it hard to relate. Evie is more of a free spirit, an artist herself, so she loves the idea."

"Evie? Another sister?" he asked.

"My mother."

"You call your mother by her first name?" He wasn't the first to ask about it.

She laughed, but there was a raw edge to it that stuck in her throat. "If you knew Evie . . . she's never really been anyone's mother."

Why had she said that? She was certain he didn't want to hear her sob story about her flaky mother. He was quiet for a moment, watching her again. She shook her head, a little appalled at herself.

"Change of subject?" he suggested kindly.

"Yes. Sure. What about you? Do you have family here?"

"Just me. Family is back in Dublin. It's just my mum and my sisters, Molly and Clara. I try to get back every year to visit."

"What brought you to the States? Did you come here for work?"

It was his turn to stall. He shrugged again, but the gesture wasn't quite as casual as it had been before. "I married an American. I've been divorced for a long time."

"Ah." He was obviously uncomfortable talking about it, so she switched tracks. "But you stayed here."

"I like it here. I'd made a life here, got my degree in graphic arts, started a career."

Why did she suspect there was something else to it that he wasn't saying? Maybe because for the first time since they'd been talking he was looking away, his gaze resting on the rain-spattered window for several moments before he turned back to her.

"Change of subject?" she suggested this time.

"Yes. Definitely."

He smiled, and she watched his tight features loosen. Noticed the merest hint of creases at the edges of his eyes. She'd always loved that on a man, for some reason.

"What shall we talk about?" she asked.

"We can talk more about you." He leaned in toward her.

"There isn't really that much more to say."

"Ah, I disagree. I find you fascinating."

"Are you flirting with me again?"

"I am."

She smiled at him. "I like it."

He lifted her hand once more and his voice was a quiet murmur against it before he laid a soft kiss there. His sea-green eyes burned into her. He had long lashes, dark and full. She could see a small scar, about an inch long, below his right eye. Which only made him more masculine. Sexier. "We have much to discuss later, then."

"Discuss?"

God, she could barely speak, her entire body feeling like she'd been engulfed by flames. He'd only kissed her hand!

He moved in even closer. "You may have guessed who—and what—I am, knowing Alec and Dylan, yes?"

"Yes."

"Then you may know that I never take a woman without negotiating first."

She straightened, pulled her hand from his. "You think you'll 'take' me?"

"I do. And I think you'll like it. I can see it in the sparkle in your lovely blue eyes. Eyes like the sky off the coast of Dun Laoghaire in the summertime."

"Dun Laoghaire?"

"Just outside of Dublin. Have you ever been to Ireland?"

"No, never. I'd love to see it someday."

How had he managed to change the subject so smoothly? Oh, he was smooth. Still, she'd never met a man who could maneuver around her. This man would be no different, despite her response to him. He could play the role of boss in the bedroom—and she knew already they'd end up there—but if he thought to pull that anywhere else, he'd be dead wrong.

She took a long swallow of her vodka, set the glass down on the table beside the square red porcelain plate. "So, back to these negotiations you mentioned."

"Ah, lass, don't you agree that should wait until after this party is done?"

He was right, of course. What was wrong with her? A totally inappropriate conversation while they were supposed to be celebrating with Dylan and Alec. But he'd talked her in circles . . . hadn't he?

She gave a small nod of her chin, sipped her drink once more. And was relieved when Dylan stopped by to chat with her for a few minutes, shifting the mood. Allowing her some time to think, to get her head back on straight.

"I'm so glad you're here, Mischa. There are a thousand things to do."

"Don't worry, sweetie, we'll get it all done. I'm completely at your disposal."

"You're sure you don't mind staying at my place without me being there? I just . . . I don't want to be away from him." Dylan ducked her head, but Mischa could see her blush.

"Oh, you've got it bad, hon," she laughed. "But honestly, I'm used to living alone. And we'll be together all the time to work on the wedding plans. You'll be plenty sick of me by the end of the trip."

"I will not," Dylan insisted. "I'm grateful you're here. I need a right hand. I've never done this girly bridal stuff."

"Me neither. But we'll figure it out."

"Thanks, Misch."

"No problem, chica."

Dinner arrived, a gorgeous array of sushi, spicy curries, noodles and rice, and Dylan went back to her seat, where she cuddled up with her groom-to-be. Mischa wondered for one brief moment if any guy would ever want to stick with her the way Alec did with Dylan—their mutual devotion was an almost palpable thing. But why was she even considering it? She'd always been fine on her own. Just like her admittedly eccentric mother had finally learned, she didn't need a man to make a happy, full life. Her life was already full with running her business, her friends, her art, her writing. Men were a pleasant pastime, and one she didn't want to do without. But anything more? No, that wasn't for her. She'd learned that lesson early on through the absence of her own father. It had only been confirmed when Raine's father had left when Evie was pregnant with her. He'd been around for Raine through the years, but Evie had been left alone again. And again and again, until she'd had an epiphany about the value of independence a few years ago. No, she was just fine on her own. More than fine. Hadn't her success as a businesswoman proved that?

"Gathering wool?" Connor asked, the deep timber of his voice breaking into her wandering thoughts.

"Hmm, yes, I guess I was."

"What about?"

She turned to look at him more fully. His face was serious. Too damn handsome. "Oh, I doubt you really want to know."

He shrugged again, reminding her of the breadth of his shoulders. He paused to eat a piece of sushi, chewing thoughtfully for several moments. "Maybe I do."

Good Lord, he did. Connor realized he wanted to know exactly what was going through that gorgeous head of hers. He wanted to know everything about her. And it had nothing to do with his usual thorough investigation of a woman he was going to play. He simply wanted to *know*.

What the hell was wrong with him? He was as taken as a teenager with his first warm tit in his hand. And he didn't even have his hands on her tits, although Lord knew he wanted to. Wanted to have her *under* his hands. Under his command. But Mischa was no quiet, passive, submissive girl. She was full of fire, this one. Which made the idea that much more tempting.

He didn't mind a little power struggle. Not as long as he came out on top. He always did, no question about it. But he had the sense that it'd be one hell of a struggle with this girl.

The idea intrigued him. Fascinated him. Hell, he hadn't been able to think of anything else since he'd first set eyes on her. With those lush curves, that fall of pale blonde hair, the way it kept falling over one eye like some old Hollywood siren. Full lips painted a wicked scarlet that was meant to imply sex. A woman as confident as she was, as cocky as any man, wouldn't go down easily. But despite what she thought—and it was obvious she thought *she* was in control, through and through—he'd seen it in her. That unconscious response that signaled a spark of submissive desire. It may only be a small spark, but he was just the man to bring it out in her. It wasn't simple ego talking. He was good at what he did in the BDSM arena. Or maybe it *was* some ego. Or just the power of his desire for this girl, which was frankly throwing him a bit. He wanted to sleep with her. Spank her. Feel her naked flesh under his hands. See what her body looked like beneath the tight-fitting black dress she wore. She looked like some 1950s pinup girl with that platinum blonde hair waving around her shoulders. Gorgeous.

He was almost getting hard just thinking about it. He had to will his cock down, to remember they were at a friend's dinner table, and not the Pleasure Dome, which is where he'd much prefer they be.

The BDSM club was where he and Alec had met, where Alec had later introduced him to Dante. Their tastes all ran in the same vein, and it was a pleasure to have friends he could be completely open with. But this was not the time and place. Not to do more than flirt with the girl, at least until after the party was over. To tease her. To gauge her reaction.

She was definitely reacting. And he was sure as hell reacting to her. Enough that he almost wanted to order another finger of scotch to help him calm down. But that was something he never did. One drink was his limit. He was as tough on himself as he ever was on any subbie girl he played with. Rules were rules. They were always there for a reason, and Lord knew he had his reasons. So why was he allowing this girl to challenge that rule, even for a moment? He'd best get things back under control.

He forced himself to talk with the others seated near their section of the table through dinner. Even though Mischa was the only one he wanted to talk to. But if he was going to be an idiot over this girl—and it seemed maybe he was—then he thought he'd at least put it off until he had her alone somewhere.

Ah, yes. Alone. Naked. Just strip that tight black dress off her and see the rise of her breasts, fill his hands with them. His mouth . . .

He groaned quietly, took the last swallow of his scotch, savored the burn as it slid down his throat.

"Was it good?"

"What?"

He whipped his head around to find Mischa's pale brow arched.

"The chicken *satay*," she said. "I haven't tried it yet."

He just sat and stared at her for several moments before he managed to collect himself. He forced his gaze from her plush red lips to her brilliant blue eyes.

"The food here is always excellent. You should try the *satay*. Here, have some of mine."

He picked up a tender piece of grilled chicken, dipped it in the small bowl of peanut sauce and held it to her lips. She flashed him a quick grin full of sensual promise before she parted those gorgeous lips and took the food into her mouth.

The woman knew exactly the power she held over men. He

wasn't immune to it—that was damn certain. But just as certain was the fact that he *would* gain control over her. He just had to wait until he could get her alone. Judging from her flirtatious behavior, that shouldn't be an issue. The only question was when?

"Mmm, that was delicious."

She licked her lips. His groin tightened.

"So are you, if you don't mind my saying so."

"I don't mind at all."

She smiled, and once more he felt that same jolt of desire he'd felt every time she'd smiled, every time she'd spoken to him. Need ran hot in his veins.

He leaned in a little closer, keeping his voice low. "Then perhaps you won't mind an invitation."

"An invitation?"

"To have that discussion I mentioned."

"The negotiations, you mean?"

Ah, she was still flirting with him. This was a fine game they were playing, but they both had some idea of how it would end.

"Yes. And after that . . ."

"After that, what?" she asked.

The look on her beautiful face was pure sex. They both knew the answer. And they both understood the small thrill in having this conversation in front of all these people, their low voices making an intimate bubble around them.

Yes, pure sex, this girl.

"After that will depend on how the negotiations go. On how you answer my questions."

"And if I have questions for you?"

"That's part of it, isn't it?" He let his pinky brush the back of her hand, watched her cheeks warm, the plump rise of her breasts flush pink. Which was exactly why he'd done it—to see that response. "Power play is all about the give and take, regardless of what those less well versed in these things may think. It's a power *exchange*. It works both ways. Except that I will be the one in command."

She blinked, her cheeks going a darker, lovely shade of pink.

"Ah, you're thinking to argue that, are you? I don't think so, my girl. Are you still in?"

She paused for one long beat, then said, a little breathlessly, "Yes."

Damn it. He couldn't get her out of there soon enough.

"Mischa, you're sure you don't mind riding with Connor? I didn't realize our car would be full of gifts."

"Don't worry about me, Dylan. It's fine."

It was more than fine. Alone in a car with Connor. Then alone at Dylan's apartment. They'd flirted all through dinner. He was every bit as interested as she was—he'd made that very clear. And she was *very* interested.

"You're sure?" Dylan asked again.

"Of course. You and Alec go relax, open your gifts. I'll see you in the morning anyway, won't I?"

"Yes, dress shopping after a late breakfast, if that's okay with you."

"I *love* late." Mischa grinned at her.

Dylan laughed. "Okay. But you have my cell if you need anything."

"Knowing you, I'm certain your apartment is lacking nothing I might need."

"There's nothing to eat . . . I haven't been home much."

It was Mischa's turn to laugh. "Like you've ever done anything other than live off takeout. Stop worrying. I know where the menus are. Go home and curl up with your man."

Dylan gave her a quick kiss on the cheek, then Alec led her out the door of the restaurant just as Connor came with her coat.

"I took a cab tonight," he said, slipping her coat over her shoulders. "Parking is hell here. I didn't mention it to Alec and Dylan. Hope you don't mind."

"A cab is fine." She was trying to ignore the way her pulse was running hot and thready again. He really was an amazing-looking man, all hard muscle and sculpted features, and eyes that seemed to look through her. "San Francisco doesn't have any decent parking, either, which is one reason why I rent an apartment within walking distance of my shop. I cab it almost everywhere else."

She was trying to have a normal conversation with him when all she wanted was for him to slam her up against a wall and kiss her senseless. Instead, she was babbling. Totally unlike her. She took in a breath of the cold air as he led her outside. It was only now that they were both standing that she realized the full extent of his towering height, how massive his frame was beneath his black wool peacoat. The acute awareness of his hulking form beside her made her shiver as much as the damp night air.

Calm down.

He was just another man. This would be just another night of friendly, strings-free sex, which was the way she preferred things. Why did he have her so shaken up?

"You haven't told me the name of your tattoo shop there," he said as they stepped to the curb.

"It's called Thirteen Roses. I've had it for almost four years."

"Business is good?"

"Really good. Better than I'd expect in this economy. Actually, part of this trip will be to discuss opening a new location here with another artist I met in the first shop I apprenticed in."

"There's a good customer base for tattoos in this town, I'd think."

"Do you have any yourself?" she asked, hoping he did. Even before she'd started tattooing herself, body art had been a bit of a fetish for her. She thought it was beautiful—when done well, of course—but she really had a thing for tattoos. For hot men with tattoos, specifically.

God, to see ink on his skin . . .

"I have two," he answered. "I'm looking for a third, once I find the right artist. Mine has moved to New York. If you're a good girl, maybe I'll show them to you later."

She laughed. But inside, she was trembling all over.

Good girl.

No one had ever said such a thing to her before. No one had dared, frankly. Not even those few men she'd let tie her up, spank her, at the BDSM clubs in San Francisco. The submission thing had never been that serious for her, and just as often she'd been the one on top. But coming from him, it was sexy as hell.

He was staring at her again. Watching her closely.

She shook her head. "What is it?"

"I'm just wondering . . ."

"What?"

"If you'll be coming home with me tonight. To have that discussion, you know." His tone lowered until she had to strain over the noise of passing traffic on the wet streets to hear him. "I'm hoping you will. Because, to be honest, I can't wait to get my hands on you, Mischa. I can't wait to feel your lovely, smooth flesh beneath my palms. To have you over my knee. To hear your breath catch when I spank you." He paused. "Exactly as you're doing now. Which tells me what your answer will be. But I have to hear it from you. Will you come with me? Or do I drop you at Dylan's place so you can think it over some more?"

Had any man ever talked to her this way? So utterly sure of himself. Despite that he was basically asking her permission . . . to what? To do things to her she'd only ever played at. But never, she was certain, as seriously as this man could play. With him, it would be a whole new world of experience. One she found herself eager for.

"What will it be, Mischa?" he urged.

He was close enough that she could smell the faint, sweet tinge of good scotch on his breath. His hand was at her waist. Somehow, even through the heavy wool of her coat, she swore she could feel the heat of his touch. She shivered.

"I'll come with you, Connor. Let's go."

Also by Eve Berlin:

Pleasure's Edge

Alec Walker should come with a warning. A man who lives on the edge, he is famous for his love of dangerous sports, kinky sex and independent women.

Dylan Ivory has come to interview him for her latest book but instead he issues her with a challenge – and the perfect way to do her research.

Part 1 of *The Edge Trilogy*, a dark sensual romantic series, perfect for fans of E.L. James and Sylvia Day, from the acclaimed author of *The Dark Garden*

Also by Eve Berlin:

Temptation's Edge

When Mischa Kennon meets sexy Alpha-male Connor Galloway at the wedding of her best friend, she finds the green-eyed Irishman hard to resist.

But while she's happy to surrender to a brief affair with him, Mischa realises Connor could easily master her heart as well as her body.

If she gives in to desire, will it be too much to handle, or will it open her to a kind of love she never thought possible?

Part 3 of *The Edge Trilogy*, a dark sensual romantic series, perfect for fans of E.L. James and Sylvia Day, from the acclaimed author of *The Dark Garden*

Want more sexy fiction?

September 2012 saw the re-launch of the iconic erotic fiction series *Black Lace* with a brand new look and even steamier fiction. We're also re-visiting some of our most popular titles in our *Black Lace Classics* series.

First launched in 1993, *Black Lace* was the first erotic fiction imprint written by women for women and quickly became the most popular erotica imprint in the world.

To find out more, visit us at:
www.blacklace.co.uk

And join the *Black Lace* community:

🐦 @blacklacebooks

⬛BlackLaceBooks

BLACK
LACE

The leading imprint of women's sexy fiction is back – and it's better than ever!

Also available from Black Lace:

The Ninety Days of Genevieve
Lucinda Carrington

He is an arrogant, worldly entrepreneur who always gets
what he wants.

And what he wants is for Genevieve to spend the next
ninety days submitting to his every desire...

*A dark, sensual tale of love and obsession, featuring a very
steamy relationship between an inexperienced heroine
and a masterful and rich older man.*

Praise for The Ninety Days of Genevieve

'This month's essential reading . . . For fans of the
renaissance of erotic fiction comes Lucinda Carrington's
tale of love and obsession' *Stylist*

'Sizzling . . . It's full of expertly written sex scenes that
will appeal to any woman who has ever fantasised about
bondage, lust, exhibitionism and voyeurism! . . .
an excellent plot, well written characters and
heaps of charm' *Handbag.com*

Also available from Black Lace:

In Too Deep
Portia Da Costa

I just want a taste of you. Or a touch. My fantasies about you plague my every waking hour. My only comfort is imagining that similar fantasies might obsess you too.

When young librarian Gwendolynne Price finds increasingly erotic love notes to her in the suggestion box at work, she finds them both shocking and liberating.

But who is her mystery admirer and how long will he be content to just admire her from afar . . . ?

Praise for Portia Da Costa

'Imaginative, playful and a lot of fun'
For Women

'[Portia] hurls dead sexy scenes and language at the reader which touches on deepest fantasy, but kicks it up so it's even better than what we could come up with on our own' RomanceBuyTheBook.com

'All the shameless shenanigans one would expect in a Portia Da Costa story' Erotica Readers and Writers Association

Also available from Black Lace:

The Dark Garden
Eden Bradley

Are you ready to surrender?

When Rowan Cassidy meets Christian Thorne in an exclusive club, he challenges everything she's ever believed about herself.

He then makes an outrageous proposal: give herself over to him completely for thirty days and discover her most secret fantasies and her true nature.

Give in to absolute pleasure with Eden Bradley's romantic, liberating and utterly addictive debut novel.

Praise for The Dark Garden

'Bradley's well-crafted descriptions help you to visualize the edgy and erotic scenes . . . strong characters surround the main couple, and a deftly handled subplot rounds out this amazing novel' *Romantic Times*

'A masterpiece' Larissa Ione

'People are constantly looking for books similar to *Fifty* . . . well look no further, I have what you need! . . . Eden Bradley writes the most sensual books I have ever read' *My Secret Romance Reviews*

Also available from Black Lace:

On Demand
Justine Elyot

I have always been drawn to hotels.
I love their anonymity. The hotel does not care
what you do, or with whom.

The Hotel Luxe Noir is a haven for hedonistic liaisons. From brief encounters in the bar to ménages in the elevator, young Sophie Martin has seen it all since she started on reception.

But as she witnesses the dark erotic secrets of the staff and guests can she also master her own desires . . .?

Welcome to the Hotel Luxe Noir – discretion assured, satisfaction guaranteed.

Praise for On Demand

'If you are looking for strings-free erotica, and not for deep romance, *On Demand* is just the book . . . Indulgent and titillating, *On Demand* is like a tonic for your imagination. The writing is witty, the personal and sexual quirks of the characters entertaining'
Lara Kairos

'Did I mention that every chapter is highly charged with eroticism, BDSM, D/S, and almost every fantasy you can imagine? If you don't get turned on by at least one of these fantasies, there is no hope for you' *Manic Readers*

Also available from Black Lace:

Wedding Games
Karen S Smith

Emma is not looking forward to her cousin's wedding: the usual awkward guests, the endless small talk, the bad dancing . . . But a chance encounter with Kit, a very sexy stranger, leaves her breathless.

Without a chance to say goodbye, Emma resigns herself to the fact their incredibly hot encounter will be just a sexy memory, but then she meets Kit at another wedding . . .

Black Lace Books: **the leading imprint of erotic fiction for women**

Also available from Black Lace:

Honeymoon Games
Karen S Smith

When newlyweds Emma and Kit speed away on their matching Ducati motorbikes, Emma knows not to expect a conventional honeymoon. From the moment they meet a biker gang and the leader takes a shine to Emma, events take a turn for the bizarre.

With hard-drinking rock bands, hunky stuntmen, booze-fuelled biker festivals and a whole lot of kinky behaviour on the agenda, Emma's taste for adventure is tested to the max – and Kit's not about to step in and save her from the wild bunch as he's having too much fun himself . . .

**A wild, leather-clad, biker orgy,
this high-octane spin across the continent
is set to send the blood racing.**

Also available from Black Lace:

Forbidden Fruit
Eden Bradley

Give in to temptation...

While Mia Curry's university students cram into her alternative sexuality class to learn about fetishes, bondage, voyeurism and much more, Mia has kept her own private fantasies carefully under wraps – until now . . .

Jagger James is everything Mia wants and everything that is taboo: he's young, gorgeous – and a student. But how can Mia resist?

Praise for Forbidden Fruit

'Intelligent, haunting and sexy as hell . . . for you people who like story and heart with your erotica, I'd definitely recommend any of Eden's books, but particularly *Forbidden Fruit* . . .' Maya Banks

Also available from Black Lace:

A Private Collection
Sarah Fisher

The chauffeur stood still for a moment, then moved his broad hand up towards the button on his tight uniform jacket. His voice was low and hypnotic.

'I can give you anything you want, Francesca,' he whispered. 'And I think I know what you want.'

When Francesca Leeman is invited to catalogue a private collection of priceless erotica she finds her new acquaintances cultured, fascinating – and intense. Yet she finds herself drawn to their intoxicating way of life and their voyeuristic games of seduction . . .

Black Lace Classics – **our best erotic fiction ever from our leading authors.**

Also available from Black Lace:

The Accidental Call Girl
Portia Da Costa

It's the ultimate fantasy:

When Lizzie meets an attractive older man in the bar of a luxury hotel, she is mistaken for a high class call girl on the look-out for a wealthy client.

With a man she can't resist . . .

Lizzie finds herself following him to his hotel room for an unforgettable night where she learns the pleasures of submitting to the hands of a master. But what will happen when John discovers that Lizzie is far more than she seems . . . ?

A sexy, thrilling erotic romance for every woman who has ever had a *Pretty Woman* fantasy.
Part 1 of the Accidental Trilogy.

Also available from Black Lace:

Threesomes
Edited by Brit M

Good things always come in threes

The Virgin Threesome

Marissa, a reluctant voyeur, becomes an eager participant after her friend introduces her to the alluring world of ménage. But can she overcome her inhibitions?

Three in Love

When Heather's two boyfriends move away to Nevada, the sudden lack of threesomes in her life unsettles her. So she follows them – but will this gamble pay off?

Black Lace Books – the leading imprint of erotic fiction for women